The Jet Necklace

by

Nelly Harper

The Jet Necklace

Published by Goblin House
www.goblinhouse.co.uk
Paperback

ISBN: 978-0-9932748-2-4

© Nelly Harper

www.nellyharper.co.uk

For Mum.
Because sometimes life gets tough

Acknowledgments

There are a number of people who I wish to thank. Katharine Smith of Heddon Publishing, your help, both literary and moral is fantastic. Kate Willis, the fastest reader ever. I can always rely on you for your honesty and input. Ciaran and Becky for being there for me, encouraging me and generally being the best.

Prologue

The last of the light was leaving the sky as Hogni finally approached his home. He scanned the entrance for the familiar sight of his beloved daughter but there was no sign. *Strange,* he thought. She was always there to meet him, he had never known her to miss his return. A sharp claw of dread gripped at his belly. Where was she? He tore their home apart but she was gone. The army would have no rest now until she was found.

Hildr was happy. Ever since Prince Hedinn had taken her away, her heart had been filled with the joy of requited love. Her steps were light as air and the birds sang with a clarity she had never known before. Her only worry was her father but she had a plan. She had stones brought from far down the mainland coast, shaped and polished by the finest craftsmen. She worked them into a multi-stranded necklace worthy of a king, imbuing it with a magical calming spell that would see the end of even the strongest hate and hostility. This token of love would surely calm even the angriest of meetings.

Finally the day came when her father arrived at the high island where they had made their home. Dressed for battle with his sword, Dainsleif on his hip and his army behind him, he was ready the moment his boat pulled up onto the shore. Whilst

Prince Hedinn and his men held back, Hildr went to meet him and presented him with the necklace. Hogni accepted the gift with a mixture of gratitude and sorrow for he had already drawn his sword as he left his boat. Dainsleif had been forged by dwarves and cursed to always kill a man once drawn.
Matters were now beyond his control.

Fighting commenced between the two armies and raged all through the day. Many bodies scattered the battleground by the time dusk arrived and the armies withdrew to their respective camps. Hildr was stricken with grief; not only were there battle dead but many men were sporting wounds given by Dainsleif and cursed never to heal. Walking the battlefield she brought the dead back to life with incantations and spells but they locked the soldiers into a battle that was doomed to repeat itself day after day.

Lost in the fierce fighting, the necklace was never found. Many battle lords wished for it over the centuries as fact and legend combined. For magic, once created, holds great power for those that keep believing.

Her insides were a turmoil of emotions, nerves strung as taut as a loaded noose. Not knowing whether to laugh with excitement, frown with anticipation, or cry with sheer panic. Somehow she had made it through the first part of the night with only short snatches of sleep before the intensity of what she was to face jolted her awake again.

In the wee small hours her mother gently shook her shoulder.

'It's time, Oonagh.'

She scrambled out of bed and silently her mother helped her into a snow-white shift. It reached to just past her knees and gathered at the wide neckline with a ribbon that her mother tied into a neat bow, letting the extra-long ends hang down almost to her waist. Oonagh sat whilst her mother combed her long, dark hair with a fine bone comb. Sections from the sides of her face were woven into plaits and tied at the back of her head with a piece of leather thonging. Her mother sighed as she looked at her, eyes glistening with pride as she fought back a tear. A quick glance over her shoulder confirmed that her husband and the other children were still fast asleep. Her hands reached out and cupped her daughter's cheeks as she placed a kiss on her brow before handing her the mask of feathers they had worked on over the last few days. Sleek black feathers of a wise raven they had found - a good omen, her mother had said. As soon as the mask was tied in place, the door was opened and Oonagh was running out into the misty night, across the village towards the forest behind.

A noise to her left startled her, another girl in her virginal shift and mask was leaving her own home. Their eyes caught for a moment and Oonagh saw her own emotions reflected back at her. She ran on, dawn was not far away and she must be well into the forest by then. Other girls appeared and disappeared as they headed into the dark Caledonian forest. Gradually the sound of them receded and Oonagh was alone. She could relax for a while now, the stags could not set off until dawn. The stags. The very thought set her heart racing again. Excitement, fear, trepidation, all fought for control. None could hold her for more than a few moments at a time. If only she knew what was to happen. Oh, she had heard rumours but they had not quelled her nerves, only caused them to strain even more. The Beltane ritual was as old as time, steeped in mystery for the young and knowing for the older ones. It was a rite of passage that sooner or later everyone went through. The morning Oonagh awoke to find a white feather fastened to her door, she knew it was her time. This was the signal a male suitor sent a female that indicated they were interested in pursuing them. The suitor, then referred to as a stag, had Beltane morning to find his doe and seduce her. Eye masks were worn to heighten the excitement and ensure the love was true, for only true love would not be fooled by a mask. Many a wedding had come from a successful

Beltane morning and many a bairn had found its way into the world ten moons later.

A noise startled Oonagh. Someone was making their way stealthily through the trees towards her hiding place. Butterflies clamoured in her stomach as she peeped around the rock she had been leaning against. Suddenly there was a squeal of excitement and a flash of white as a girl ran across Oonagh's field of vision, closely followed by the jubilant roar of the approaching stag. Their laughter could be heard disappearing further into the forest. Oonagh's heart thumped in her chest. The laughter eased her concerns a little. It didn't sound like there was anything to be frightened of, maybe that girl had done this before? It had been too quick for her to see who they were, though most of the people around here were known to her. Numerous small villages inhabited the valley the river Nabaros ran through, known locally as Strathnabaros, though probably only people from near the northern shores of the loch would be in these woods today. She turned back and stepped away from the rock and jumped suddenly as she realised a silent stag was standing before her.

He was wearing a dark kilt and mask of dark brown buzzard feathers. His bare chest bore a light covering of dark curly hair that gathered together to form a line running down his stomach and disappearing beneath the top of his kilt. Hazel eyes shone out through the feathers and Oonagh could feel them travel the length of her body. The sun had found a way through the dark canopy and as a shaft of light rested on her, the snow-white shift revealed to him the secret of her naked body beneath.

A strange feeling was growing in the depths of her belly and with it rose the fear of the unknown. Her nipples began to tingle and harden and parts of her pulsed with a sensation she had never known before. She suddenly felt extremely vulnerable and exposed. She wanted to run and hide but a treacherous part of her wanted to reach out and stroke the dark hair before her and trace where it disappeared to. Her fearful eyes looked up to meet his, which were shining with arousal. She was frozen to the spot as he stepped forward and traced a light finger across her forehead and down the side of her face. Her pulse quickened.

He was so near to her, she could smell him. She closed her eyes and breathed deeply. His finger was sliding down her throat towards the bow of her shift. In one deft move he had pulled the ribbon and the shift fell to her feet, leaving her standing naked before him. She gasped with shame and moved to cover herself, mortified, but he grasped her wrists and held them out to the sides. She could feel the heat rising up her cheeks as his greedy eyes took their fill of her before he lifted her left hand and kissed the palm. Her stomach lurched, unknown sensations were filling her body. Slowly he took her hand and guided it to his kilt where he had her take hold of the pin holding it fastened and pull.

The cloth fell to the floor and he stood before her proud and erect. Suddenly she knew what was about to happen and she felt a moment of panic. She started to struggle, to try and push him away, but he caught hold of her body and pulled it close to him. Lowering his face to hers he kissed her firmly on the lips. She felt herself melting and the panic dissolved. He lifted his head, took a step back and held his arms wide, letting her know she was free to leave. Whatever happened, she would need to be a willing participant. A smile played on his lips as she stood there looking at him. She smiled shyly back, realising she didn't want this moment to end. She felt her knees go weak as he gathered her back in his arms. The next couple of hours passed in a blur of pleasure she had never realised was possible.

Oonagh watched the leaves on the branches overhead as they danced in the light breeze; her insides felt just like that. Slowly her breathing returned to normal. Next to her she could hear her stag calming too. She stole a glance sideways at him. His mask was still in place but she was sure she recognised him as Donal, son of the Maor who lived a short way from her village in the tall stone broch by the side of Loch Nabaros. As she watched, he rolled onto his side to face her. Reaching for her, he caressed the side of her face but before he had a chance to speak they heard the sound of someone moving noisily through the wood. Quickly they grabbed their discarded clothing and scrambled to get dressed before they were discovered.

A stag and doe passed closely by, their arms entwined around each other. Oonagh recognised the stag as one of the young men of her small village, the doe was from Grumbeg further along the loch. The pair grinned at them as they passed but did not stop to talk. Soon enough they were out of sight again, leaving Oonagh and her stag alone once more. He gathered her up in his arms and placed the gentlest of kisses on her forehead.

He broke the ancient tradition and spoke, 'Will you meet me here again?'

'Yes,' she exhaled the word, quickly followed by, 'When?'

'In two days' time.'

Her heart raced at the thought and she nodded in response. Whoever started the idea of being silent certainly knew what they were doing. It heightened all the other senses and made them notice things they may otherwise have missed. Like the way his heart thumped against her ear when she rested her head on his chest or the feeling of his naked skin against hers. She slid her hands up his arms, loving how the hair felt under her palms, and groaned in pleasure as he kissed her neck. Her breathing began to speed up again as her arousal grew once more but it was time to go. She inhaled his raw scent, determined to commit it to memory, and sighed as they pulled apart.

Together they turned and walked hand in hand back towards home. The man next to her took up all her awareness. For the first time ever, Oonagh didn't notice the birds in the trees or the flowers by her feet. She felt as if she was floating on air, only held down by the firm anchor of her hand within his.

Once they got within sight of the first houses, they kissed again. Then he was off, skirting the village, keeping out of sight of any prying eyes. Oonagh hugged her arms around herself. Grinning, she made her way back home.

Her mother looked up anxiously as her daughter entered but even before she had removed her mask, Doada knew she was happy. Oonagh flushed a little at the sight of her but needn't have worried. This tradition was as old as anyone could remember, a ritual everyone went through. Her mother had no intention of prying. She gave her daughter a quick hug then left her to change whilst she finished preparing her herbs.

'Katiana McFergus has gone into labour,' she called. 'You're just in time to come and help me.' Quickly they sorted what they would need and before long they were heading across the village to the McFergus home.

***

The rest of the day passed with frustrating normality. It was Katiana's first birth but the labour was surprisingly short. After a few hours the baby was born healthy, with a fine voice and strong limbs. Oonagh removed the soiled sheets and took them to the burn to wash.

She let her mind wander back to the morning. A flush coloured her face as she remembered the sensual feeling of skin on skin. Was she shocked at what she had done? She smiled. Shocked or not, she couldn't wait until they met again.

'I see your morning went well,' her father said, reaching down and grabbing a clean sheet.

Oonagh jumped. She smiled at him and took an end. They twisted the sheets until all the excess water had been forced out. Angus eyed her carefully. He had been hovering about the village all day, waiting to find out how she was. Even though he was an easy-going man by nature, one hint of upset and he would not have stopped until he found the culprit. It was clear he needn't have worried. He said no more about the matter. He and Doada had agreed to give their daughter her space. She would talk to them in her own time when she was ready.

Oonagh's siblings, however, were another matter. Their little home rang with singing voices.

'Oonagh's got a boyfriend, Oonagh's got a boyfriend,' they sang at every opportunity, though only Moira was old enough to have any idea what had gone on. A year younger than Oonagh, she was half hoping to be given a feather herself next year. She tried to pry more information out of her big sister when they were alone.

'You know I'm not supposed to tell you anything, Moira.'

'But I need to know,' her sister had insisted. 'Everyone knows Martha came home in floods of tears last year. She wasn't seen again for ages. If something can go so wrong I need to be ready. What if I get my feather next year?'

Oonagh sighed. Her sister was a worrier as well as a dreamer. She herself had never really bothered about Beltane until this year. Down-to-earth and practical, Oonagh preferred to spend her time learning herb lore from her mother and helping tend to anyone who needed healing. Taking a husband had never really occurred to her before. Now in her seventeenth year, she had spent as long as she could remember following her mother as she tended the sick, the dying, and those giving birth. Moira was usually left to tend their younger brothers and sisters. Young Angus at fifteen was fast becoming a man, spending most of his time out with their father tending the family's cattle. Next came the twins Taran and Sionagh, fourteen and rarely seen alone. They tended to the house and any odd jobs that needed doing in the village. Finally there was little Ffiona who, at twelve, was the youngest. She adored her big brother Angus. Whenever she went missing it was usually him that brought her home, having caught her trying to follow as they herded the cattle to fresh ground. She was a tomboy, afraid of nothing, and the cause of more worry than the rest of the children put together. Despite all their differences, she and

Oonagh were extremely close. Now though, she giggled each time she looked at her big sister.

'Imagine kissing a boy!' she said, screwing up her face in disgust. Suddenly she became serious. 'If you're going to get married you will have to kiss him, you know.'

Moira laughed at her. 'I think she has already kissed him, Ffiona... now she just has to work out who it was she kissed.'

They fell about laughing and soon the whole family had joined in. Oonagh tried to be cross at them but soon she too was smiling. She hadn't let on to anyone who he was. It was her secret and she was going to keep it as long as possible. In a family of this size, secrets were hard to keep and privacy was even harder to find. She wasn't going to tell anyone about her plans to meet up in the forest again, either.

Soon they got bored with teasing her and talk moved on to other things. Later though, Ffiona flung her arms around her neck and whispered, 'I will miss you if you get married and go away.'

Oonagh hugged her and whispered back, 'I promise not to go far away.'

A couple of days later, Oonagh made her excuses and slipped out of the village. She walked by the burn a good way up the hill and into the trees then she veered off to the left and carried on up the rise. Her heart was beating heavily in her chest, she hadn't been able to manage anything to eat. In fact, she had barely eaten anything since Beltane morn.

A tall oak came into sight, one half of the tree was lush with new leaves but the other was blackened and dead where a lightning bolt had ripped the trunk in two. The local children claimed it was the witches' tree, scared by the strange deformity. The little glade behind it was the perfect place for a private meeting.

She checked to make sure no one was around. As she did, she heard a low whistle coming from up ahead. She froze, her eyes searching for a sign of anyone. Then there he was, stepping up onto a boulder so she could see him clearly. With her heart in her mouth she almost skipped the last few paces. The look on his face told her he had been as nervous as she was. There were no masks to hide behind this time, no chance to pretend. They stood facing each other for the briefest of moments before they were once again in each other's arms.

'You came,' he managed in between kisses. 'I was so worried you wouldn't want to.'

'You were worried?'

'I thought I might have frightened you off, after all you have never looked at me twice before.' Donal squeezed her bottom in reproach.

'I never thought about it... About anyone.'

'Never? Not even once?'

Oonagh blushed, 'Not once. I guess I was so busy helping Mother, it never occurred to me someone would be interested in me.'

'Well I am,' he told her. 'Very much so.'

The next few weeks passed in a blur of joy. Oonagh had never felt so happy. Her mother was not fooled by her sudden interest in jobs that would take her out of sight, especially as those jobs were taking longer and longer for her to complete. The young lovers met as often as they could, usually up in the clearing by the witches' tree but occasionally they would go further afield. Walking hand in hand or sitting talking for hours. When they made love their souls mingled, melted, and returned that little bit stronger, until they could no longer think of a life without each other. The only thing that clouded their plans was Donal's father, Dungall. He had barely been at the broch over the weeks they had been together and when he was he was blinded by worry.

The life of the Maor was usually a calm one. He oversaw the local area for the Maormar, sorted small disputes and presided over celebrations and funerals. Now, however, the area was coming under increasing pressure from the north coast. Vikings had begun attacking settlements near to the sea in flash raids and it was no secret that where the Vikings came, Norse settlers would eventually follow. They had seen it happen time and again on all the islands off the Cait coastline.

Dungall was called on more and more to help plan for the expected invasion. When that day arrived he would be responsible for the safety of his area and for supplying eligible men to fight in the Maormar's army. It was not a task he took lightly. Trying to spare his people for as long as he could, he kept the news to himself but his shoulders were weighed down with the pressure. Donal's mother, sympathetic to his problem, counselled him to wait. There was nothing the pair could do but keep their relationship quiet and continue to meet in secret.

2

'The Norsemen were seen in the area again, sire.'
'When?' the Maormar barked, slamming his hand down on the ledge in front of him. In the distance the Bay Mountain could be seen rising high above its surroundings. The mountain stood as guardian to the south but it was from the north and east that the true threat lay. His patience was wearing thin; only yesterday they had received news that one of their barrows had been ransacked. Now this.
'Word reached here this morning. Three of them, seen scouting the moors not far from the looted mound. It makes sense to think they are the thieves.'
Moddan, as Maormar, was responsible for a wide area. The people looked to him for protection and support, especially now the Vikings were becoming more troublesome. They arrived quickly to pillage and decimate before disappearing with their spoils. The fact some had stayed after breaking into one of their ancient tombs only served to fuel his concern.
'Did no one think to challenge them?'
'They were seen by a child, sire, a little girl playing too far from home. She ran screaming when she saw the men but by the time a search party went back...'
The informer's voice trailed off as Moddan began to pace up and down the small chamber. The air was thick with his rage. The yellow-haired Scandinavians were getting bolder year on year,

even raiding their own kinsmen on the multitude of islands off the mainland. As if that was not bad enough, word had also begun to filter through from the south that the kingdom of Dal-Riata was sending more and more Scots priests into their adjoining lands, spreading news of their strange new religion. Men apparently plain but gifted with extraordinary talents for miracles and healing were telling people to throw down their own beliefs and worship in fear of their angry, vengeful God who demanded complete devotion. Moddan had no intention of being told how to worship, any more than he had of letting the Norse scourge gain a foothold in his lands.

'Send word to every Maor in the province,' he told the waiting man. 'I want them found and brought here alive, no one raids our dead. Viking, Norse, or whatever they are, they will answer for this. I want what they have stolen found and returned to the grave as soon as possible and I want a watch put over the tomb. Tell Lutrin I will meet him there, we need rites performed to appease the gods. The last thing we need right now is a fore-bearers' curse.'

***

The tomb lay to the east of Moddan's stronghold. It was one of a group of small ancient burial mounds that were held in reverence by the Picti, for they were the tombs of their ancestors. No one knew exactly to whom they belonged, it was said they were the first of men. The ones who had

17

carved a living out of the inhospitable land, calming the gods and the elements that had forged the landscape around them. In doing so they had paved the way for all who followed.

The Maormar and his men arrived to see the damage for themselves. One of those burial mounds now lay ripped open, revealing the capstone of the central cist smashed and its pieces thrown to the side. The bones of the body were scattered as the thieves had rummaged around for whatever grave goods they could find.

Moddan knelt by the edge of the wound and bowed his head in respect. Silently he sent out his words of sorrow and regret for the act of sacrilege that had been committed there, along with his solemn vow to bring the perpetrators to justice. A hand reached out and rested on his shoulder. He looked up to see the druid, Lutrin, standing over him. His shoulders were uncharacteristically hunched, his eyes dark with anger. In his other hand he held the remains of a skull.

'This was thrown into the trees,' he said.

Bending, he placed it back into the cist and began to rearrange the bones as best he could. Together the two men replaced the pieces of capstone and began to rebuild the earthen mound. Too important a task for just anyone, the work had waited until the two great men had been able to attend. They worked in silence whilst others checked the surroundings for further signs of the thieves.

'It looks like they were going after more graves, sire,' one of the men told Moddan as they gathered back together again. 'There are signs of disturbance on one of the other mounds.'

Lutrin nodded, as much to himself as to the others. 'It makes sense. There is no way to know what might be inside each one.' He shifted his weight uncomfortably. 'This strikes me as more than a random act. No one would desecrate the elders in such a way without good reason.'

He looked at the red-haired leader in front of him, watching as his left eye twitched. Only someone who knew him extremely well could see just how concerned he was. 'We need to prepare, I have a feeling we will know the reason soon enough if these men are not caught.'

'I will have the place watched along with all the other mounds in the area, I have already sent word out to all Maors.' Moddan gripped forearms with the druid. 'This is the work of the Norse, of that I have no doubt.'

Lutrin let his own composure slip for a moment. 'I understand that they have their own gods,' he almost spat. 'But that does not excuse this.' He waved his arm, indicating the freshly built mound. 'Nothing excuses such disrespect.'

***

Autumn was marching ever closer. The shorter days brought with them the heightening threat of the Norsemen loose in the Cait countryside.

19

Dungall was under immense pressure to ensure the Vikings did not slip through his fingers and as a result more work fell to Donal. Everyone in the village was on high alert, children were kept close, and no one strayed far from home. Dungall had set up frequent searches of the local burial mound at Grumbeg, along with the forests surrounding the villages. Donal took Oonagh with him whenever he had to check near Grumg-Mhor but their times together were all too brief.

Donal's mother hated to see her son so conflicted. She tried to bring the subject up with Dungall but the Maor was having none of it.

'My son has no time for such things, Sheilagh,' he told her. 'He has duties to perform. I will not have my lands playing host to the Norse. If they are here we will find them. Nothing else matters.'

Sheilagh sighed and shook her head. In a home full of testosterone she longed for some female companionship. She prayed that the men would be caught soon and everyone could relax but this was not the typical raid and retreat they had become so used to hearing about. Every omen pointed to bleak times ahead and rumours were rife that a full-scale invasion was imminent.

Just in case, Sheilagh had been busy preparing. As always, the lower level of the broch held enough grain to plant again next year should that year's crop be destroyed. Her main concern was making the broch ready for a siege. She had some of the local sheep and cattle slaughtered and smoked early. The rest of the live animals were brought into the enclosure surrounding the front of the broch to ensure a safe supply of milk and meat. Fish they would have to live without. Though a staple food, it was hard to keep fresh for any period of time.

As much room in the upper two galleries as possible was made to house extra people, though many would have to make do with the small space between the broch's substantial outer and inner walls. This double wall gave about a three-foot space between, helping with both the security and the airflow of the tower. Anyone that couldn't fit would have to make do outside with the animals.

Just now the courtyard rang with the sounds of the blacksmiths hastily forging new swords and spear tips. Wood was cut from the surrounding forest to provide the poles for new spears. Those which didn't receive a metal tip were sharpened to provide a defensive fence around the courtyard walls. All around the area, similar preparations were being made. Moddan had no intention of giving the Norse an easy time of it.

***

Mid-August, not long after daybreak, Oonagh was busy rinsing washing in the little burn that ran to the east of Grumg-Mhor. The morning was bright and the linens would dry quickly in the sun. At the sound of a low whistle she looked up to see a man trotting up the rise towards her. She smiled as Donal rode by with a sneaky wink in her direction.

Quickly she laid out the linens on the rocks and raced into the woods before anyone had time to notice she had gone. He was waiting only a short way away and helped her up onto the pony behind him. With her arms tight around his waist, more for closeness than balance, they set off up the forested hillside towards their clearing.

'Father has gone to Dun Yrredell to meet with the Maormar again so I have more time than usual,' he told her as the stocky piebald made his way carefully over the rough ground. Oonagh giggled and squeezed even tighter. She would have think of an excuse for why she had left the laundry on the way back.

Later, as they lay wound in each other's arms, they got to talking about the future.

'You will marry me, won't you?' Donal said.

Butterflies danced inside Oonagh. 'Yes,' she answered. 'But I will still be able to keep up my healing, won't I?'

'I would have it no other way.'

His fingers traced circles on her bare skin, sending frissons of electricity to mix with her excitement. 'You won't mind living at the broch, will you? I am sure Mother will love the company and we can make our room on the top level.'

Oonagh was overjoyed, she would be living right next to the water's edge and not very far away from her family.

'When would we marry, though?'

Donal frowned and his fingers stilled, 'I cannot say just now, darling. Father is very worried, he won't hear of anything else other than the Norse. It is as if the rest of life has stopped for him.'

Oonagh wriggled around in his embrace until she was lying along his body, looking down at him. 'We have all the time in the world.' She kissed his nose and watched the gold flecks in his eyes shine again in their hazel beds.

He pulled her face down to his and kissed her, deep and searching. Then he broke away. 'Alas, we have no more time for today though.'

She groaned as he slid out from underneath her and began to pull on his clothes.

They made their way slowly back down the path hand in hand, leading the pony. Each was lost in thoughts of marriage and never having to make this journey any more. It was always sad leaving the wood, they never knew how long it would be before they could meet again. The pony whickering alerted them to the fact someone else was nearby. His ears pricked up and he blew out a couple of strong breaths. Immediately Donal held his hand up to warn Oonagh to be wary. He walked the pony back up the path and tied it to a tree, he didn't want it giving them away. Together, Oonagh and Donal moved slowly forwards, listening for sounds.

They found the men at last, three of them in a small clearing a short way from the path, all with the distinctive blonde hair of the Norse. They made to leave. The settlement had to be warned but something stopped Donal and he held back. The sunlight was glinting off something one of the men held in his hand, it looked like a necklace of polished stone. Why would these men have such a thing?

'What is it?' hissed Oonagh.

Donal pointed to the man and whispered for her to get back to the village. Before she could stop him he was creeping forward.

Whilst he edged nearer, the man placed the necklace back into his saddlebag then moved back to sit with the others. They were clearly not happy about something. Their voices began to rise, disagreeing as to their next move. Keeping low to the ground, Donal eased himself carefully towards the horse, willing it not to startle. His luck held, the horse carried on eating, ignoring him. It was easy enough to use the horse as a screen whilst he slipped his hand into the leather bag and pulled out the necklace.

'That is all very good and well, Skuli,' one of the men's voices rose as he jumped to his feet. 'But just how are we going to be managing that now, eh? Everyone is on the lookout for us.'

The man named Skuli stood to face him, 'We are supposed to get the information as well as the grave goods. What will it look like if we fail, eh?'

'We have already failed. Every inch here is being combed in the looking for us, men are preparing for us coming. We need to get to the coast and be away while we still can.'

The third man stayed quiet, letting them argue between themselves. He had no intention of letting them know the real nature of their mission; the

fewer people that knew that, the better. He bent
and picked up a twig and used it to prod some ants
crawling around his boots. As he did so a
movement next to his horse caught his attention.
Somebody was moving away in the trees.

The man jumped up and roared to the others. 'Get
him!'

Donal, cursing his stupidity, turned and raced away.
He hurled the necklace as far into the trees as he
could whilst he ran. For some reason it was
important to them and he did not want them
getting it back. The ground was uneven, full of
rocks and hidden roots. It was hard to keep his
footing. Behind him he heard one of the men curse
as he fell heavily. Risking a quick glance over his
shoulder, Donal's luck ran out and he tripped over
a rock. Before the men had gained much ground he
was up and off again but pain shot through his big
toe. Hobbling, he didn't get very far before one of
the Norsemen leapt on his back and brought him
down again. His head was forced backwards by the
fistful of hair Skuli had grabbed and he found
himself staring into the bright angry blue eyes of
the enemy.

'Who are you now?' the man spat, 'What were you
doing near our horses?'

Donal glared back. He was the son of the Maor. He
would not be intimidated easily. Holding his silence
he allowed himself to be dragged to his feet and
hauled back the way they had come. All three men
had chased him, much to his relief; it meant that
they had no idea he was not alone. He prayed

Oonagh had got away to safety, she would be able to raise the alarm and bring re-enforcements.

Back at the clearing the quiet man went to the horses to check them and soon found the necklace was missing.

'Ivar, he has the goods.'

Ivar kicked him hard. 'Where is it?'

Donal grunted in pain but held his tongue.

Skuli pulled at Ivar, 'You might damage it you fool.' Roughly he yanked at Donal's clothing while Ivar held him firm. On finding nothing he turned to his friend, 'Now you can kick him.'

***

Oonagh, still hiding in the trees, stifled a cry as she watched her man beaten. She was frozen to the spot with fear. The man whose name had not been mentioned stopped them before Donal lost consciousness and shouted a string of questions at him in a heavily accented voice.

'What did you do with it?'

'Where are you coming from?'

'What is your name?'

Each refusal to answer was met with yet another foot or fist.

'Are you here alone?'

'Is there a village nearby?'

'How did you get here?'

On and on it went until Oonagh thought it would never end. She watched through blurry eyes as the face she had stroked so tenderly only a short while before was bloodied and bruised beyond all recognition. Finally they had finished their sport and the body that had once been the man she loved was dumped on the ground. The final humiliation being the long knife Skuli thrust through Donal's chest.

'Do you think anyone else is with him?' Ivar asked, looking around.

'Not now,' Skuli laughed 'But it won't be long before someone wants to look for him. I think they will be getting the message when they find him.'

***

Suddenly Oonagh was forced into action. If the men were to start looking they would find her easily. Terror drove her to think. If she could get back to the pony she would have a chance of getting to the village and warning everyone. It was already mid-afternoon, people would surely be looking for her, she had to stop them from getting this far. She crept slowly back from her hiding place.

Once she was back on the path, Oonagh raced up the hill. It was the wrong direction but she needed the pony. She hadn't got far when she heard sounds of the men starting to check the area. Praying they did not head her way, she pushed on. She felt something give beneath her foot. Looking down, she saw what must have been the necklace Donal had died trying to steal. It was made of shiny black jet stones intermixed with strands of polished coal. Her shoe had broken some of the middle strands and cracked the large central pendant. There was no time to gather the fallen stones. She stuffed the necklace into her tunic and set off again. The piebald pony was standing impatiently, still tied where Donal had left him. Jumping astride him, Oonagh urged him down the track towards Grumg-Mhor. His hooves clipped on the stony path but she was too frightened to slow down.

'There!' she heard one of the men cry. 'Get the horses, catch her. If she runs to a village, burn it. Kill them all. No word of us must escape!'

Panic rose with stinging bile into her throat. Home was no longer an option. She must lead the men away from the houses. Images of her young sisters and brothers flooded her mind. She could not risk anything happening to them. The men's horses were bigger and would be faster than her pony but maybe not as sure-footed, hopefully that would make them an even match.

Soon enough she heard them gaining ground behind her. She needed to lead them off the path and away from the village. Luckily she knew the woods well. Not far away the path split and if she crossed the Grumg-Mhor burn onto the Grumbeg path she could divert off and lead them up to Coire Buidhe. She would just have to improvise before she reached the houses there; it was far enough away to give her time to think. Thanking the gods that the burn was not in full spate, she clung on as the pony leapt the narrow stream. She turned his head back up the hill, making sure she made plenty of noise. Sure enough, she heard them follow her

For over an hour Oonagh continued to lead the Norsemen further and further away from the people she loved. The pace had slowed now as the hill took its toll. Her piebald was used to these conditions but even he couldn't carry on indefinitely. The village of Coire Buidhe sat in a small hollow and would have been the perfect place to hide but she was too afraid of what the men chasing her would do if she was found there. She needed to lead them from the path before they got too near. If she remembered correctly there was a path somewhere nearby that led east. There were a number of small lochs and villages that way but if she was careful she was sure she could keep far enough away from them. She should then be able to make her way further over towards where the Nabaros river ran out of the loch and north towards the sea. From there she hoped to be able to double back down the valley and get herself home.

There had been no sign of anyone following her for quite a while so she took the chance to stop and relieve herself, making sure to hide herself out of sight should the men come upon her without warning. As she straightened out her clothing, the necklace fell to the ground. Stones blacker than night arranged like a half moon to lie on the wearer's throat. This was what Donal had died for. She had no idea why he had taken it or why it was so important but the sight and feel of it filled her with revulsion. She hated it for what it had cost him, and her. Hated it for its beauty and perfection. She was glad she had damaged it, she wanted to smash it to tiny pieces. Finding a large rock, she made to hit the necklace but something stilled her arm. For some reason, Donal had risked everything for this. Who was she to destroy it? Her mind set firm, for his sake the Norse must not get it back. She knew if they caught her they would, she needed to make sure it was safe.

There was an old marker stone a short way back down the path. Oonagh made up her mind. Leaving the pony tied where he was, she ran back to the stone. Once there she dug down and buried the necklace, carefully covering it over and hiding the fresh earth with loose stones. Now she would easily be able to find it again.

Not daring to stay and rest, she mounted the pony and set off straightaway. She heard a few noises behind her in the distance and knew the men were getting nearer. When she found the path that would take her east she tore some of her tunic and left it caught on a branch where it could not be missed. Coire Buidhe should be safe now.

The new path was much easier going, the ground was flatter and the pony happily picked up speed again. For a few minutes she relaxed slightly, until she realised that the Norsemen's horses would also be able to move faster. Filled with renewed dread, she pushed on. The hardy pony was soon flecked with foam.

By early evening she had pushed him as much as she could, they both badly needed to rest. Dark wouldn't arrive any time soon and when it finally did it would not be here for long. This far north, the summer nights lasted only a few hours. There had been no sounds behind her for a long time so she pushed her way through the trees and found a small clearing hidden from the path. She hobbled the horse and lay down nearby. It didn't take long for her grief to catch up. So far she had been too frightened to cry but now her adrenaline was easing and the reality of what she had witnessed soon gained hold.

How long she wept, she never knew, she was asleep before her eyes dried. Her dreams were filled with Donal, of living with him in the broch and long, happy days without a care. She woke a few hours later, stiff and hurting. The panic in her chest was there to meet her before her eyes were even open. It was almost dark, she had slept too long. Creeping back to the path she looked for signs of the Norsemen. There were none. Relieved, she made her way back to the pony. It made sense to stay put now, until first light at least. Her trackers would surely be doing the same and there was no way for her to know if they were still behind her, or if they had passed by as she slept.

3

A cacophony of birdsong woke Oonagh just as the first light of dawn was starting to show. She blinked, unable to work out where she was, then her stomach tightened and fear flooded back. She bolted to her feet and went to check the path. Still no sign of the Vikings but it did not put her at ease. Her stomach was rumbling and she realised she hadn't eaten in almost a day. There was mallow growing in a patch of sunlight nearby so she picked some flowers and leaves to chew on. The gummy flavour was not to her taste. Close to where the pony stood, she spotted some meadowsweet. The medicinal taste mixed with the mallow made her wince even more but beggars couldn't be choosers and it would put her on for now. Mounting the piebald, she headed off towards the valley.

Sounds from behind her urged her on. She pushed the pony to a slow canter. The close-growing trees inhibited anything faster. Her heartbeat raced and thumped against her chest. Ducking under the low branches, it was all she could do to stay on. More sounds came to her; laughter and children. Realisation dawned and she slowed her pace, she must be near to a village. Her panic eased slightly, should she go to them for help? Or would that bring danger for them? The voice echoed in her mind, screaming *burn the village she goes to*. She rode on, not daring to risk sanctuary.

The sun had reached its highest point in the sky when it became clear the ground was heading downwards. Providing no one caught up with her, she should hopefully be able to head for home once she reached the river. Her luck at avoiding people ran out a short while later when a drover spied her. She had come further north than she had realised and was closer to the familiar village of Rosal than she had intended to be. Having never approached it from this way before, she hadn't recognised it. The drover took in her dishevelled, dirty state and shook his head.

'Have you escaped the burning, lassie?' he called to her. ''Tis a dreadful thing they did, all those people gone and for what?'

Oonagh eyed him suspiciously, she had smelt no smoke or heard of any burnings. The drover mistook her confusion for shock.

'Will you come away wi me lassie, I will see you to a nice warm cuppa and a safe place to rest.'

She shook her head but the drover had hold of the pony's reins and started off towards his shieling.

'No, I must go,' she tried to tell him but he simply glanced at her and carried on.

'I had a brother at Grumg-Mhor,' he told her. Sadness filled his voice. 'Canny tell whether he is alive or dead yet. Twas said some folks managed to get out into the trees before the worst was on them. Only time will tell.'

Cold dread crept over her. 'What do you mean?' Oonagh begged him. 'Please tell me.'

The drover looked at her strangely. 'You be the healer lassie from Grumg-Mhor don't you?'

She nodded. 'I had some problems up in the forest, I haven't been home since yesterday morning.'

The drover shook his head once more and slowly patted her hand.

'You'll no be knowing yet then, lassie.' He sighed.

The shieling was in sight now, low turf walls and thatched roof caused it to blend in well with the surroundings. The drover helped her from the pony and tied it to a long tether so it could graze.

'Sit you down lass and I'll get the kettle on.' He nodded to some stools by the cottage door. 'You'll be needing the brew. Aye and mebbies a piece too by the look o you.'

Oonagh wasn't too sure, besides the mallow and meadowsweet early this morning she had only managed to grab a few handfuls of hawthorn leaves. She had been starving but now dread was making her nauseous, even as the mention of food made her stomach growl. Why wouldn't he just tell her?

The kettle was soon boiling on a small fire and the bread and cheese the man had given her had been eaten.

'Tell me,' Oonagh asked. She was getting frightened, the man seemed to be avoiding the moment when he had to explain himself. He sighed again and poured the brew.

'Tis like this, lassie,' he began. 'News came to us late last night, Grumg-Mhor was burning. Fierce it were. We raced over. Every man around went but there were nowt much we could do 'cept wait for the worst to burn through. Few came back from hiding in the woods to try and help. Said Vikings did it.'

The cup fell from Oonagh's grasp, she gulped at the thickened air as her vision swam. After all her running, leading the men away up the hill. How on earth had they found her home?

'Easy there, lass.'

The drover was on his feet and patting her back in a futile attempt to help. He had lost his wife many years before and children had unfortunately been denied to them. He understood grief all too well. He knew nothing would make this right for her apart from time.

She looked at him with glassy eyes. 'My family?'

Drover shook his head. 'Couldn't say for sure lassie, but I cannae mind seeing any o them.'

He saw no point in lying to her, she would have to face the truth sooner or later. 'I'm away back there the morrow. I will search for you.'

Oonagh looked up expectantly but the drover shook his head. 'Best you dinnae come this time, lass. It'll no be a sight you'll be wanting to see.'

'But I am a healer,' she insisted. 'I could help.'

'Aye lass, no doubt as you could. But there are other healers and they will manage just fine. Your time will come but not now.'

The drover settled her into his home and ordered her to rest, shock was good for no one. She thought about sneaking out the moment his back was turned but he was no fool. He brought in one of the stools and sat down at the foot of the bed. Closing her eyes, she was overtaken by sleep before she had a chance to form another plan. This time no dreams came, only the deep sleep of exhaustion. The drover left her alone, all being well he would find some of her family tomorrow and be able to re-unite them.

He never got the chance.

***

The evening was dry and clear. The drover was busy preparing his cart for the morning. It would be needed to move bodies but he didn't tell the girl that. He worked methodically until something made him look up.

'Did you hear that, lass?' he asked Oonagh as she emerged from the shieling. She shook her head. Not many minutes later, he looked up again. He could smell smoke, surely it was too far from Grumg-Mhor for the smell to have reached them? There was barely a breeze. Something didn't feel right. Then he heard it, Oonagh had heard it too and her blood ran cold. The sound of screaming was filtering through the trees from the settlement of Rosal along with the increasing smell of smoke. The village was burning.

At that moment a figure crashed through the trees and into the clearing. Blond, fearsome, and terrifyingly familiar.

'Run, lass!' the drover shouted. 'Now! and dinnae you look back.'

He grabbed his axe from the wood pile and rushed forward.

Oonagh ran. There was no time to grab the pony. She dived into the trees and raced up the valley away from the horror. When she could run no more she collapsed to the ground, her breath coming in ragged gulps. Reason told her she could not stay there, she had taken no care in her mad flight and the tracks would be visible to anyone looking. She forced herself to move on even as every inch of her shattered body screamed in protest. This time she took care to cover her tracks. At last she found an ancient oak, its bole split and hollow. Crawling in through the low opening she found just enough room to fit. Managing to perch on the lumpy wood still remaining, she wriggled around until she could peek out of the split. It was just wide enough to see out of whilst still keeping her hidden from all but the closest of looks.

Her second night out in the open wasn't to be as comfortable as the first.

***

Once more the dawn chorus woke her, it had been a very long night and she was cramped and sore.

37

Slowly, she tried to ease the stiffness from her body, not yet knowing if she dared to leave the safety of the trunk. It was lucky she waited, the birds were not the only ones abroad early. Silently she watched as two riders came into the clearing. Surely they could hear her breathing? She willed them to ride on and not look too closely, just in case her feet were showing, but they drew their mounts to a halt. Their coarse voices were clear.

'I tell you she will not be coming this far, Ivar.'

'And you told me you would catch her when we left you on the hill,' Ivar answered. 'We are needing that necklace back and I am wanting my sport while we are at it.'

Skuli grunted, 'You had sport enough last night. There is no one left alive for miles. We should be leaving here before word gets out.'

The third Norseman rode into view. 'False trail,' he announced. 'What about you?'

'Looks like the same here,' Skuli answered. 'What now?'

The third man straightened his back and threw the others an arrogant glare.

'She is bound to show herself to us sooner or later. Until she does we continue. I want this area and I am damn sure she is not going to be stopping me.'

He wheeled his horses around and headed back down the way they had come. The two others shrugged and followed. Oonagh waited a while longer before easing herself from the tree. She didn't know what to do. If everyone was dead, there was nothing to go back for. Besides, she had no idea what the Vikings' plans were, she could be walking into a trap. She wanted to panic, to cry and to scream, but where would that get her? A hollow feeling crept its way into her heart as she sat thinking. Two days ago her life was wonderful, her future stretching out before her like a joyous path. Now everything and everyone she knew and loved was gone. Wherever she went she would be with strangers. The only people that knew her now were the three Norsemen and she had clearly heard one of them say he wanted this area. Nowhere here would be safe for her.

Silent tears traced pathways down her face, her grief was too much for her to acknowledge. The thought of being so truly alone was a nightmare come true. She had always been part of a bustling community but now no one was left but her. Even if they were, last night had proved beyond doubt that nobody would be safe helping her. She thought of the drover and imagined his body lying crumpled and bleeding beside the cart he would have used to bring her family's bodies back to her. She had dealt with many bodies in her capacity as a healer, her mother had trained her thoroughly. She began to shake as she thought of Doada. So practical and calm, she would know what to do. All of a sudden a comment her mother used to make popped into her mind.

The best place to hide something is often in plain view.

She smiled at the memory, it was like her mother was still there guiding her. Telling her she should go to the one place the Norse would never think of looking. They would be expecting her to stay hidden amongst her own people, to find solace in distant relations or friends of the family. Instead she needed to find somewhere well away from anyone they may target.

The Norse had taken over all the islands off Cait's shores years before. The nearest to them were now known as the Sudreyjar. Many tales had come to them about the constant troubles between islanders and Norse. Oonagh shivered, she would not go there. To the northeast though, they had taken Orkas Islands and changed their name to Orkneyjar. The area had been peaceful for a long time now. Locals had mixed happily with the incomers and the islands prospered as a result. That was where she would go, she would be right in the heart of the enemy - the last place they would look for her.

Her resolve hardened, she jumped to her feet and made to set off but Ffiona's whispered words came back, twisted to haunt her. *I will miss you if you go away.* Her steps faltered but it was the memory of her answer that really undid her. *I promise not to go far away,* she heard herself say.

She collapsed back onto the grass. How could she ever bear to leave? Everyone and everything she had ever held dear was tied to this place. They wandered unbidden through her mind, reminding her of all the precious times they had shared together. Oonagh felt she would go mad with the pain, her little sister's face kept grinning up at her, pleading for her to play. She felt Donal's hand holding hers and closed her eyes to smell the scent of his skin. All things she would never experience again. The light was failing again before she found the energy to move. She found a stream and drank, too weak to look for any food.

She spent the night curled by the base of the hollow tree, waking and crying regularly. In the morning she was weak with hunger and feeling no better. A noise startled her, it was a small group of sheep wandering into the clearing. They eyed her warily as they fed. Their fleeces were matted and full of briars and two of them were limping. They looked a sorry sight. Oonagh was reminded of the drover, maybe these were his sheep? Well there was no one left to look after them now and whilst they were frightened and dishevelled they were still busy getting on with the business of surviving. Something stirred deep within her, turning the great tear in her heart into a hard lump.
She could not afford to look back, if she were to survive she would need to put all her efforts into focusing on her plans. Her parents had brought her up to be practical, not to fall apart when things went wrong. The feelings of loss were too great to ever leave her but she knew that wherever she went her family would come too, locked in her heart and her memories. It was time to move on, to leave Cait behind and start a new life.

4

Haey looked very much like parts of Cait. It had enormous cliffs, home to thousands of nesting seabirds. Dark guillemots and razorbills jostled for nesting space on the rock face, while funny little tammie norries with their rainbow bills and jolly little walk nested in burrows in the soil. Close by a huge double stack of red sandstone, known locally as the Old Man, stood slightly apart from the island's edge. Red-throated divers flirted with the waves offshore and large bonxies dive-bombed unsuspecting gulls to steal their food. Seals and walrus basked on the shores whilst wading birds picked their way in between them. Harder to see were the sea-loving otters that foraged along the shoreline and played in the foamy waters.

Unlike many of the other islands there was a good expanse of forestry, taking advantage of the protection the hills gave from the often unforgiving wind. Moors headed up the heights of the high hills, creating a haven for hen harriers, grouse and plover. Coat-changing hares, white in the winter and brown in the summer, flourished. Sheep and boar wandered throughout the island, along with a few wild horses that occasionally swam over from the main island of Hrossey.

It was here that Oonagh chose to settle. Almost as soon as she had arrived on Hrossey she had learned that Haey was desperately in need of a healer. There was even a home supplied by the Jarl, complete with its own physic garden and well. Sitting to the east side of the highest of the island's three hills, the small cottage sat hidden away and surrounded by the forest of Berriedale. Not too far away lay a valley known to the locals as Trowie Glen. So named for the spirits of the dead that were supposed to live there. It was said the Trows would steal away babies, leaving a sickly changeling in their place.

The hill was known as the Ward and it too had its own protection. Two enormous rocks on the slope nearest to Trowie Glen were reported to be the entrance to the home of a particularly bad-tempered giant. Anyone foolish enough to venture into Trowie Glen or even onto the Ward at night would soon wish they had not. Folk wandering the Ward at any other time had to beware of the Faerie rings of darkened grass that would appear indiscriminately. Oonagh made sure to watch her step and never had any problems.

Unlike the locals, Oonagh had no fear of spirits. As she saw it, all her family were dead and so living in the spirit realm. She could never be afraid of them. Besides, the Trow sounded very much like the Shidhe, the faerie folk who inhabited mounds and caves all over Cait. They had never been a bother to Oonagh. Rather, she had thought of them as friendly beings who were only malicious if provoked, which was exactly the same as most people. For a young woman who needed to hide herself away and start again it could not have been more perfect. For the first few weeks people kept their distance whilst she settled into her new life and tried to come to terms with her losses.

She found the island could easily offer her all she needed to survive. Wild food grew readily if you knew where to look and there was a small area around the cottage that had been cultivated before. She set to work clearing the ground and preparing it for planting, taking refuge from her grief in the physical labour. Her main problem was getting meat; sometime soon she would have to start mixing with the locals. Until then she would make do with whatever she could get her hands on. Between two large cliffs not far from her home was a secluded bay with a sandy beach and access to the rocky base at the foot of the cliffs. It was the perfect place to forage for muscles, even limpets if she could hit them quick enough to loosen them from the rocks. She had managed to form herself a small basket similar to those she had seen fisherman use in the Nabaros back home. Leaving it in a deep rockpool on a long rope tied to a boulder, she checked on it every few days.

After a stormy night, Oonagh was making her way down to the rockpool when she heard screaming. There were a handful of cottages near to the bay but the sound didn't appear to be coming from any of them. She scoured the shoreline looking for anything unusual. Near the bottom of the cliffs she spied the man. Fishing basket forgotten, Oonagh rushed over to help.

'What is your name?' Oonagh asked.

'Erelend,' he answered through teeth gritted firmly against the pain. 'I slipped from the path up there,' he inclined his head towards the cliff, his face had a nasty grey look to it and she noticed a slight tremble to his hands.

'How long have you been here?'

The man's breathing was shallow and he didn't answer. She looked at his leg, it was a mess. The broken end of the bone was protruding from a nasty gash down the shin. Blood was already beginning to congeal around the wound, he had been there quite a while.

'Right,' she continued, keeping her manner calm but firm. 'Give me a moment.'

Oonagh rushed back to the shoreline where kelp was growing freely. Taking a handful, she made her way back to the injured man. She balled some of the seaweed and placed it into the cut, knowing the saltwater would also help to wash away any dirt. There was no way for her to set the bone out here. She wrapped the rest of the kelp around his leg like a makeshift bandage. Her patient was not looking good and she was worried he was going into shock. She felt his forehead, it was clammy and hot.

'Do you live far away?' she asked him.

Erelend shook his head. 'Up above the bay... by the waterfall.' He gasped.

Oonagh groaned to herself. There was no way she could get him up the hill by herself.

'Right, this is going to hurt some but we are going to have to get you moved, the tide is on the turn.'

Erelend nodded and readied his hands on the rock.

'One, two, three!' she called. With as much force as possible they managed to heave him onto his good leg. Erelend roared in agony. The effort brought a new sheen of sweat to his brow.

It wasn't easy but together they managed to make it the short way over the stones to the edge of the sandy beach. He was heavy and the stones were slippery in places. Oonagh nearly went over on more than one occasion but they managed to get to the sand where they collapsed, breathless. After a few moments he managed to speak.

'You're the Pict.'

She nodded her head in response, now was not the time to be wary. 'My name is Oonagh.'

He struggled with his words. 'Thank you lass, I don't know what I would have done without you.'

Oonagh grinned at him, 'Well I could hardly leave you there, scaring all the birds with your noise. I don't know how we are going to manage now, though.'

Erelend pointed to the fishermen's cottages hugging the side of the bay, the nearest one was not too far away. She was there within minutes. The fishermen, Anlaf and Harald, had been busy repairing nets. They needed no introduction as the new healer told them what she needed. Helga, Anlaf's wife, rushed for a blanket and some strips of linen whilst the men found some sticks to use as splints. By the time they arrived back down on the beach, Erelend was barely conscious. They took advantage of this and whilst Helga sat at his head, Oonagh directed the men to pull his leg until she felt the bone fall back into place. His screams tore through the air and it was all they could do to keep him still whilst she added more kelp. Finally, with the two sticks either side of the leg to hold it straight, she tightly bandaged it all in place.

'That is all I can do for him here, we need to get him on the blanket so we can carry him home,' she told them. 'He is going to need something for the pain and honey to stop the wound getting infected when we get him there. The salt water should help for now.'

They looked at her with respect. Anlaf pulled a leather bottle from beneath his tunic and handed it to her. She took a grateful swig and coughed as the liquid burned her throat. Anlaf grinned.

'Fire ale,' he told her with a wink. 'Only fit for the best.'

He encouraged her to take another drink. This time she sipped carefully and was rewarded with a warming glow, complete with heady kick. It made her laugh. Harald clapped her on the back.

'You're one of us now, girl,' he told her. 'Anlaf don't give that stuff out to just anyone.'

***

For the best part of two weeks Oonagh made the journey to the cottage above the waterfall every day to tend to Erelend's leg. She became good friends with his wife, Thora. The couple had two young children, a three-year-old boy named Barth and a little girl called Groa who was only a month old.

Their cottage had a fantastic setting with an amazing view over the bay. Just a little lower down the hill was a picturesque waterfall cascading over a sharp stone ledge. Low birch trees arched overhead and lush green ferns covered the stream bank. The bed of the stream was a collection of water-worn pebbles, smooth and rounded.

It was there Thora first brought up the subject of Oonagh's health. She had been sick a number of times but thought she had managed to hide it from them. Sipping mint tea as often as possible and keeping her food light, she had put it down to grief. She told Thora it was from the stress of the move. Her new friend, however, had another suggestion. She looked at Oonagh with a knowing smile.

'Could you be pregnant?'

At first Oonagh firmly denied the possibility. True, she had missed her last monthly courses, but that really was down to stress, surely? Over the next few days, however, she began to realise that Thora could actually be right. It had never occurred to her that she may have conceived. It was as if fate would not let her forget what might have been.

Despite her calm outward appearance she had been fighting a constant battle with her grief. Even Thora had no idea just how devastated she was. The fear of reprisals for anyone who knew her real identity kept her from confiding the truth. Almost every day there came a time when she couldn't block it out and the pain would sear through her. Then it was all she could do to keep one breath following another. In slowly. Out slowly. Think of nothing else. Don't let it in. Often though, there was nothing she could do to hold back the tide. Grief and panic would overwhelm her and she would be reduced to a wreck.

The day she accepted she was actually pregnant, she hit her lowest ebb. The thought of having Donal's baby without him was more than she could handle. She shut the world away and hid inside her cottage. Faces swam in her mind; her mother, Donal, Ffiona. She could hear Moira's voice asking her, *What does it feel like? I need to know, it could be me next.* The lump that had formed in her heart when she decided to leave Strathnabaros shattered, leaving behind a void so black that nothing mattered any more but seeing everyone again. They reached for her with outstretched arms, calling her to join them.

It would be easy enough to do, one step from the top of the cliff and she would be with them before she reached the bottom. In a daze she left the cottage and made her way through the wood. Once up on the high moor she headed straight for the cliff edge.

Her hand reached for her belly, imagining the life that was growing inside her. Something clicked into place. Her baby, Donal's baby, needed her. She staggered back from the edge. She must snap out of this mire of depression. Find a way, any way, to get through this. Tiny steps would do it. Just put the life growing inside her first.

She began to spend more time on the cottage and garden, making up for the neglect it had suffered whilst it stood empty. The work kept her attention focused on the present for long periods of time; without it she would never have coped. Mint and nettles had run amok and were threatening to choke out the smaller plants. She tackled these first and whilst she was careful to remove the nettles by their yellowy-orange roots, she still managed to get stung a number of times. The mint was much easier to handle, the roots did not snap so readily. Once she had these in order she tackled the morning glory in the hedge, taking care to remove every last piece of vine to stop it growing right back.

In the evenings she would go out walking, keeping well away from the cliffs. She soon learned to keep an eye out for the dive-bombing bonxies up on the moors. At first she mistook the large brown birds for the harmless buzzards she was used to seeing back home but the tell-tale flash of white feathers in their wings soon had her running for cover. There were times they had her reduced to laughter despite herself. Slowly she emerged from the blanket of pain that had smothered her.

***

For the first time in the three months since she had escaped to Haey, Oonagh was to meet the Jarl of Orkneyjar, Sigurd the Powerful, given the role by his power-hungry brother Ragnvald who had his eye on far too great a prize to be stuck on these distant islands. She was feeling stressed, worry played with her growing stomach and teased the back of her throat but there was no getting out of it. Known to the Norse as The Thing, the bi-annual gathering was where the community got together to go over pressing matters and pay their skat, as the local tax was called. Any wrong-doing was dealt with and punishments meted out, rivalries sorted, and new laws decreed. Afterwards there would be celebrations and dancing as people enjoyed the rare chance to all be together. It was held at the skali, the main hall on the island and home to Thorstein the Red, an important ally of Sigurd. Oonagh was yet to meet him, he had not been there all the time she had been on the island. It was said he was away a lot on the Jarl's business and would not be back any time soon.

The November morning was crisp and bright as the small group made their way between the Ward and its neighbour, Cuilags. Autumn was in full swing with rich browns and reds on the trees. Nuts and berries were ripe for harvesting. Many of the walkers, including Oonagh, had brought baskets to fill on their return journey. The pace was steady to accommodate little Barth and his father. Erelend's leg had healed well, though he still walked with a slight limp and tired easily.

Normally one to find solace in a good walk, Oonagh found the slow pace only served to heighten her apprehension. She could not shake the worry that had held her in its grip since the early hours. Covering the cause of her anxiety with feigned apprehension at meeting the whole of the island in one go, she forced herself not to ask anything about Sigurd.

The group arrived with plenty of time to spare. Slowly the skali began to fill and they took their place inside along with everyone else. Oonagh could see Sigurd seated at the front in a large wooden throne, the arms of which terminated in matching carved dragon heads. As he sat waiting for the room to settle, he absentmindedly caressed the dragons as if they were well-loved pets. He scanned the room with mild interest and Oonagh felt her heart leap into her mouth as he turned her way. She let out a long, slow breath as he passed over her without even a flicker. He wasn't looking for her at all. Her imagination slowly crept back into its little box, taking with it all the scenarios she had been worrying about. So long as she did nothing to draw attention to herself, she would get through this.

The Thing got swiftly underway and Oonagh was surprised to find it very interesting. Sigurd was a capable and bright leader, well organised and amenable. The main matters were quickly dealt with and he moved on to any misdemeanours and disputes. These were few and soon sorted and the floor was then given over to islanders' comments. To Oonagh's horror, Erelend limped forward. As the blood drained from her face she heard him introduce her to the hall and ask everyone to give their new healer a warm welcome. All eyes turned to look at her. A hand at her back gently urged her forward. Glancing sideways she saw Thora smiling encouragement.

'Go on,' she whispered. 'Introduce yourself.'

Another hand patted her on the shoulder and she turned to see Helga and Anlaf at her other side. Beyond them she could see all the faces of her new friends, smiling and encouraging her. Taking strength from their support, she stepped forward. She needed these people to accept her. Murmurs of interest scattered around the hall as people strained to get a better view. Sigurd lifted his hand to indicate silence and watched with interest. Holding her head high, Oonagh focused on her story and tried to ignore the sweat forming on her palms.

'My name is Oonagh,' she said, willing her voice not to shake. 'I have trained in healing all my life. My mother was a healer, as was her mother before her. I come to you to share my skills and find a home amongst you all.'

'From where do you hail?' a voice called from the crowd.

She was ready for this. 'I hail from the Sudreyjar, the Southern Islands. There has been much fighting there of late. People will not settle and accept peace. We tended the sick on all sides, taking no part in the quarrels, but a small number of men did not like this and turned on us for traitors.' Oonagh paused. She did not like to lie. She rested her hand on her rounded belly and felt a reassuring kick beneath her hand. The baby needed protection, the lie was not so far from the truth in a way and she certainly did not have to pretend her grief. The people watched, waiting eagerly for her to continue. The baby kicked again, urging her on.

'My parents were killed by the angry men and I managed to escape and run. I had nothing with me but my love of the islands and a need for peace.'

'What of your husband?' another called through the listening hush.

Both hands covered her bump protectively. The crowd wanted the story in all its detail but at the thought of Donal, she was becoming overwhelmed. 'He...' she faltered.

Through a veil of tears, Oonagh saw Sigurd rise to his feet. Heart in mouth she watched as he raised both hands for attention.

'Good folk,' he began. 'We have heard many tales of the unrest happening in the Sudreyjar but to turn on healers? This is shocking to us all. It is clear our new arrival has been through hard times. We are not ungracious enough that we need to put her through the memories as well.' He turned to Oonagh. 'Stories of your skills have reached my ears. Erelend here speaks most highly of you. As do one or two others you have helped. I am glad you felt able to come to Orkneyjar and trust in our peaceful ways. The Sudreyjar will be tamed in time and the people shall once again live in peace. Alas it is not only the Pictish but also Viking pirates from our own homeland that are causing trouble. But worry not, we will be your family now. Here you will be safe and your skills appreciated.' His smile was genuine. She nodded in response, not yet ready to trust her voice again.

Sigurd turned his attention to the crowd. 'Let no one here bother the healer with gossip from the past. A Pict who can see us for the good and peaceful people that we are must be respected.'

The people cheered their agreement. Oonagh and Erelend melted back into the crowd. Relief lightened her spirit at the knowledge she was safe, though her heart sat heavy in her chest. Talk of her family had rekindled her sadness, she wanted them with her so badly. On top of this she had come to realise how much she needed her mother to help her birth the babe. Her new friends has eased the burden of the long, lonely life stretched out before her but they couldn't keep her longings from burning beneath the surface.

After the meeting, the folk piled out into the crisp autumn sunshine. Feasting followed, during which Oonagh met most of the islanders. All were pleasant and polite. She relaxed more and more as the day wore on, then as the afternoon crept into evening, the revelry picked up. Drink flowed freely and someone began to tap a beat on a drum, a whistle quickly followed, and soon people were dancing and laughing. Oonagh was dragged up to join in. For the first time in weeks she found she was actually happy. The night wore on, the elderly, children and young families began to head to nearby houses or into the hall to sleep. Those that were left huddled nearer to the fire as the air chilled under the star-filled sky. Bears, hunters and dragons battled for space in the heavens and the moon shimmered inside her frosty orange halo. Peace descended for a while as the drum and whistle took a break, the silence broken only by the low hum of voices.

Before long, the melancholic sound of wooden pan pipes filled the air. The lilting melody rising and falling as it told its tale of woe. People snuggled close together, wrapped in heavy woollen cloaks. Many a festival night back home, Oonagh had huddled under blankets with her sisters down by Loch Nabaros, watching the very same hunter walk the night sky with his two dogs beside him. A tear slid its way down her cold cheek as she remembered. There would be no siblings for her baby to huddle up with in future years, it was going to miss out on so much. Laying her head down, she drifted off to sleep with the light of the fire dancing wildly across her face.

5

A loud knocking cut through the quiet of the early summer morning, someone was hammering on the cottage door. Oonagh rose quickly from her bed and went to answer it. On the doorstep was a boy of about twelve, he had clearly been running for he was out of breath and doubled over with a stitch. She recognised him at once.
'Your mother?' she asked. 'When?'
'She sent me soon as she was sure, just like you told her,' he said between pants. 'I've run all the way.'

'Bethoc,' Oonagh called into the main part of the house, 'I'm going to need you, Afreka's time is here.'
Afreka was an older mother, she had struggled with her last two pregnancies and lost the babies as a result. Oonagh was determined this time they would have a happy ending. Her daughter Bethoc, just like herself, had grown up shadowing her mother to learn the healing ways. At seventeen she was growing fast. Already she was tall like her father, with an abundance of dark curly hair. She had his hazel-coloured eyes too, even down to the tiny gold flecks. It made Oonagh proud to see Donal shining within her. Though the gutsy, stubborn streak Bethoc had been developing lately she could do without.
Over the years they had become an integral part of the small community. Bethoc was as much an

57

islander as the rest of the younger folk. Oonagh led a quiet life and kept to herself much of the time, though her friendship with Thora remained strong. The cottage she and Bethoc shared had become known as Picts Well. It too had blossomed under Oonagh's careful hand, no longer resembling an unloved victim of superstition and Trowie stalking. Oonagh smiled every time she remembered people warning her of the Trows and how they would take her baby away and leave a sickly changeling in its place. Bethoc had proved them all wrong in that. She had come out a healthy, squalling baby and barely had a day sick in her life.

Before many minutes had passed they were ready to leave and the three of them headed around the base of the Ward and into the valley that ran across the island. The lad took his leave of them and raced off towards the harbour loch to pass the news on to his aunt. Oonagh and her daughter hurried on past the great giant's stone where the dwarfs were said to hide and across into the Trowie Glen, heading between the stone cliffs they called the Hammers and up to the Knap. They skirted around the top of the Knap and crossed over the Pegal Burn, taking care not to see any horses by the waterside. The Nuggle was said to live here. A magnificent equine beast that would wait patiently by waterways for an unsuspecting person to mount it. Once astride, the horse would plunge into the water, drowning the sorry rider.

Not far from the burn under the protection of Withy Gill stood the little cottage. Oonagh noticed the thin spiral of smoke rising from the chimney. She smiled; hopefully that meant there was already water on the boil. Inside the cottage, Afreka was pacing, one hand on her cramping side and the other reaching out for whatever she could hold onto. Two girls aged about eight and ten were with her. The eldest had busied herself tearing an old sheet into large rags. She had a cauldron of water over the fire and a stock of firewood at hand to keep it going.

'My brother got the firewood ready last night,' she told them. 'I have done everything you asked, Oonagh, the water is boiling and the bed is covered in old blankets. I made sure they were clean as you said.'

The girl's chest puffed up with importance. She knew her mother was old for childbearing. She would always remember seeing the lifeless body of the last babe, so small it was hard to believe. The pasty white coating that covered its skin was streaked with birthing matter. She shuddered every time she thought of it but it was her mother's wail that had affected her the most. The keening had gone on for many hours, long after the little corpse had been laid to rest under the hazel tree by the back of the house.

Her sister was too young to remember, though she was bright enough to realise that everyone was doing their best to pretend they were not worried sick. She paced the floor with her mother, her little hand rubbing at the base of her back. Every time her mother stopped for another contraction she murmured soothing words and exaggerated her breathing as if to guide her.

'You are doing wonderfully,' Oonagh assured them with a smile. 'It's a wonder we will be needed at all.'

Bethoc nodded her agreement, 'It certainly is. How about I make us all a drink to keep us going?'

She set about making a pot of tea, using some of the collection of herbs they had brought with them. Rock rose to ease their worries, betony wood to drive away nervous exhaustion, wild chamomile for its calming effect and roseroot to give them endurance. For Afreka she made a simple infusion of raspberry leaf which they encouraged her to sip.

The day wore on and the pains grew closer together. A little after midday the expectant mother gave a deep groan and her knees buckled. They got her onto the bed and Oonagh checked her.

'You're nearly ready Afreka, now remember how we said? Nice and slow with the pushing. If the cord is in the wrong place again I am going to need time to move it.'

The two girls sat with wide eyes as their baby brother battled his way into the world. Bethoc held a stick for Afreka to bite down on so her energy wasn't wasted screaming in pain. As the head emerged Oonagh was able to get her fingers to hook the cord and slip it over the baby's head, removing the noose that had cost the last baby his life. One last push and the cottage was filled with the glorious sound of the baby's first cries. Faltering at first then growing stronger, louder and more urgent. His little hands splayed at the air, unsure of their newfound freedom. As soon as the cord was cut Bethoc swaddled the baby and passed him over to his exhausted mother. She helped her put him to the breast whilst Oonagh dealt with the passing of the placenta.

'You have a new baby brother,' she announced to the sisters, sitting holding hands with fingers tightly crossed.

'Is he..?' the older girl began but Bethoc cut her off. 'He is fine and healthy, didn't you hear those lungs?'

The girls both nodded, their eyes wide and bright.

'You will be fed up of hearing that noise soon enough.'

Oonagh came over to them with a ball of bloody rags in her hands. 'Your mother is fine too. Let's just give her a moment with the baby then we can get her all cleaned up and you can meet him yourselves.'

She put the bundle on the fire. Bethoc fished around for some aromatic herbs to throw on the flames and sweeten the smell. Then she got to work making a broth. They were all hungry, no one had bothered with food for hours.

It was evening by the time they made their weary way back home but it had been a good day. Babies died often but to lose two in a row had been especially hard for Afreka. At her age this was probably the last chance she would have. Oonagh understood that feeling all too well. She was not old but she had known when she was giving birth to

Bethoc that she would never have another child. No one could ever come close to filling the space Donal had left. She had felt relief when her baby had been a girl. Hardly daring to acknowledge it even to herself, she had secretly dreaded having a boy in case he was a mirror image of his father. She took hold of her daughter's hand and squeezed. 'You did well today, love. The girls really needed someone to keep them calm. I was proud of you.'

Bethoc grinned and squeezed back. The praise meant a lot to her. She couldn't think of anyone she would rather please or be like.

As they passed through the end of Trowie Glen they noticed the light shining at the top of the Ward.

'The Trows must be partying tonight,' Bethoc said.

Her mother answered with a grimace, 'Just don't tell Afreka or she will think they are coming after the baby.'

***

For the next week Oonagh visited the family every day. The baby was thriving and Afreka herself was recovering well and getting all the rest she needed. The girls had taken all her advice seriously, the chores were being done without complaint and they were fussing endlessly over their mother and new brother.

'I can see you are in good hands,' Oonagh told Afreka at the end of the week. 'So I will leave you alone now but if you have any trouble at all or you are worried, send the boy for me.'

She left the family content and made her way down to the burn to sit awhile under the trees that overshadowed the water. The Pegal burn reminded her of the little burn at Grumg-Mhor just before it left the woods and headed past the village. She sat down and let the water run over her hand, remembering a hot summer's day many years ago with her brothers and sisters. The twins were soon soaked as they challenged one another to various contests. Who could make the largest splash? Who could kick water the furthest? Serious Angus was always the judge of such games. Ffiona kept getting in the way, wanting to join in until Moira and Oonagh steered her away. Oonagh smiled as she remembered how they had piled stones across part of the stream to form a small pond. Here they had tried unsuccessfully to teach Ffiona to skim pebbles. As always though, eventually the happy memories were infiltrated by the unbidden thoughts of how her siblings' lives must have ended. She would hear their screams in her mind and see them gasping for breath in their smoke-filled home. Failing that, she imagined them being beaten or stabbed by the long sharp knife that had finished her beloved Donal.

Half blinded by her tears, she left the stream and began to make her way back over the moor. She failed to hear the warning cries of the angry bonxie as she strayed too close to its nest. Before she knew what was happening the bird had clattered into her, knocking her to the ground and clawing her scalp. She arrived home dishevelled and annoyed at herself, snapping uncharacteristically at Bethoc when she voiced her concern.

How much longer would the ghosts of the past torment her? She had thought they were buried safely at the back of her mind but just lately they seemed to want their freedom again. Poor Bethoc hadn't deserved the sharpness of her tongue. She had never told her daughter what had really happened to her and why she had fled to Haey, sticking instead to the story everyone else had been told. Bethoc had grown up believing her to be an only child just as she was. Oonagh sighed, she would have to make it up to her.

***

The boy arrived late one afternoon only a few weeks later. The baby was sick and Afreka desperate. Oonagh raced off to help, warning Bethoc she may be gone a long time. She had still not returned the following morning so Bethoc set to work scrubbing the floors. They were almost dry when Erelend called through the open door.

'There has been a bad accident down Vagaland,' he said. 'When will your mother be back?'

Bethoc shook her head, 'Not for a long while. Afreka's babe has the fever. What has happened?'

'Folks were quarrying rock when the stone face came away and buried a number of them.'

His face was grim, he shuffled his feet, unsure what to do next. Bethoc thought quickly, there was no time to wait for Oonagh or even to head off and get her. Her mother could not help but she could. She had learned enough now to be able to do her bit. She bid Erelend wait until she gathered together the supplies she thought she would need.
'I will just have to do what I can until she can get there,' she told him.

Vagaland was a small island just off the southeast coast of Haey, like a tail to the larger beast. It was much quicker to get to by boat than cross country and over the Giant's Causeway, which was only accessible at low tide. Erelend kept the boat close to shore as he navigated the way. Bethoc had a clear view of the tall cliffs. Much steeper here than further north, by the towering Old Man with his two legs striding to form a giant archway. There the cliffs were intermixed with grassy areas perfect for tunnel-loving tammie norries. Here kittiwakes and guillemots held sway, clinging to the cliff-face on precarious ledges splattered with droppings. At the bottom of the cliffs a scattering of selkies basked in the warm air, holding their tails up high. Bethoc watched them, fascinated in case one should start to shed its skin. Everyone had heard the stories of how the selkies came ashore to dance and ensnare unwary people with their beauty.
Erelend smiled, 'You're alright while you can see them. They never change in front of you.'
'Oh... was I that obvious?'

He pulled on the oars, keeping the boat steady ahead. 'I used to watch them all the time, wishing one would turn into a beautiful woman and dance just for me.'

He laughed at the surprise on her face. 'I might add, it was long before I had met Thora and yes I have had my fair share of ribbing from her about it.'

They rounded the southern tip of the island and Erelend guided the boat in past the ness and into the quiet bay. Bethoc could see right over to Cait in the distance. Sitting quietly in its bed of unpredictable waters between the mainland and Orkneyjar lay the island of Straumsey. The castle on the stack was very clear today, the pillar of rock was joined to the mainland by a narrow, rocky bridge. The first Norsemen had used this vantage point to build a stronghold to watch over the maelstrom waters that could either push a boat away or drag it towards its doom on the island's rocky coastline. Today the waters appeared calm and content, the white-tipped waters known locally as The Merry Men of Mey were hiding. Even the huge sea beast known to frequent the waters in calm weather, with its huge gaping mouth ready to swallow anyone in its way, was not in sight. A call from the shore brought her attention back and Bethoc readied herself as the boat bumped into the landing point. Two men were waiting to catch the rope and haul them in. She saw great swathes of kelp at the water's edge and asked Erelend to gather as much as he could, keeping the strands as long as possible. They left him to it and raced towards the quarry. Bethoc's heart was in her mouth, anxious as to what awaited her. She had never dealt with such an emergency before. One of the men brought her up to speed with the news. The quarry face had come away, killing one man and injuring two others. A further man was half buried and a lad of ten and his father were still to be found.

The quarry cut into the ground like a great mouth full of huge stone teeth. It formed a horseshoe shape, the far end of which was a bustle of activity. Two men gingerly lifted stones from a great mound of fallen rock, a chain of others then ferried them out of the way. In the middle of the quarry lay the body of the dead man. His head had taken the brunt of the fall; what remained was barely recognisable. Bethoc fought to control the churning in her stomach, moving quickly to the injured man a short distance away. A woman was sitting with him, she looked in shock at the pale-faced girl that came to help.

'Where is Oonagh? This is no place for a girl such as yourself. We need the healer.'

She made to push Bethoc away. Stubborn as ever despite her nerves, Bethoc swatted at her hand and knelt down by the patient.

'My mother is busy dealing with another emergency. Until she can get here I am all you have. Now are you going to fight me or help me?'

She glared at the woman, willing her not to hear the thumping of her heart. The woman harrumphed her disgust but didn't try to stop her any more. Bethoc checked the man over. His side was giving him a lot of pain and numerous dirty cuts covered his face and arm. He most likely had a rib or two broken but other than that he was not too bad. The sound of a man's agonised screams nearer to the rock fall told her others were not so lucky. She needed to prioritise.

'I am going to need hot water,' Bethoc told one of the men who had brought her up from the bay. 'Can you boil some for me?' Fishing in her bag, she found a jar of lady's mantle and yarrow salve and passed it to the woman.

'When the water is ready can you use some to clean his cuts then apply a little of this to them? Try not to move him too much until I have time to look at his ribs.'

She didn't wait for an answer. Grabbing her bag, she rushed over to where the screaming man lay with his arm trapped underneath a huge boulder. Her nerves vanished, there was work to be done. Everything she had learned from her mother came to her without effort. A quick glance at the situation was enough to see that she was going to have to cut the arm off. The boulder was far too big to lift and all efforts to roll it had failed and caused the man unbearable agony. It was clear the men around him had already realised this. They looked at her with horror.

'Right, I need a fire lit here and something clean,' she told them, fishing around in the bag for her tincture. 'Flat and metal with a wooden handle.'
'Miss, where is your mother?' the eldest one asked. 'This is no job for a lassie.'
The trapped man looked at her with pleading eyes. Bethoc gave him a reassuring smile before turning a cold face to the old man.
'Well, this lassie is all you have, so either you stand there complaining or you shut up and help me!'

She scanned the ground, looking for something. Finding it, she grabbed it and dropped to the ground beside her patient. 'I am going to give you something for the pain and then we are going to get you free,' she explained in a clear, calm voice. The man nodded his head and let her drip some tincture into his mouth, curling his nose up at the smell.
'It's the valerian in it,' she said. 'Smells like rotten, sweaty feet but it works wonders, especially with the other ingredients. Though it will take some time to take effect.' She kept a hand reassuringly on his good shoulder, she didn't want him to start panicking. She looked at the men. One had already got the fire started and another pulled a trowel from his pocket. The rest were standing, not knowing what to do.
'Have you got what is needed?' she asked them, willing them to understand. At first they looked puzzled then the old man clicked and nodded.

'Give me a minute,' he answered and rushed off. The rest hovered, ashamed that a girl had more courage than they did.

'Can you clear these rocks away to give us more room?' she asked them.

They set to work, eager for the distraction. The bustle gave the injured man something else to focus on whilst the minutes passed.

Bethoc watched him carefully. His eyes were starting to look slightly glassy, a sure sign the tincture was beginning take effect. She must keep him calm at all cost.

'Can you count for me?' she asked. 'Count up to ten slowly and the medicine will start to work.'

Together they counted to ten, then they counted again. The tincture was the strongest she had, it would make most people sleep but with the amount of pain he was in it would not knock him out completely. He would still feel what she was going to do but the more relaxed she could get his body, the less he would feel and the easier it would be for all of them.

Someone patted her on the shoulder and she turned to see the old man had returned with a saw, holding it behind his back where his friend couldn't see. She nodded at him.

'I gave it a wash first, miss,' he told her. 'Thought that would be best.'

Bethoc smiled at him, he had some sense. 'Do you think you will be able to help me?'

The man gulped but nodded his head firmly. 'Can't say as I have had any real practice, mind.'

Not wanting to admit that she hadn't either, she busied herself getting ready. She pulled some leaves of bugle, gypsywort and plantain out of her bag and prepared a quick poultice. Next she tied a strip of linen tightly around the top of the man's arm. He winced.

'You are still going to feel this, I'm afraid, but it will be over quickly. I promise.' She placed the stick she had picked up earlier between his teeth. 'Bite down on this if it gets too much to bear.'

She looked up at the other men, they had cleared a wide space around them and were hovering, unsure.

'Ready?' she asked. 'I'm going to need you to hold him still and can someone put that trowel in the fire.'

Mollified by the young girl's determination, every man there nodded and got ready, despite the white faces and looks of dread. Taking the saw, she began to cut. The man screamed and writhed. Someone put the stick back in his mouth and held it there for him to bite on and the others did their best to hold him steady. She started to struggle as the saw hit the bone and the old man took over. Using long, deft strokes he made short work of the grisly job. Wrapping her hand in rags, Bethoc grabbed the handle of the trowel and pressed the metal onto the wound. The man's screams curdled in his throat but his movements were weakening. The smell of cauterising flesh filled the air and one of the men turned away, gagging.

'Did Erelend bring the kelp?' she called to no one in particular.

'Here,' someone cried and rushed over with a handful. It was the woman. 'He has gone back to wait for your mother.'

Bethoc covered the stump with the poultice, wrapped it all in kelp, and covered it with linen bandages. She cooled the man's brow with water and fed him some more tincture. All the while she kept talking to him in her softest voice, telling him how well he was doing and how brave he was. Finally he closed his eyes and let the herbs ease him to sleep.

'You did well, lass,' the old man commented. She nodded, not trusting her voice, but there was no time to talk. A shout had gone up near the rubble pile. Someone had been found.

Over the next two hours the boy and his father were gradually freed from their temporary graves. The boy had been alive when they found him, clinging tightly to the hand of his father. Despite everything she tried, Bethoc could not save him. Exhausted, she sat down with the rescue team and tried not to look at the three bodies, covered with blankets. Someone pushed a hot drink into her hand.

'I am sorry lass, I was wrong to doubt you,' the woman told her. 'No one could have done more than you today.'

'Aye,' the old man joined in. 'You've sure showed us a thing or two.' He gave a wry smile. 'There's no many round here would have spoken to me the way you did but I deserved it today.'

Bethoc said nothing, now the adrenalin rush of the afternoon was wearing off the shock was setting in. She was shattered, filthy, and could not get the young boy's face out of her mind. It was with great relief she heard her mother's voice as Oonagh rushed into the quarry with Erelend.

6

The tale of how Bethoc had fought to save the boy after taking off the quarryman's arm, saving his life in the process, was told to Oonagh many times. The people of Vagaland had found a new heroine and she couldn't be more proud of her daughter. That day would be remembered for a long time to come. She herself had come home from the cottage at Pegal burn, tired but happy. The baby had pulled through and was going to be fine. She was looking forward to putting her feet up and having a drink with her daughter. Instead she found Erelend waiting and her emergency supplies missing.

Despite all the praise, it took Bethoc some time to get over the events at the quarry. The young boy's face continued to haunt her long after the stories had faded.

'I learned something interesting at the cove this morning,' Oonagh told her weeks later as she removed her cloak. She moved over to the fire and held her hands out to warm. There was a definite touch of autumn in the air.

Bethoc looked up from her sewing. She had avoided the cove for a while now, not wanting to see the boats and be reminded of her trip with Erelend.

'It turns out the boy was at the quarry because his mother died the year before,' Oonagh said. 'He and his dad were inseparable, they went everywhere together.'

'Oh...' Bethoc didn't know what to say. Wasn't it wrong to be relieved that someone had died?

Oonagh gave the cooking pot over the fire a stir and sat down. 'Like I have been trying to tell you, sometimes people die for the right reasons.'

Bethoc felt the weight of blame fall from her shoulders. She looked at her mother and smiled, 'I would still have tried to save him if I'd have known, though.'

Her mother nodded. 'Of course you would,' she replied. 'Everyone deserves a chance to be saved. You just have to accept that sometimes there is another path for them.'

Bethoc sighed. Fate worked in strange ways but at last she could see that it had worked out right for the boy.

By the time the next Thing came round, Bethoc was more than ready for a night of fun.

However, when the time for announcements came, Bethoc was shocked to hear her name mentioned. The one-armed quarryman hailed her achievements for the whole island to hear. Everyone cheered and clapped both Bethoc and Oonagh on the back. Two new faces in particular watched all this with mounting interest. Thorstein the Red was back on one of his flying visits, this time bringing his son Olaf with him.

That evening Bethoc received more attention than ever. She mingled along with Groa, laughing and joking. Olaf especially was very keen to get to know her. Oonagh smiled as she watched her daughter joining in the dancing. She deserved some fun. This was most likely the last chance she would get to catch up with everyone for many months. The abundance of berries on the trees and bushes was a sure sign of a harsh winter to come. Company would be in short supply for the girls until spring. Oonagh, on the other hand, kept herself away from the limelight as usual. Though it was a long time since she had worried about her safety, the reclusive lifestyle had become a habit. She had her close friends and was more than content to sit quietly near the fire.

***

The signs had proved correct in every way. Winter was the harshest they had seen for many years. Birds perished in the trees and the shoreline was littered with washed-up corpses of sea life tossed up from the constantly angry sea. Oonagh and Bethoc were kept busy with a nasty winter virus that laid low almost every islander on their side of Orkneyjar. Imbolc came and to everyone's dismay the day was bright and sunny. Nature's warning of six more weeks of winter. By mid-April everyone was well and truly sick of the weather and looking forward to Beltane and the hope of finally getting some sun.

***

The feather fluttered in the breeze, the quill firmly held in place by a small, flat stone. Bethoc squealed when she found it, racing inside to show her mother.

'Who can have sent it? Did you see anyone?'

Oonagh shook her head, her insides a turmoil. The feather was like a key, unlocking the iron door in her mind behind which she had hidden the bittersweet memories of her own Beltane morn all those years before. She hastily shoved the thoughts away.

'I saw no one, darling. Who do you think it is from?'

'I have no idea, do you think Groa has one too? Oh Mother, would you mind if I go and ask her?'

As the dusk fell later that day, Oonagh sat on Cuilags Hill looking out over the sea. It was one of her favourite spots for quiet contemplation. Every so often the peace was interrupted by the funny clapping noises of the tammie norries' wings slapping together as they came into land on the clifftop below. They always made her smile, such strange little birds with their black and white feathers and bright rainbow bills. If she turned her head left and looked out over the waves, she could imagine Cait and her old home. She wondered what everyone would look like now if they had lived. Even little Ffiona would be a mother and the twins would have settled down with families of their own. She grinned as she realised that her mother would be an old woman now. She had always refused to become one. Regularly telling her children that, should she become old, they had to finish her off with a big stick. Of course no one had agreed.

The merry dancers lit up the sky to the north, pulling Oonagh's mind back to the present. Green and purple light flitted across the sky like a bright halo. It was as if the sky was smiling down on her. This was her daughter's time to shine, she would not let her sadness spill over into Bethoc's happiness and mar it. With a last look over towards Cait she set her resolve and headed back towards home.

***

On Beltane morning, Oonagh helped an over-excited Bethoc into her white dress and helped tie on her mask. Just as her mother had done to her, she kissed her daughter on the forehead and held the door open. Watching as she sped off into Berriedale forest. In cottages all over the north, mothers were doing exactly the same thing. Feeling exactly the same mixed emotions as their daughters embarked on their first forays into real adulthood. Luckily there were no young males on Haey that worried Oonagh, or on Vagaland for that matter. She doubted her daughter's stag could be from any of the other islands.

Bethoc was filled with excitement. She had dreamed of finding true love for as long as she could remember. She didn't want the life her mother had, all alone. She wanted what Groa's parents had. Every time she saw them together she realised just how lonely her mother must be. Oonagh would not even contemplate looking for another man. Whenever the subject came up she would say Bethoc's father was the most wonderful man she had ever met and no man could ever take his place. Then her eyes would become so sad and she would excuse herself for a while. Bethoc would hear the quiet sounds of her mother weeping.

Thora and Erelend were always touching and kissing. Their love had never diminished over the years, if anything it had grown stronger. They were the best of friends and the most committed people Bethoc had ever met. Her friend's father was just how she imagined her husband would be with their own children, how she imagined her own father would have been with her.

She didn't want to hide away in the trees waiting to see if fate would drive her stag to find her. She wanted to stretch her arms out in full view and race to meet him.

Impatiently, she waited for dawn to break.

She had found the perfect place, mayflower blossomed all around and a soft carpet of grasses covered the floor. A brook gurgled away happily nearby and the air was full of dawn chorus birdsong. She sat down to wait, daydreaming every possible perfect scenario she could.

He stood behind the tree for the longest while watching her, letting his anticipation grow. Loving the way a shaft of sunlight broke through the trees and danced with her hair. Stepping out from his hiding place, he slowly walked towards her. She had her eyes closed, smiling. Her face radiated beauty, pale skin with pink cheeks and a rosebud mouth. He bent and lightly brushed her lips with his own.

She had heard him coming but for a moment nerves had got the better of her and she had hidden behind her closed eyelids. At the touch of his mouth on hers, her eyes flew open and she saw with amazement that it was Olaf behind the mask. She had forgotten all about him since the Thing, not even realising he was back on the island.

He took her hands and pulled her to her feet. Then he kissed her knuckles and looked deeply into her eyes. She felt her soul touched and the tiny hairs along her spine stood on end. Her heart raced, pumping the blood through her veins so fast she could almost hear the rushing sound in her ears. He dropped her hands and brought his right hand up to her throat, stroking the smooth skin until he reached her chin. Gently, he lifted her face as he brought his mouth down on hers once again. This time the kiss was not so light, it was searching, probing. Finding every nerve ending and melting it until her insides were a fused glow of joyous awakening. Sliding her hands around his neck, she pulled him deeper. She felt his hands searching her body, feeling every inch. Eventually they broke apart and she reached up and pulled at the tie holding her shift.

Naked, she stood before him, watching his eyes as they travelled downwards. New feelings she had never experienced before bubbled up inside her. Intimate feelings, shocking feelings, and a strange new awareness of her own personal power. Power over the man that stood before her, shedding his own clothes and revealing his reaction to her. She longed to take him in her arms and feel him the way he had felt her. They stepped together again before falling to the ground.

Afterwards they lay looking up at the shaft of sunlight still breaking through the leafy canopy overhead. Bethoc knew her life had changed forever. Her fingers intertwined with Olaf's when finally he spoke.
'I am never leaving Haey again.'

***

She skipped back to the cottage much later. Ignoring tradition, they had spent the rest of the morning talking. Getting to know each other, feeding more fuel to the fire of young love that was starting to burn within her. Oonagh noted the grin stuck to her daughter's face and her heart swelled with pleasure. Pushing the fingers of memories back into their confinement, refusing firmly to let them taint this precious moment. History would not repeat itself, her daughter would have her happy ending. She busied herself making a lavender and chamomile tea for them both then, focusing her attention solely on her daughter, she sat down

at the table and listened as Bethoc told her all about
Olaf.

In the weeks that followed Olaf became a regular
visitor. Always polite and respectful, treating
Bethoc as though she was the most precious girl in
the world. The weather picked up and the young
lovers spent hours walking hand in hand around
the island. Bethoc would return from these walks
with a handful of wildflowers or a bag of foraged
herbs for her mother. The smile never left her face
and there was a new lightness to her step. Her life
stretched out before her with new meaning.
In the times when he wasn't with her she imagined
what her future would be. Olaf as her husband,
father of their children and the soulmate she never
knew she had needed. Her life felt complete, secure
and whole. Finally she realised just what her
mother must have gone through when she lost her
father. Bethoc could not imagine the pain of losing
Olaf, the very idea filled her with cold dread. She
tried to include Oonagh as much as possible,
pleased that Olaf was more than happy to oblige.

By the time the Summer Thing came round,
Bethoc was brimming with excitement. The whole
island would see them together. Not only that,
Olaf's family had made a special trip to meet her.
With Oonagh at her side, Bethoc made her way
over to them. Thurid was a dowdy-looking Norse
woman with a strong chin and fierce eyes.
'My mother,' Olaf introduced her.

She spoke in a clipped voice and kept her welcome brief. Her eyes flickered over Oonagh and she gave her a slight nod.

Olaf's many sisters giggled before Thurid silenced them with a glare. Olaf's father, Thorstein, was more polite. He took Bethoc's hand in his and gave a slight bow.

'I am honoured to meet with you at last my dear.' Glancing to Oonagh he added, 'Both of you. It is a great shame our paths have never crossed before this time but I am afraid I am seldom in the islands any more.'

A slight shiver prickled at the back of Oonagh's neck. She disregarded it quickly. She really must stop being so funny with strangers.

'Olaf tells me your work for Sigurd takes you all over.'

'Indeed it does, though I have high hopes my life will be much more settled soon.' He smiled at his son. 'Olaf is taking the lead in that department, aren't you?'

His son nodded. 'The farm is starting to come along nicely now I have taken control for you.'

The girls started to giggle again, quickly hushed by their mother. She nodded to Bethoc and Oonagh and led the girls away to find their place at the top of the hall.

Thorstein watched them go before speaking again.

'You must excuse my wife,' he explained. 'She does not like it that her son is so far away from her.'

Bethoc sat with Olaf and his family, she would be spending the next few days with them. Taking the opportunity to get to know them before they left the island again. Oonagh made her excuses and went to sit in her usual place. It was strange not having her daughter beside her but she was going to have to get used to it soon enough. She was sure that it was only a matter of time before wedding plans were announced and she would have to face her future alone. All evening she watched the proceedings with a strange sense of unreality. The sudden feeling of being an outsider again was overwhelming and she found herself eager to return home and hide herself away. She waited until everyone's attention was focused elsewhere then slipped away, unseen.

***

The sky darkened in a matter of minutes, they had been too distracted to notice the warning signs. A few tentative drops of rain landed but before they had even risen to their feet a torrent of skyfall ensued. Drenched, they sought cover in the nearby woods and hastily struggled into their soaked clothing. Olaf helped Bethoc straighten her tunic.

'It won't always be like this,' he told her. 'When we have a place of our own we will be able to make love whenever we want in our own bed.'

'But I can't leave my mother, Olaf, I am all she has.'

Olaf stroked her hair and pulled her close. 'She can live with us too, darling, she can help take care of all our children.'

She pulled back to look him in the eye, her insides somersaulting. 'You want lots of children?'

'Don't you? I thought you would love the idea, you always say it has been lonely growing up without brothers and sisters.'

She grinned, 'I would love a big family. I cannot believe just how perfect we are for each other.'

'We are bound together throughout eternity, my darling. Every life we have lived, we have found each other and so it will continue.' Placing a kiss on her wet forehead he added, 'But now you are getting cold and we must get you home and dry.'

***

Days passed in a dream. Olaf started to spend more and more time at the cottage. He took care of all the maintenance that had been overlooked down the years, tidied up the parts of the garden not used for herbs or crops. He even went down the well to check everything was in order. He was kind and generous, always polite and well mannered. Nothing was too much trouble for him. Today he had his head and shoulders up the chimney. Oonagh tried voicing her concern over how much time he spent helping them when he had his father's farm to oversee but he would hear none of it.

'Well I am very grateful for all your help, Olaf. Bethoc is certainly a very lucky girl having you. And so, for that matter, am I, that chimney has needed looking at for ages now.' Olaf ducked his head back down and looked into the room.

'I think it is just some loose stones and plenty of soot. I will have it cleared in no time.'

'And I will have the job of getting you clean again,' Bethoc said as she came into the room and saw the sight of him. She laughed and glanced at her mother, a frown clouded her brow. 'Mother, are you feeling unwell?'

Her mother rarely suffered with her health but today she looked tired and her skin was even paler than usual. It was typical that she hadn't mentioned it.

'I must admit I have been feeling a little under the weather,' she confessed. 'I am so tired and I ache all over.'

Bethoc fussed around, preparing a herbal tea. Chamomile, yarrow, mint and lemon balm steeped in a pot before she poured it into a mug and made Oonagh sit and drink it. She put the back of her hand to her mother's head and was surprised at how hot she was.

'Mother, you are close to a fever, I think you should take your tea to bed with you and get some rest... I can sort out everything here.' She added when Oonagh made to argue, 'Let me look after you for once.'

'Yes, do,' came a muffled voice from the chimney.

Knowing she was beaten, Oonagh retired to bed. She really did feel awful.

By the next morning the fever had taken a firm hold. Bethoc cancelled her plans with Olaf and stayed to nurse Oonagh, she had never seen her mother so ill. Delirium clouded her words and Bethoc struggled to understand the strange snippets she raved about. She heard Grumg-Mhor mentioned a number of times and fire and running. She laid cool cloths on her mother's forehead, replacing them every few minutes as they quickly heated up. Between short periods of blissfully calm sleep, the ramblings continued. It upset Bethoc greatly.

'I just can't understand it,' she confided in Olaf when he called in later with fresh eggs. 'I have never heard her talk like this. It sounds like she is having a nightmare and she keeps talking about a Grumg-Mhor? I have no idea what that is.'

'I am sure it's the fever,' he reassured her. 'Do you want me to sit with her for a while?'

Bethoc smiled, 'You are a dear but no, Mother would never forgive me if I let you see her like this.'

Reluctantly, she chased him from the cottage and returned to her mother's bedside. All through the night and the next day they barely got any sleep. Oonagh became more and more distressed, clinging onto her daughter and screaming at her to run. Through her tears, Bethoc struggled to calm her until finally the fever broke and her mother fell into a dreamless sleep.

Morning broke and with it Oonagh's senses returned. Bethoc approached the subject of Grumg-Mhor with trepidation. Her mother looked shocked but recovered her composure after a sip of water. Her face fell to one of resignation as she held out her hand.

'There are many things I have not told you about my past,' she admitted, 'I had intended to take them with me to my grave.'

Bethoc pulled over a stool and took her mother's limp hand in hers. Until then she had told herself her mother was just locked in a bad dream and that none of it made sense but her reaction gave no doubt that whatever had caused her such distress was in fact real. 'You can tell me anything, Mother dear. You sounded so distressed yesterday, I cannot bear the thought of you holding all that in.'

Oonagh tried to squeeze her daughter's hand in reassurance but the effort was feeble and barely felt.

'It was a very long time ago and I must confess I rarely think of it nowadays so you must not upset yourself.' She paused for another sip of water then began her tale.

'I was really born in Cait and lived in a small place called Grumg-Mhor in Strathnabaros, a valley that runs down from the sea to a big loch near to our village. We all lived in a small house. My father, mother, and my brothers and sisters. I had three sisters, Moira, Sionagh and little Ffiona. And two brothers, Angus, and Sionagh's twin Taran.'

Bethoc held her breath and forced herself not to interrupt with the multitude of questions now running through her mind.

'Then one Beltane I received my feather and that was how I met your father.' She paused for a moment, a smile playing in the lights of her eyes. 'Oh, he was a handsome man and so perfect, just like your young man is for you. I loved him so very much. We used to meet up the hill in the woods as often as we could. Only my mother suspected. We had to keep it quiet you see because Donal was the Maor's son. There was trouble in the area, Vikings were trying to invade and some had been seen not far away. Donal was kept very busy with his father, searching for the men. Then one day we found them. Up in the woods.' Oonagh paused for another drink. Bethoc helped her to sit up whilst she sipped then laid her back down again and waited eagerly as her mother remembered. Oonagh's eyes glazed over and she was back in the forest.

'It was a perfect day and I was so happy. My love had just proposed to me and the world was bright and cheerful. As we walked back down to the village we heard the men. Donal made me hide but they caught him. They killed him right there before me.' Her voice broke as she said the words and a tear escaped her eye, trickling slowly down to the pillow, but she didn't stop.

'I grabbed our horse and ran. They chased me a long way and I heard them behind me. They were going to burn my village with me and everyone else inside. I could not let that happen, so I turned away from home and led them far away over the hill. It took me two days to get back. I stopped at a village further along the strath first and that's when I found out.' This time her voice faltered to a stop. Bethoc's blood ran cold, she was not sure she wanted to hear what came next. She stroked her mother's trembling hand and waited.

A great heaving sob wrenched from her mother. 'I found my whole family had been killed, burnt by those butchers. The whole village gone. Whilst I was staying with the man who was going to take me back they came again, looking for me. He made me run again. I didn't know where to go. Everywhere I went would be unsafe for everyone. I had to hide, I could have gone up the strath to the sea but what then? So I came to Orkneyjar where the Norse already were. I thought they would not look for me here and I would be safe. And so I was, we were. For I found out not long after I came here that I was carrying you.'

The questions froze in Bethoc's mind. Each time she picked on one to ask, it shattered into a myriad of new ones. Finally grasping at the only thing she had ever known about her mother she asked, 'But what about the islands, the Sudreyjar?'

Oonagh shook her head. 'Just a story. I needed them to think I was from a Norse place then they would accept me. I couldn't trust anyone and once

the story was told it was easier just to keep on with it.'
'But your family. Were they all gone?'
'The man who told me, the drover. He said everyone was dead. Some may have escaped to the trees but before they could go and look they were all killed as well. I heard the screams myself. So I did as he bade me and ran.'

A rap at the door interrupted them. Olaf was there, looking agitated.
'Your mother is needed on Grims Isle. Is she well enough?'
Bethoc shook her head. 'She cannot go,' she explained. 'What has happened?'
'The old fisher wife on the island had a fall and passed away in the night.'
Oonagh was often called on to prepare the dead. It was one of the over-riding beliefs of the islanders and a matter of deep importance; if a body was not immediately laid out and bound, the deceased could return and haunt the living. This particular old woman was known for her disagreeable nature and threatening such an act had been common in her final years. Having no family of her own, the job fell to the healers.
Bethoc had no choice. Never before had she left the house to work with such bad grace.
Before leaving, she sorted out her mother so she would be comfortable until she returned. Her eyelids were already heavy and it would not be long before she was asleep again. Kissing her on the

forehead, Bethoc left the cottage with Olaf. Together they raced over the island to where a boat was waiting to take Bethoc across the narrow stretch of water to the neighbouring island. Olaf left her at the shore, a crisis at the farm had to be dealt with. He had already left it as long as he could. For once Bethoc was relieved, her mind was a confusion of thoughts and she needed time to sort them all out. Besides which, she wasn't ready to talk about what she had just learned yet. They were her mother's secrets and until she had spoken to her again she would not discuss them, even with Olaf.

Cleansing herbs in the water filled the room with their heady scent. Bethoc wondered absently who had washed the bodies of her mother's family, *her* family, she realised with a shock. She looked at the old lady and the dried blood at the side of her temple and her mind was brought back to what she was supposed to be doing. Clearing her thoughts, she began to wash the body, wasting no time. Once it was dried and re-dressed, she got one of the neighbouring men to help her lift it into a crude wooden coffin. She sprinkled the chest with salt then stood back whilst the man drove the stake through the body, securing it to the coffin. Now the local people could relax. So long as no one spoke her name until after the burial she would not be coming back. Bethoc really should have done more, afforded the woman the respect of cleaning up her home and keeping an aromatic fire burning overnight, but her mother was far more important. Apologising to the corpse, she broke with tradition and left.

7

The door creaked slightly as he eased it open. Stepping inside, he glanced quickly around the room. It was just as they had left it a short while before. Good, she was still in bed. He crept towards the bedroom and slipped inside. She lay there, eyes closed but with the residue of tears still clinging to her face. Disgust filled him, it had been so hard to feign niceness to this woman, all the while knowing who she might be. Now though, he had finally got the proof he had been sent to find and he would pretend no more. He hooked one of his feet around the leg of the stool and pulled it towards him. Her eyes flew open at the noise, startled. She eased when she saw who it was but looked puzzled as he sat down.

'I thought you had gone with Bethoc?' Oonagh asked.

He nodded, 'I did but now I am back.'

His tone threw her. Gone was the caring voice, the understanding and concern she had learned to associate with him. In its place was a harder, abrupt air of what she could only interpret as... hatred.

'Oh, you can look at me like that,' he told her, keeping his voice calm and low but full of animosity.

Oonagh felt a frisson of fear run up her spine. In her weakened state she could not understand what was going on.

'Where is Bethoc?'

'Where is the necklace?' came his retort.

Oonagh's head was foggy with fatigue. 'Olaf, I don't understand. What is the matter? Where is Bethoc?'

'Your daughter is on Grims Isle where I sent her.' He snarled. 'I needed her out of the way whilst I talked to you.'

'But I thought a woman had died?' None of this was making any sense. Was she hallucinating?

'Oh she died alright, most obliging of her considering I held her neck until she did. There are ways of making no marks.' He chuckled, 'And there are ways of making marks good enough to fool anyone else into thinking it was just an unfortunate accident. Something you had better remember, Oonagh.' Her name twisted from his mouth, laced with derision.

Now she was scared, the frisson of fear had developed into cold, hard dread. She struggled to lift herself from the bed but he pushed her back down and leered over her. He tapped his fingers sharply into her collarbone.

'Where... is... the... neck... lace?' he staccatoed with each jab.

'What necklace? What do you mean?' What on earth had happened to the lovely young man they had welcomed into their family?

His voice rose slightly, 'You stole the necklace from my father and you ran away with it.' His hand hovered menacingly close to her throat.

The assumption shocked her. 'Olaf, I have never stolen anything in my life.'

He grabbed a handful of her hair and hung on tightly. 'You stole the necklace from my father after he killed the miserable oaf you were in love with. He had to burn five villages to try and find you. I know it's you, you talk when you have a fever. Did you know that? And your stupid daughter told me all about it.'

Wincing at the pain, Oonagh tried to think. It was amazing how easily fear drove away the fog. Bethoc was far away and safe for now. That was good. She tried to remember about the necklace. It was hard after so many years. She had never given it a moment's thought after she buried it. Somehow a broken piece of jewellery did not compare to losing everyone she loved so dearly.

'I don't remember a necklace.'

Olaf kicked the stool away from him and marched around the room, his temper rising with every step.

'Do you have any idea what that necklace was, woman?' he chided as she shook her head. 'It was the lost necklace of Hildr, with the power to render any opponent tamed. It was lost in the battle of Prince Hedinn and King Hogni on this very island hundreds of years ago. Somehow it found its way into a Pictish leader's hands years later. He gave it to his wife, who tried to take it to the afterworld with her. But my father found the grave and took it back. With it he would have subdued all of Cait and your ignorant people. We should have been leaders, commanders, instead of battle-weary fighters. And now here I am pretending to the likes of you and your girl. Crawling here instead of being home with my wife.'

The venom with which he spoke shocked Oonagh to the core. He had pretended so well, been so helpful.

'So that is why you have done all that work here at the house?' She needed to keep him talking while she thought of a way out of this. She needed to buy them enough time so they could get away. Far from the islands, far from the north this time.

Olaf spat on the floor, his lips curling in distaste. 'My father knew it must be you the minute he heard about Bethoc at the quarry. The brave daughter of a Pictish woman who had arrived on the island almost twenty years ago? He knows Sudreyjar very well you know, it didn't take him long to prove you were never there. You did well keeping quiet for so long. He had begun to think you had died. Very clever coming to live here. You think you are very clever, don't you. You Pictish scum.' He grabbed her hair again and leaned close.

'I miss my wife,' he hissed, spittle spraying her face. 'I miss her in my bed. Now, where... is... the... neck... lace?' This time his words were punctuated by her head being rammed against the cottage wall. Pain coursed through her, chasing all thoughts of escape away. Blood ran down into her eyes and she tasted its metallic tang in her mouth.

'Please,' she begged. 'I don't know.'

He hit her across the face with the back of his hand, sending her hurling from the bed onto the stone floor. She lay sobbing, muttering over and over that she did not know. For so long she had kept her secret, so long she had kept them safe. Never realising it would all be undone by the ramblings of her fevered mind and the callousness of Thorstein, sending his son to catch them out. She remembered the cold feeling she had when she had met Thorstein at The Thing. He must be the man who had been in charge of the three who had killed Donal; she never had heard his name. Pain dulled her memories, she could not picture what he had looked like other than the typical blond hair of the Norse.

What a fool she had been, thinking she could ever be safe from these people. She had led her daughter into a trap. Dismay fuelled her resolve. She had taken the necklace because it was important to Donal. She would stand by him until her dying day and she would never tell Olaf where it was. She screamed as he stood on her hand, feeling the fingers break beneath his weight.

'Maybe we should wait until Bethoc returns?' he asked her.

Terror stilled her heart for a second until it lurched back into life, threatening to burst out of her chest.

'Alright,' she whispered, lifting her head to squint at him through her blood-filled eyes. 'I threw it into the forest when I ran.'

He roared his anger, drew back his foot and piled it into her stomach with all the force he could muster. There was an explosion of pain and she knew he had done her serious damage.

'Where?' he yelled, bending and grabbing her face between his fingers and thumb, nipping as hard as he could.

She looked him straight in the eye, using all her will to play for time. 'I don't remember. I was too busy running.'

Everything went dark as his fist slammed into her face.

***

Bethoc found her there a few hours later. The door was swinging in the breeze and she was immediately alert, knowing she had closed it securely when she left. Inside she found the cottage ransacked. Crockery smashed, furniture overturned. Bethoc burst into the bedroom, yelling for her mother, and found her curled in a bloody heap on the floor. She was breathing but only just.

'Mother,' she cried. 'What happened, can you hear me?'

Her mother groaned and her eyes twitched. Bethoc grabbed a cushion for her head and raced for a damp cloth. Gently she began to tease the blood from her face, giving her mother more time to regain her senses.

Suddenly Oonagh grabbed her hand. 'Olaf,' she started. Her voice struggling through her swollen mouth.

Bethoc shook her head. 'No Mother, he isn't here, he had to go home to work. Do you need me to get him?'

Terror filled Oonagh's eyes. 'No!' she mumbled. 'He... did this.'

Bethoc didn't even pause in her response. 'No, Mother – you're mistaken. Olaf would never do this.'

Oonagh's hand squeezed tighter, nipping her daughter's skin. 'Listen to me Bethoc, Olaf is a bad man. His father killed Donal, your father. He's found me. He sent Olaf to find the necklace.'

Blood trickled from the side of Oonagh's mouth as she struggled with the words. Her daughter watched the crimson line grow longer. Reason danced with reality and Bethoc found herself unable to connect the two.

'Mother, Thorstein is a good man. He liked you when he met you. He asked me all about you later, and Olaf, he has always been concerned for you.' The hairs started to prickle at the back of her neck as unbidden memories tugged at her.

She had tried to ignore how uncomfortable she felt when Thorstein and his family were at the Skali. Olaf's mother, aloof and condescending, had barely said a word. The girls too had giggled behind their hands, watching her with thinly veiled curiosity as though she were an object for their entertainment. Thorstein himself had always been polite but all his questions, now she came to remember, had been about Oonagh not herself. She tried to shake away the doubt that was starting to creep into her veins.

Thorstein may have been too inquisitive but Olaf was her soulmate. Together throughout eternity, he had told her. How could he possibly have done this? Yet here they both were, huddled on the cold stone floor of their wrecked cottage, covered in her mother's blood. Someone had to have done it.

Then as if she could feel her blood turning to icicles and stabbing right into her heart, she realised. She had told Olaf all about her mother's fevered ramblings. Never guessing for a moment that she was feeding him everything he needed to hear. Oonagh's voice was failing fast and came out barely louder than a whisper.

'The necklace, it was more important than I realised. I hid it and they want it.'

 Olaf had asked about a necklace. Bethoc recalled the day, not long after they had met. He had told her that her neck was so perfect it should be highlighted with something of beauty. When she admitted she owned no jewellery he had insisted her mother must have something she could wear. Reason and reality almost fused.

'What is the necklace, Mother?' she asked.

'Your father stole it from them. It is... shiny black stones... half-moon shape... broken.'

Bubbles of blood were appearing now and Oonagh's words were becoming harder to discern. Bethoc grabbed her drink of water and eased some into her mother's mouth. Oonagh swallowed gratefully.

'Let me get you comfortable and give you something to ease your pain,' Bethoc urged but her mother shook her head.

'Under the marker stone, up the hill away from Grumg-Mhor.' She forced the words out. 'That is where I put it. Even though I broke it, I didn't want them to have it. I told him I had dropped it, they must never find it.'

A noise from outside made them jump. Oonagh's eye were wide with fear. Bethoc ran to check but it was only the door swinging in the wind. The catch had been broken off, so she pushed a stone against it to hold it still and raced back to the bedroom. Gathering her mother back into her arms, she was alarmed to hear the ominous rattle of Oonagh's breath. A film was beginning to form over her eyes. The effort of staying conscious long enough to pass on the warning was ebbing away the last of her strength. She needed one last thing before she could go.

'You must leave this island, Bethoc, it is not safe for you here. I am so sorry.'

A tear cut a lonely line down her face as she spoke, she knew oh so well how frightening it was to leave everything and everyone you had ever known behind. 'Leave now, tonight.'

The words rocked through Bethoc like barbs. 'I cannot leave you, Mother. You need my help.'

Even as she said the words she knew her mother was lost but she could not bring herself to accept it. 'Dying now... Promise me,' Oonagh insisted, her words little more than breath.

The bright red blood from her mouth contrasted starkly with the pale greying pallor of her face. Yet more blood pooled in her hair and crusted around her forehead. Bethoc wiped the blood away one last time but more appeared almost immediately. Through her tears she nodded, stroking the side of her mother's face that was not so badly damaged. Her tears dripped down to mingle with the blood.

'I promise.' They were the hardest words she would ever have to say.

How long she sat there, she couldn't tell. It could have been minutes or hours. She never heard her mother's final breath. At one point she looked down and realised her mother had simply ceased to live. All she was left with was her battered and bleeding body.

***

Cold and stiffness eventually forced Bethoc into action. She placed her mother's body gently down onto the floor and eased herself to standing. Numb with shock, she could not think straight. Burrowing her face in her hands she felt an unusual roughness. She looked at them and realised they were covered in her mother's dried blood. Not only her hands but all down her front. Her stomach recoiled at the sight and she had to rush outside before she heaved, kicking the stone from the door on the way. The well water was cold as she washed herself down. She watched the water running from her arms in red rivers and thought that this was the last time her mother's blood would ever flow again.

She was still outside when movement in the nearby trees alerted her to Olaf's return. Quickly she pushed herself into the bushes that grew along the

103

side of the cottage wall. From her hiding place she watched him stride in through the gate and up the path before disappearing from sight. Above her head the window of her mother's room stood open and she heard him enter. His voice sounded different, gone was the gentle, loving tone she was used to. In its place was a harsher edge that she was astounded to hear. Bile rose in her throat at his words. 'Where is Bethoc, you old hag? Is she not back yet?'

A dull thud sounded as he kicked the corpse still in a heap on the floor. 'Not speaking, are we? Don't tell me you went and died, now where is the fun in that? Looks like she's got more work to do when she gets here. Still, it will keep her busy till I come back.'

Finally reality and reason fused solid. There was no room left for the tiny spark of hope that had clung to Bethoc's heart. She willed him not to look out of the window, even though the sounds from within told her he was busy tearing the room apart. He let out a roar of frustration as he found nothing.

'I hope you realise what you have done, woman,' he raged as if Oonagh could still hear him. Like a madman he ranted on. 'But even without the necklace we will still win. We will take all of Cait and your people will be defeated.'

He laughed. 'Oh yes, they are still there. Hiding in the hills, thinking to outwit us and drive us out. Painted scum that will not let go and to think, all this time you never even knew.'

The noises came to a halt and there was a moment of silence before his footsteps sounded his retreat. The door banged and Bethoc shrank down against the wall as she watched his back disappearing into the woods. In a state of shock, she crept out of the branches and made her way inside.

Her mother's body had moved slightly where she had been kicked but the greatest change was the state of the room. Olaf had been through every trunk and storage space. He had upturned the cotbed and smashed into the base to check inside. All possible hiding places had been searched. As numb as she was, Bethoc was spurred into action, she hadn't much time. Olaf had said he would be back. She must be gone before he was. Her two biggest problems were what to do with her mother and the fact that there had been the distinct hint of storm clouds in the distance when she was heading back from Grims Isle. She would rather be off the island before Olaf came looking for her but she couldn't risk leaving during a storm.
Being rational, she figured that Olaf would not return before daybreak the next day. The storm and the dark would keep him at home for the night. That gave her a good few hours to get prepared. She set about cleaning up her mother as best she could. She warmed water over the fire and carefully washed away the worst of the blood from her face and head. Carefully she combed out her hair and tied it how her mother preferred to wear it. Lastly

she removed her ruined nightwear and managed to get her into her favourite clothes.

The bed was all but ruined for sleeping on but she pieced it back together as best she could and covered it in skins and a woollen blanket. Then, using all the strength she could muster, she lifted her mother's body onto the bed. After resting for a few moments she disappeared into the garden, coming back with an armful of flowers. These she scattered around the bed. By the time she had finished it was almost shrine-like. She smiled to think how pretty she had made it. Oonagh had loved the garden flowers.

It was now getting late and there was a lot still to be done. Everything was strewn all over the floor, making her task of finding the essentials she would need on her journey all the harder. A change of clothes, knife, wash things, comb, tinctures, some food. Eventually though, she had a bag packed, ready and waiting at the door. She paused for a moment to say her final farewells to the peaceful figure in her flowery resting place. There would be no stake for her mother, Bethoc could not face doing it. She just had to hope that her love for Donal would be strong enough to keep her spirit heading in the right direction.

It was now the middle of the night and at that time of year it was only really dark for a few short hours. Time to go. With a heavy heart she lifted a burning brand from the fire and touched it to various piles of kindling laid out ready. Then she turned, picked up her bag, and walked away. Behind her the only home she had ever known was quickly engulfed in flames.

8

The men tramped back to their homes, shattered and defeated. Unable to settle, they came out with their families and gathered at the top of the beach around a hastily-made campfire. Tears were shed and someone started a throwing game to help relieve the frustration. The sound of stones clattering off the rocks kept the wading birds from their evening foraging at the water's edge. All around the air of sombre reflection permeated everything.

Bethoc watched, detached and unfeeling. She knew they had been up at the cottage ever since the storm started abating. The fierce winds that had raged throughout the early hours would have whipped the fire up into a frenzy. By the time the lashing rain had arrived, most of the cottage would have been consumed. She imagined they had found the charred remains of her mother's body in the smouldering ruins and hoped that when she could not be traced they would believe she too had perished. From her vantage point further up the hill she had huddled in her hiding place and spent the day going over her options. She knew she must leave the island without being seen. That meant a dangerous boat trip in the dark; last night in the storm it had not been possible. She had been soaked to the skin out on the hillside but she had found protection against the worst of the winds in an area of prickly gorse bushes. They had torn at her flesh as she crawled inside but they ensured no one would find her. From there she had grabbed what little sleep she could and spent the rest of the time formulating her plan.

It was a long boat ride over the strait to the mainland and she was not used to rowing very far. She had already decided she would need to take Erelend's small boat. It was the only one she stood a chance of managing. Everyone in this small bay went to bed early so they could rise with the dawn and head out fishing. That should give her enough time to be well out of harm's way before anyone noticed the missing boat. Now the storm had passed she was relying on having a window of calm weather. The strait was notorious for whirlpools and freak tides but as long as she stayed away from the islands between Haey and the mainland she should miss the worst waters.

Her mother had raised her to be self-reliant. To set her mind to a task and not stop until it was done. Oonagh had learned the hard way and she had made it her duty to teach her daughter to rely on no one but herself, it was paying dividends now. She focused all her attention on the task before her, whenever her thoughts started to stray towards her mother or Olaf she dragged them back to the plan. Her meagre rations of food sat untouched in her bag but her thirst was growing. In her haste she had forgotten to pack any water. Not daring to creep out of the bushes until everyone had settled down for the night, she sucked at the damp cuff of her tunic and waited.

Gradually the folk started making their way inside. Bethoc waited until all the doors were closed and the dogs shut away before carefully extracting herself from the gorse and making her way to the nearby stream. After quenching her thirst and emptying her bladder she crept between the cottages and down onto the beach. Then came the hardest part, the boat was pulled well up out of the water's reach. She needed to move it without making any noise or the dogs would bark. Inch by inch she heaved the boat, pausing every few minutes to listen for anyone coming. When the waves were lapping around her calves she jumped in and readied the oars. Keeping her eyes firmly on the shoreline she eased the boat out into deeper water. Now she was at the mercy of anyone on the headlands either side of the bay. She pressed on, praying that no one would be on the cliffs.

Bethoc was conscious of not using up all her energy too soon, the crossing was a very long one and the going would be arduous. Keeping her breathing slow and even she focused first on her arms. Letting them take the weight of each stroke for the count of ten. Next she moved her attention to her shoulders for ten strokes, then her back and finally her legs. She kept this up for the first hour then as boredom started to sink in she tried to concentrate on different muscles, buttocks, stomach, even her feet. Anything to keep her mind strong and her body paced.

Erelend had often told of this crossing when she was visiting with Groa. He would tell them of the sea monsters he encountered on the way. Most would stay well away from his boat but sometimes a group of smaller creatures, each with three shiny pointed wings on their bodies, would jump and dance in the bow wave. One of their wings pointed to the sky and helped them leap in a graceful arc right out of the water. Dolphins, he had called them. She kept an eye out for them but so far they were proving elusive. She hoped the rest of his descriptions were correct. If so she should reach the mainland at a peninsular known as the Nose. All she had to do was keep rowing due south. This would ensure she missed the stretch of troublesome waters the strait was famed for.

A brisk breeze was getting up the farther out she went and the swell was beginning to rise. Bethoc looked up and to her dismay saw storm clouds over the horizon to her west. Glancing behind her all she could see was the vast stretch of open water, with no sign yet of the main shore. Doubling her efforts she pushed on, hoping the storm would not come too soon. After another hour she knew she was in trouble. Her muscles were starting to burn with the effort of fighting the swell. The breeze had become a strong wind, driving her little boat way off course. She knew if she was forced too far east she would be powerless to break free of the notorious tide the fishermen called the Boars of Dunscaby. She would be dragged onto the rocks of Straumsey Island. Rain had begun to fall, barely registering on the erratic waters of the strait, but once more Bethoc was soaked to the skin. Fighting with the oars she made a valiant attempt to free herself from the treacherous currents but her arms could not keep up the pace and her wet hands slipped on the wooden oars.

Storm clouds filled the darkening skies, making it even harder to see. Grabbing her bag, Bethoc shoved her head and arm through the strap. She was not going to risk losing it as the swell rose, threatening to tip her into the brine. Her hair clapped to her face and whipped in her eyes, she dashed it away but as she went to grab the oar again it was torn from her grip and off into the sea. Tucking the other one into the bottom of the boat, Bethoc clung onto the sides and tried to keep her balance. She should have been frightened but she was too busy fighting for survival.

The cliffs of Straumsey loomed up ahead of her and just as she thought she would be smashed straight into them, the boat started pulling back to the north. The Boars of Dunscaby flowed both sides of the island and it seemed she had been dragged into the northerly course. Her heart sank even further as she recalled with dread the tales of the Swelkie to the top of the island. Of all the whirlpools that haunted these waters, the Swelkie was the worst, powered by the water forcing its way through the two giant quernstones under the sea that gave the water its salty tang. Rumour had it that two giantesses powered the turning of the stones and kept the Swelkie alive. They could only be soothed by gifts thrown into the pool. All

Bethoc could spare was the one remaining oar. She could not see a way she would survive such a fate.

The deafening roar of the waves crashing onto the rocks at the base of the cliffs filled the air, drowning out the noise of the wind. The boat was now at the mercy of the gods. It was not going to make it around the northern tip of the island. Tossed and tipped in the tumultuous water, slowly the bottom began to fill as the waves crashed over. A sickening crunching noise sang of the rocks' teeth biting the underside of the little vessel. Bethoc was flung forward and smacked her head on the gunwale.

***

The sound of sea birds slowly clawed at her senses, mingling with the incessant throbbing pain at her forehead. Her mind swam in thick fog, oblivious to anything else. A light spray kissed at her face, washing away the fog. Blinking against the morning light, her eyes took in the towering, algae-covered rocks forming the huge cave above her. Beneath her the stone was slimy and only a few inches above the water. As her senses awoke more she could see the remains of the wooden boat, smashed beyond repair. Her body screamed in protest as she tried to move and the water-soaked bag weighed heavy on her shoulder. A quick check told her most of her belongings had survived but her food was ruined. The thought of food brought with it the realisation how thirsty she was. Pain lanced through her leg as she made to rise, her right thigh had a deep gash down it and her ankle felt as if it was made from sharp blades. Trying to keep her weight on her toes, she limped to the cave wall and tipped her head under a rivulet of water running down from above. Only then did the realisation hit her.

There was no way she could leave the island and make it to the mainland now, she was stranded. Panic threatened to overwhelm her but she forced herself to be practical. By the tide mark on the walls it was clear the rocks she was standing on were only visible at low tide, she could not stay there long. Already the rock she had woken up on was under water. Using the cave's wall as a crutch, she edged further into its depths, hoping there would be a ledge she could be safe on. Instead of finding a dead end she found that the back of the cave formed a tunnel to an area of light where the roof opened up to form a large sinkhole. She was relieved and frightened to see a pair of small boats tied up there, along with a well-worn path winding its way up to the surface. Clearly this area was well used. Further caves ate their way deeper into the bedrock but there was no way of getting round to them with her leg in the state it was.

She had to think fast; should she stay where she was until her ankle felt better or should she risk climbing the path? Judging by the light, it was still very early. Fishermen would be heading out to sea but there was nothing nearby to indicate these boats were used for fishing. Surely there would have been ropes, baskets and nets? She sniffed the air, there was always a distinct aroma around where Erelend and the other fisherman landed their catch. She could make out no such thing here. Her heart pounded as she imagined someone coming down the path, where could she hide? There was nowhere.

Decision made, she took a deep breath and dropped to her knees. Crawling up the incline would be far quicker than hobbling with nothing for support. Plus, it would keep her low to the ground and harder to spot. Bracken started to grow about halfway up and nearer the top, bushes gave even more cover. If she could make it that far, she stood a chance. Concentrating on the bracken, she set off. The pain in her thigh was bearable but the gravel tore at her knees. Her face was wet with tears by the time she reached the ferns and was able to duck within them and rest. She did not wait long. Dashing away the tears with an angry hand, she ploughed on towards the bushes.

As the path opened out onto the island she got the first proper view of where she was. No trees grew but there were numerous bushes. Though not enough to hide the outer walls of a structure not far away to the north. This area was definitely not safe but she was hurting too much to go very far. She grabbed a handful of vetch growing nearby and shoved some in her mouth, stuffing the rest into her bag. It would allay her hunger for a while, which in turn would help her to think clearly. What did she know of the island? She had seen it every time she had been near the southern coastline of Haey.

There were a number of Norsemen living here, she remembered, even though it was only a small spit of land it held at least three large homesteads. The castle on the Stack known as Mestag she knew was to the southwest of the island. Built to oversee the swell tide that she herself had been caught up in. When it wasn't dragging boats onto the rocky shoreline the swell thrashed around and formed the white-tipped Merry Men of Mey. The shipwrecks were a constant source of treasure, making the lonely homeland a lucrative place to live. The promontory to the northwest held a small fort where Valthiof lived which, she assumed, must be what she could see. She had only met the man once at the Summer Thing and he had given her the shivers, more than living up to the reputation the Straumsey people had of him being the toughest in the whole of Orkneyjar. Who else would want to live in such a turbulent stretch of water?

She knew there was at least one other settlement on the island though she had no idea where. She could only guess it must be over to the east. Noises were coming from the fort now, was someone coming? Keeping low, she hurried away as fast as her leg would allow.

✳✳✳

The smell hit her before she reached the cliff edge, the unmistakable combination of stale fish and musky scent left behind by the hundreds of sea birds who colonised the cliffs in the breeding season. The red sandstone cliffs might be impressive from the sea but from the top they were hugely disappointing. Stretching as far as she could see in both directions, it was clear there would be no way to descend to the caves below. Even if it were possible, they would probably fill up whenever the tide came in. Barking sounds below assured her this place was home to selkies only, until the guillemot and fulmar returned in the spring. She would have to find somewhere else to shelter. Haey was a hazy blur in the distance, she felt a pang of regret as she looked over towards it.

With the prospect of yet another soaking, Bethoc turned her back to her old home and set off inland. At least the rain should keep the islanders from venturing out too far.

The terrain to the east offered more cover than the west. The land here was more fertile and plants grew in abundance, she found many tiny strawberries hidden amongst the grasses and soon her fingers were stained red but her belly was happier. Still, there was a distinct lack of trees and the ground had a tendency to be boggy. More than once she stumbled into wet ground and soon she was muddy as well as wet. Her leg seared with pain whenever she put her foot down and the unrelenting pounding in her head never let up. After what seemed to be an age but was really little more than the distance between her old cottage and that of her friend Groa's, the ground began to slope downwards towards the sea. Here she was able to hobble right down to the rocky shore and rinse the worst of the mud from her legs.

The shoreline to the south looked the most promising. There the ground rose into cliffs and offered the chance of a cave or two. Sure enough, just as the rain began once more, she struggled into a deep cave and slumped, exhausted, to the floor.

Shivering woke her a short while later, she badly needed to dry out and get warm again. Foraging in the cave she found enough dry flotsam and old nesting material to start a small fire. It was dry enough to start at the first spark from her flint. The sticks snapped and cracked as the flames licked them into white, powdery ash. The noise was comforting and the resulting heat eased her shivers away. For a while she watched the smoke making shapes in the air before it dispersed readily inside the cavernous shelter before finding escape almost undetectably amongst the rain.

Forcing herself to endure the pain in her ankle once more, she set about collecting as much firewood as she could. The cave penetrated the island a good way, too far for her right then. To make it easier she stayed near to the front part where she could see without needing a torch.

It was clear no one had been there for a very long time. Debris had built up in the nooks and crannies and a dense mound of pungent guano covered part of the floor. She studied the area above and saw where the cave reached sideways into a narrow slit that cut up through the rock, creating a long, dark passageway. An involuntary shiver rippled down her spine. Bats! Guardians of giant's lairs. That was surely why the cave was deserted. Her mother had always discounted the Norse rumours of giants but even Bethoc shuddered at the thought of the leathery-winged creatures. *Well,* she thought, *I am well and truly in the hands of evil now so I might as well get used to them.*

Settling herself down at her fire she watched, mesmerised by the flames. Her mind made pictures as they flickered and danced. Before long the pictures turned into a pair of eyes. Olaf's face swam into her mind and her stomach lurched. She loved him so much, *had* loved him, she corrected herself angrily. She thought of how he had told her they were soulmates, lovers to the end of their days, however many lives they lived. She could feel the tender touch of his hand as it stroked her face. His lips on hers as her heart melted into him and his hands sliding lower onto her breasts...

'No!' she willed her mind to break the thought. She shook away the image and her head responded with even deeper pounding pain. Nausea danced in her stomach and she tasted bile in the back of her mouth. Yet still her mind taunted her with a cruel mixture of love and hate. Time fused with her sorrow, waltzing through the hours, leaving her weak and defeated. Eventually reason cut through her grief and hardened her with its clarity. It didn't matter how long she sat there crying or how distraught she became, the truth could not be changed. He had deceived her, broken her trust and done everything in his power to cause as much hurt to her as possible. Where was the love she had believed he felt for her? How could it all have been an act? She would have defended him to the ends of the earth only a day ago and she would have been a fool! If it hadn't been for her stupidity, her gullibility and longing desire for someone to love her, well then her mother would still be alive.

'Ohhhh.'

The cry escaped her and the tears she thought had all been used returned to flow once more. Her poor mother. How could she sit here keening for a love that had never been true when her mother's life had been so cruelly ended? Her mind dragged her back to the moment she had washed the blood from her dead mother's face, her precious mother. Battered and flung to the floor like a used rag all because of a damned necklace. The very same necklace that had caused her father's death all those years ago. Both of them dying because of a string of stones. Now Bethoc was the only one who knew where those stones lay. The only one who knew why her parents had died and who had killed them. The people from the villages had also died, all so Thorstein could assure himself of victory.

Suddenly she knew what she was going to do. Olaf had said that some of the villagers had survived. He had goaded her mother, thinking himself unheard. Thinking himself superior in every way. He expected he was going to return to his father and go about his life as if nothing had ever occurred between them. Well, he had vastly underestimated her. She was going to find the survivors, find the necklace, and make sure they never got their hands on Strathnabaros.

9

Overnight she slept fitfully, waking early to a curtain of rain across the cave entrance. The unforgiving rock had not helped the pain in her thigh and she winced as she stretched her leg out. Mercifully though, the pain in her head had eased, to a dull ache. She shivered. The fire was well and truly dead, even a quick prod of the ashes couldn't raise a spark. Gingerly she rotated her ankle and was relieved to have more movement than the night before, raising her hopes that it was just a sprain.

There was enough wood left to re-start the fire. Keeping to her hands and knees, she set it going. Once again the tinder-dry twigs took the spark readily and she was soon enjoying the satisfying chatter of burning wood. A deep sigh escaped her. What now? Last night she had fallen into an exhausted sleep with her new plans ringing in her ears, but now she must be practical. First things first, she needed to heal. She took a look at her thigh, the wound was deep and long but the sea water had ensured it was clean. She found her jar of salve in her bag and dabbed it onto the cut. It should heal well given time.

Her ankle was the main problem just now; even if she was lucky and nothing was broken it was still going to hinder her mobility for a few days. What she really needed was some fresh comfrey leaves. The damp ground by the entrance to the cave was the perfect place for it to grow, could she really be that lucky? Hobbling over, she searched around, finally finding some just out of reach up the rugged cliff. Cursing under her breath she balanced all her weight on her good leg and jumped, managing to grab a handful of leaves before landing with a yelp. Back by the fire she wrapped a few of the furry leaves around her ankle and bound them in place with a sodden linen bandage. They would help to reduce the swelling and ease the bruising that was starting to show. Elevating her foot, she found herself back at her starting point once more. What now?

She knew she could not get off the island until she was fully mobile again. Even then she would need to acquire a boat and wait for the unseasonal storms to abate fully. Until then she had to make the most of what she had. Looking around her she realised that wasn't much. She had gathered a good supply of edible leaves on her way there yesterday, so she wasn't going to starve.

Water was also in good supply, rivulets of rain water ran down the walls near the entrance and collected in rock pools where the sea water could not reach to contaminate them. Her immediate concern had to be the possibility of being found. For that she needed to explore outside the cave. She really needed to rest and keep her foot raised but knowing she would not settle until she was sure she was safe, she gathered herself and stepped out into the rain.

***

The tide was out, exposing a run of skerries along the shore. No boat would attempt to land there but the cave was still visible to passing vessels. Cautiously she made her way down onto the exposed rocks. Her ankle protested at every step, driving daggers of fire up her leg. She pushed on. Every few paces she would turn and check the clifftop, aware someone could be watching her from above but she saw no one. When she reached the water's edge she looked back at the cave entrance. The larger boulders near the base of the cliff obscured the fire and she was pleased to see the smoke had dispersed enough to not be visible above. However, she realised that anyone near the top of the cliff would easily smell the smoke and come looking. The thought nagged at her whilst she gathered more driftwood. She stowed it back in the cave to dry out, banked up the fire and began to make her way painfully up the cliff.

The slope was not sheer like the west side of the island and she was able to crawl most of the way. By the time she got there, her hands were grazed and bleeding and the pain in her leg was making her nauseous. Gorse bushes clung to the clifftop, making it impossible to get anywhere near the area above the cave. Their stunted bodies, bent over time by the prevailing wind, reminded Bethoc of little old men looking out to sea. She grinned to herself as she realised what they were telling her.

Unless the wind changed from its usual course the smoke would be blown out to sea.

Even that knowledge could not let her rest easily. The hunger pangs of an empty stomach were nothing compared to the emptiness she felt inside. Needing to keep active to block it out she thrust a long brand into the fire and waited for it to catch light. Raising it above her head she went to investigate the back of her refuge, using another stick to help bear her weight. The bat roost was quiet, last night they had poured out of the cave above her. Covering her hair with her arms she had willed them not to land on her. A ripple of revulsion overtook her. She had no idea when they had returned, the thought of them flying over her as she slept made her skin crawl. The feeling, however, roused the lump in her stomach where her grief had settled. Her mind clouded as she tried to drive away the feeling and she stumbled over a loose stone on the floor, sending pain shooting up her leg.

Tears filled her eyes and she bit down hard on her lip. So much for taking care.

A black hole teetered at the edge of her mind, threatening to open up and engulf her. She pushed it away and pulled down her mental shutter, forcing herself not to feel anything. Gritting her teeth, she made herself keep going.

The cave went back much further than she had originally thought but it was dank and wet. Fissures in the rock let water pour down before seeping through hidden cracks in the floor. Algae and slime covered the walls and the air was stale. Bethoc returned to her fire and thrust the torch onto the flames. She had done all she was capable of for now. Her leg hurt and her enthusiasm had died. She sat in a stupor, staring at the rain and imagining it washing her whole life away. The shutters broke and with a wrenching sob she let the grief in. Losing herself to the loneliness and desperation she had been determined not to accept.

Images of her mother broken and dying tore at her heart. The guilt that she had not been there to protect her cut deep into her soul. It soon turned to hatred. Hatred aimed at Olaf for taking away everything she had held dear but also hatred for herself, for allowing it to happen. Well, she thought, she was paying the price now. She was so lonely. All her life she had been part of a loving family, even it was only her and her mother. Her whole reason for being had been to love other people, to be just one part of the whole picture. How was she ever going to learn how to be the entirety of what she had? Oh, how she missed that feeling of belonging. Without those she loved around her she no longer knew who she was.

There was only so long she could remain so distraught. Gradually her mind worked its way through the mess and began to focus on the few positives she had. Somewhere in Cait she had a family, people she belonged to even if they didn't know she existed. She needed to get onto the mainland and try to find them before the weather

126

became too bad and she was trapped there for the winter.

Eager to make the most of her positive state, she braved the rain again and made her way down to the water's edge. It was much closer now the tide had come in and she had only a small area left to forage in but she managed to detach a few limpets with a quick sharp tap from the handle of her knife. The seaweed she left for now, she had no container to boil it in and she had never really liked the texture.

Back at the fire she placed the limpet shells down in the embers so they could cook in their own juice. The much needed protein would help give her strength. Tomorrow she would need to do some serious food gathering.

***

For the next few days the storms battered the island. Westerly winds predominated as usual, leaving the cave reasonably sheltered. Every once in a while the winds would whip around and drive straight into the entrance. Then Bethoc would gather her few belongings and retreat further into the cave. The smoke would soon fill the space, clinging to her clothes and stinging her eyes. She knew it would also be blowing over the island and she would scatter the wood and pray it burnt out before anyone could smell it.

Huddled in the dismal space, she alternated between eager planning and the depths of despair.

Slowly the stiffness and pain in her leg eased, the wound was knitting together nicely and the swelling in her ankle was almost gone. Whenever the weather let up enough she took to exploring the area around the cave. This improved her diet no end as she harvested wild garlic and sea beet. In the rockpools along the shore she found small crabs, muscles, and even an eel.

On the fifth day she saw her first islander. A short, stockily-built man with wild dirty blond hair and a rugged complexion well used to the biting salt-laden winds. He appeared to be checking his livestock and enclosures for storm damage. She watched as he mended a section of broken fencing where a stunted hawthorn had come down and split one of the rails. Whistling, he set about dragging the tree out of the way and replacing the rail, tossing the broken pieces to one side. Job done, he gathered his tools and headed along the fence line away from where Bethoc was hiding. She crept out of the bushes and edged nearer, the discarded fencing would make a useful addition to her firewood stores.

The next day she set out to find where the man was from. She still had no idea where the eastern settlement was but if she was to get off this island she would need to steal another boat. She really didn't fancy going back to the sink hole and risking the current there again. Keeping to the cover of the bushes that lined the fence, she followed the direction the man had taken. The ground rose steadily the further south they went and with it came a sinking feeling. High ground meant more cliffs, she knew from home that fishermen preferred a bay to bring their catch ashore. She had been banking on the fact she would be able to find a boat on the south of the island. It would mean a much easier crossing to the mainland.

She was almost upon the longhouse before she realised. Nestling in a slight dip in the ground and surrounded by large shrubs and a few hardy hawthorns. Smoke rose from the thatched roof, people were at home. Like the thief she had become, Bethoc scrutinised the dwelling, searching for anything that would help her. She noted the pathway worn into the mud, heading from the doorway over the rise to the south. A collection of lead net sinkers sat in a pile alongside a lethal looking fish spear. Her heart leapt - fishermen! Next to the path the vegetable garden was neat and well-tended. Her mouth watered.

The wood pile stacked neatly against the end of the building caught her eye, an empty bucket and stool stood next to it. She assumed it had been placed there to protect the user from the worst of the wind. Beside the bucket was a pile of dishes waiting to be washed. Could she risk it? Creeping closer, she watched as a woman emerged from the doorway and made her way round the far side of the house. After a moment or two she disappeared back inside. Quickly, Bethoc raced forward, grabbed a cooking pot and spoon, shoved them in the bucket and fled. Tonight she would have her first hot meal in a week.

***

The hot water was bliss. Using the rag and scrap of soap she had brought with her she took her time to wash. She had missed being clean. Combing out her wet hair, she waited for fresh water to heat so she could make a start on her clothes. For the first time since she left Haey she had a smile on her face. Even the thought of the theft made her giggle, she just hoped she hadn't started a search party looking for the culprit.

Tomorrow she was going to follow the southern path and hope it led to a cove.

Following the path proved more difficult than she had anticipated. She hadn't considered there may be further houses over the rise which she had to loop around before picking up the path on the other side. Not daring to get too close to it in case she was seen, she kept to the dense bracken, ready to drop into the curly fronds should anyone appear. The run of storms had still not abated; the rain pelted her, driving deep into the fibres of her clothes. Soon she was soaked through but she kept on, knowing it was unlikely she would meet anyone in this weather.

Her hunch about finding a boat on the south of the island proved right. A short way from the hamlet, the path began to dip down and the sea came into

130

view. With it came the welcome sight of the mainland across the water. Wonderfully close and far nearer than she had realised it would be. Below her she could see a natural inlet, housing a number of fishing vessels. The ground between her and the harbour was devoid of all cover; as much as she would have liked to go further it was just too risky to cross in the daylight. She made her retreat just in time to avoid two fishermen heading down to check on the boats. Her mind burst with ideas.

Back at the cave she changed into her clean, dry clothes and laid out the wet things to dry. Tonight she was moving nearer to the cove. She wanted to be ready to go as soon as there was a clearing in the weather. The fishermen would be looking for the same clearing and she wanted to watch where they went and which boats they used. That way she hoped to slip out of the bay and away from the island unnoticed.

***

The watercolour sky slowly lightened, changing from shades of grey and violet to gentle pink. A warning sky, the fisherman would not be out long today. Two boats made their way out of the harbour refuge, one carrying a single man, the other carrying two. Both headed eastwards, keeping fairly close to the shoreline before disappearing from view. From her vantage point overlooking the bay, Bethoc watched them go. Down below she could still make out two smaller boats bobbing on the slight swell. Another hour reassured her that no one else was coming. Quickly she skirted round the bay, keeping well south of the hamlet, and made her way to the headland. From there she could see a good way up the sheltered eastern side of the island. Sure enough, both boats were there. The smaller of the two still hugged the coastline whilst the larger one had ventured further out to sea. She breathed a double sigh of relief. Not only had they kept out of the strait but if she had stayed in the cave for another night she would have been seen for sure as the boats passed.

Her bed had been softer out on the hillside above the bay but she had no real shelter. The few bushes that braved the incline were scant and windswept. She had made herself comfortable in a low ridge halfway up the slope where a number of the stunted bushes grew, along with plenty of bracken. It provided perfect cover as long as she was careful not to make tracks when she moved around.

The rest of the morning she spent away from the bay, foraging for food. As she did so, she wandered west until she could make out the top of the castle on the stack and from there she crossed back to the southern cliff edge. Down below her was a large skerry jutting out into the sea, like a crooked finger pointing out across the water to the mainland. Today the sea looked calm and serene. Sea birds hovered on the light breeze, occasionally crying out their presence.

Further out she noticed a flock of gulls low over the water. She gasped as she saw dark shapes lifting up from the depths. Triangular fins cut through the air and every so often a whole tail would reach up and slap back down. All of a sudden one of them broke free in a graceful arc before disappearing again. They must be the dolphins Erelend spoke of. She smiled, he had been telling the truth after all.

She wondered what he was doing now, what all of them were doing, especially Groa. Her friend had been hopeful of an autumn wedding and Bethoc could imagine the scene. A small intimate group of them gathered over onto Hrossey watching as the happy couple clasped hands through the hole in the Odin stone. Most of Haey would celebrate with them afterwards, all except for Oonagh and her. Bubbles of sadness rose up from deep inside her, finding escape in the tears that crept down her face. The joy from the day was gone along with the dolphins. The seagulls dispersed and white tips started to show on the roughening waters. Bethoc took a gulp and forced the sight of the battered body from her mind. This was what life here meant now, she must never forget. She had a purpose, to make sure her mother had not died in vain. Both her parents had been killed for a cause and she, Bethoc, was going to end that cause whatever it took. Like a mantra, she reminded herself she was going to find the Grumg-Mhor villagers, find the necklace and bring peace to the homeland she had never seen.

Further along the clifftop she looked down on a huge selkie colony covering the flat rocks at the water's edge. Yet more heads bobbed in the shallows; large, fluid eyes watching. She remembered Erelend's assurance that they would never change whilst anyone was looking. Imagining them all shedding their skins and partying on the beach, she hurried on, not sure if she believed in the tales but not wanting to risk finding out. A slow pitter-patter of raindrops accompanied her walk back, gradually settling into the steady drenching rain more typical of the time of year than the previous week's storms. Back at her base she watched as the larger fishing boat made its way back to the harbour, the smaller one having arrived back before she returned. A number of men and women were waiting, ready to haul the catch up the slope. Voices drifted up to her in broken sentences as they headed up the path. One in particular caused a jolt of alarm.

'Thorstein... tomorrow... Mestag... before winter... feast... plenty fish.'

She really needed to shift her position so she could hear better but she was afraid of drawing attention to herself. Did it mean Thorstein was coming tomorrow? Or was he already there at Mestag? Her mind was racing with the possibilities. Either way, tomorrow there was to be a well-stocked feast and in some way Thorstein would be involved. It meant only one thing. Her time had run out, she could wait no longer. Tonight, no matter what the weather, she was going to take one of the smaller boats and leave the island. She would rather die at sea than be caught and beaten like her mother.

It was impossible to sleep. Though the rain had stopped, everything was wet. The bracken showered her with drops every time she moved and the ground seeped water into her clothing. As soon as the sky grew dark enough she put her bag over her shoulder, took her stolen bucket and made her way down to the bay. It was so much easier than last time, the houses were too far away to hear any noise and the boats were already bobbing in the water. She stored her belongings into the smallest one, untied the holding rope and slung it in before jumping in herself. Using her hands to push the boat past the others she was soon clear enough to start rowing.

Darkness seemed to cloak her as she pulled away from the shore, reassuring her that she would not be followed. Further out though, the darkness felt more smothering. She twisted her head around her but all she could see was the all-encompassing inky blackness weighing down on her. By the time she had reached the middle of the strait she was the most claustrophobic she had ever been. Panic took hold of her, like a sea demon reaching over the edge of her boat and threading its probing tentacles deep into her mind. She stopped rowing and frantically searched the gloom for anything that could give her a point of reference. There was nothing but the gentle slap of water on the hull of the boat, like a friend letting her know she was not alone. She focused on the sound and willed herself to calm down and think. The sound had always come from her right but now it was coming from the stern, the boat must be turning. It was impossible to tell without anything to anchor her vision. Gathering the oars, she pulled the boat back around until the waves slapped once more to her right. Satisfied, she began to row once more and the sea demon's grip loosened slightly.

A point of light blinked overhead, the clouds were beginning to clear and she could make out the north star. Slowly, as if the night sky was waking up, more and more stars appeared. Bethoc could make out the big scoup and the zig zags above it. The sea demon's grip was broken and it slipped back into the watery depths. So long as she kept these in her sights she would reach the mainland.

The stars dipped and shone as the last stray clouds chased their way across the sky. She had watched these pictures in the sky all her life. She could never lose her way whilst they were shining.

Slowly the stretch of water she had to cross shrank and the mainland loomed ahead. The stars gave enough light for her to see she was heading into a wide bay. She stored her oars for a while and studied her options. The shoreline appeared to be a continuous stretch of shallow beach backing onto grassland. A noise to her left startled her and she jumped to see something disappearing under the surface. It reappeared a few moments later on her right. Similar to the dolphins she had seen earlier but as far as she could see this was all alone and eager for her company. There was something slightly different to what Erelend had described but she could not immediately put her finger on it. Only when the creature opened its mouth did she realise it had no snout. Instead, the face ran in a smooth curve from eye to lip. The result was a cheerful, happy face with a wide, smiling mouth. As Bethoc floated, he played around her. Popping his head out of the water frequently before diving for a few minutes and coming up in a different place. She was held mesmerised until he suddenly dived from view only to break the surface much further out to sea, then he was gone.

She turned and realised the beach was almost upon her. Using the oars again, she steered onto the pebbles. As they crunched beneath the hull she gathered her belongings and jumped out. She pushed the boat back off the shingle, hopefully the outgoing tide would carry it back out to sea and hide her journey. A yawn escaped her. She badly needed sleep and for that she needed cover. She was dismayed to see that the area was extremely flat. Even in the starlight she felt exposed.

10

She woke to the sound of sheep bleating as they grazed nearby. By the look of the sun, it was around midday. Bethoc yawned and stretched, wincing as she caught her hand on one of the gorse bushes she had hidden next to. Sucking the scratch, she checked her surroundings. Over the water she could just make out Haey in the distance. The sight was both frightening and saddening. The sheep, startled by her sudden appearance, fled, calling to one another in alarm.

Where there were sheep it followed that men would be nearby. Time to move on, she was too near to Orkneyjar to be caught here. She had decided it was better to keep the coastline in view and work her way along the top of Cait. Her mother had said the strath opened up to the sea, so if she could find the right river mouth, all she would have to do was follow the river down to the loch. This way it almost felt as if her mother was still guiding her. She took one last long look at the island.

Goodbye Mother, she thought sadly as she turned and walked away.

The next couple of days were a blur of walking and hiding. Her legs ached and her feet were blistered. She ditched her bucket the first morning, it was too cumbersome to carry. The cooking pot she tied to her belt; hot water was a luxury she did not want to miss out on again. She had seen a few people as she travelled but a number of them had the telling blond hair of the Norse and she quickly moved on. Slowly they petered out and the only people she saw were dark-haired Picts. She began to relax a little.

On top of a low hill she came across a pair of long cairns a short distance apart and at right angles to each other. The ends of each cairn terminated in a rounded head with banked horns forming a courtyard. They sat like huge grass-covered serpents waiting for their next meal. At the end of one she noticed a small gathering of people, all dark-haired she was relieved to see. She was quietly making her way past so as not to draw attention to herself when a voice called out to her. A woman was making her way up the hill along a track Bethoc had not noticed before.

'Aiy,' the woman repeated with a wave of her hand. She was short and middle-aged, puffing slightly at the exertion, but her face was friendly and Bethoc risked stopping to talk. The way was getting more mountainous and still she had no real idea where her mother's homeland was. It was about time she trusted someone. She flicked her head towards the group at the cairn.

'What is going on?' she asked.

'The end collapsed in the storms,' the woman answered. She shrugged her shoulders, 'who can say whether the gods are angry or if it was just the weather? The men are trying to find any bones to re-bury them just in case.'

She stopped as she reached where Bethoc stood. 'You feart of the Shidhe folk in the hills?'

As Bethoc shook her head she nodded and laughed. 'Aye, you look too sensible for that. I've no seen you round here afore, are you just passing through?'

'I am actually looking for the mouth of the Nabaros,' taking a leaf out of her mother's book, Bethoc already had her cover story ready. 'My father was from those parts and still has family there, I have bad news to give them.'

The woman gave her a shrewd look and shook her head. 'You won't be reaching there today lassie, it's another full day's walk and this day is almost done.' She eyed Bethoc's shabby appearance and her features softened. 'You can rest down at the stead tonight, it will save you having to risk the Shidhe running loose and catching you in your sleep.'

Bethoc thanked her and waited until she had spoken to the men then together they set off down the hill. The farmstead was basic but it was warm and the woman's family was friendly enough. Her daughter was busy attending a large pot over the fire.

'The men will be down shortly,' the older woman told her. 'They only found one bone so it looks like we will be safe enough now.'

'You shouldn't laugh so, Ma,' her daughter scolded.

'Pah, I'll have no truck with such nonsense.' The woman pulled up a stool for her visitor and poured them both a drink of water from a large pail in the

corner of the room. 'My daughter would have us believe in sprites and kelpies and the like.'
Bethoc gave an apologetic smile to the daughter, she had no wish to be dragged into the dispute.

***

By the time the men came in to eat, they were tired and rowdy. Plenty of ale was drunk as they ate their stew and Bethoc was drawn into a conversation about the recent weather and how it had affected where she was from. She jumped on the chance to strengthen her story.
'My Da was killed by a tree brought down by the winds,' she told them. 'As soon as the rites were done I set off to tell his family. There was no one else who could go, I have only younger sisters and my Ma is not so healthy these days.'
The men nodded their approval, one of them raised his tankard and called out a toast to her father.
'The only direction my Ma could give me was to head north for the sea then follow the direction of the setting sun until I reached the mouth of the Nabaros.'
The eldest man, who Bethoc believed to be the father, clapped one of the others on the back, 'Fergus here can tell you all you need to know. He was along that way a while back, weren't you son?'
The young man nodded and turned to her.
'You will reach it before nightfall tomorrow, you canna miss it, tis the only river mouth you will see past midday.' His tone changed as he added a

warning. 'I wouldn't be hanging about long there, though. That place has been troubled for years now, the Vikings took over the area and they are spreading their hold all the while. Even Moddan has been chased from his home at Dun Yrredell. It is no place for a long visit.'

Bethoc felt her blood run cold, she had no idea who Moddan was but it was never more clear that her task would not be an easy one. Her concern must have shown on her face because he added, 'You will be alright for a short visit, though. They pretty much leave the people be as long as they do as they are told or unless there is trouble. The Norse want to hold the area for themselves, not clear it.'

The woman topped up everyone's tankards and her husband proposed the next toast to Bethoc and her safe return. She thanked him then stayed silent, she had no intention of coming back this way.

***

The next morning she left them, thanking the woman for her hospitality. Fergus had given her a rough idea of the journey ahead, reassuring her that she would not be going anywhere near to Dun Yrredell since it sat further west. By midday, when a promontory took the sea from her view, she knew to just keep straight on the path and trust that the sea would return. Fergus's warning had saved her a good deal of extra walking and when the sea returned for the third time she knew she was almost upon the mouth of the Nabaros. Warily, she slowed her pace, she wanted to avoid the fishing village that straddled the inlet. As soon as she caught sight of it she altered course and headed south, keeping the river in sight. In this way she managed to avoid any unwanted attention from the locals. As soon as she was a decent way from any houses she looked for somewhere to make camp for the night. A sheltered area on a small rise above a tiny lochan with good views all around her seemed the perfect place. Relieved the worst of her journey was over, she lit a fire and dabbed salve on her sore feet.

It was peaceful here, she wanted to make the most of it, not knowing what tomorrow would bring. As she had so many times before, she went over all her mother had said about the area. It wasn't much, there was a loch and a heavily wooded hillside next to it. Her father had been the Maor's son so that would mean he had a large home, possibly even a broch, but she had no idea where that had been or even if it was in Grumg-Mhor. She wondered how long it took a burnt village to disappear. Would there still be any trace? Her mother had said more than two villages were burnt, how many more had been put to the torch looking for her? Olaf had said people were hiding in the hills, that meant they had not gone back and rebuilt. Maybe Norsemen had taken over those villages? She puzzled for a long while until eventually her eyelids drooped and she fell asleep.

***

The next day was cold and wet, rain found its way under her cloak and down her neck. She turned a blind eye to the discomfort, knowing the atrocious weather had helped keep her hidden for so long. Today it should drive most people inside, thus giving her the chance to have a good look round any ruins she found.

There were many. The first she came across, a short while after midday, was a tumbled-down stone building. Charred markings still clung to the fallen stones. She paused and rubbed more salve onto her feet, she really would have to rest and let them heal properly soon. From the old broken sheep pens a short way off, she guessed it was an isolated farmstead. She left it behind and carried on. Before long she came across the first village remains, just a handful of houses from what she could see but there was no sign of the loch her mother had mentioned. Trees had sprouted up amongst the circular impressions in the ground that marked where homes had once stood. Blackened remnants of wood littered the floor, held in place by angry blackberry stems, weighed down with the promise of a bumper crop of fruit later in the year.

She did not linger. Further on she came across another, larger village. Here she also found grave markers by the side of many of the houses. The whole area had been kept tended and the weeds held back by regular maintenance. Her heart lifted; people must be nearby if they could risk coming to pay their respects. She tried to find evidence of tracks or pathways leading away but there was nothing. Only the well-worn pathway that ran adjacent to the river the whole way down the strath. Not risking actually walking on the path unless she was forced to, she had been keeping well to the side to avoid the risk of being seen.

A fair way on and she came across yet another village. Here and there more substantial footings of buildings could be seen, lonely stones forming the blackened bases of what were once well-loved homes. Again she saw signs of attention, a few neat graves and the odd rag tied to branches of a gnarled old hawthorn tree growing near the river. *Wish rags,* Bethoc thought to herself. The rags themselves were in various stages of decay, showing clearly the tree had been used for many years. Interestingly though, on closer inspection, a couple of them - although torn and ragged - were clearly recent additions yet she had seen no signs of life nearby.

The river was beginning to widen, banks giving way to stony beaches. Loch Nabaros, it turned out, was a long, narrow body of water nestled in the valley floor. The area to the north was heavily forested and Bethoc started to feel excitement grow. Somewhere not too far away, her mother and father had lived. She pushed on quicker but was soon driven further up the hill and out of sight of the water by the dense undergrowth. Frustration was beginning to mount as she struggled to keep her bearings. Eventually she found a narrow track winding its way through the trees. Throwing caution to the wind, she followed it. Rounding a corner, she came across remains. Her heart leapt into her mouth, was this Grumg-Mhor?

In the heart of the ruined village stood a circular cairn surrounded by a stone bank. She walked around it, moved by the realisation that her mother would have also looked on it when she was her age. Even if this were the wrong village, she would surely have visited here. Looking around, it was obvious someone had kept the place clear of new tree growth. She wandered through the various house remains, trying to get a feel for the people who had once called them home. So focused on her find, she didn't hear the approaching horse until it was almost too late. Just in time, she managed to dart into the cover of the nearby trees. Crouching low behind one, she watched as the rider came into view. He jumped from his horse and led it around the site. Just as he neared her side of the cairn, the hood of his cloak blew down, revealing his rain-soaked blond hair. Bethoc had to stifle a gasp. Olaf!

She froze, her back against the trunk, willing herself to shrink down. She could hear him talking to himself, cursing the weather. The tone of his voice cut through her like dry bracken through naked skin. It was so hard to associate this man with the one she had believed loved her so deeply only a few days ago. Something unfroze at the back of her neck and flowed like cacti down her spine; she realised it was fear.

Her legs threatened to give way. She screwed her eyes closed. She had come so far, she was not ready to fail now. She risked another peek at the village. Olaf was just disappearing around the far side of the cairn. Quickly she bolted to the next tree. He was still out of sight so she moved again, this time diving behind a cluster of holly bushes. Before she had even caught her breath a hand clapped over her mouth.

'Don't make a noise,' a man's voice whispered in her ear, she could feel the hot breath on the side of her face. He held her low down to the ground and waited, not speaking. After a few moments a low whistle was heard, coming from the trees at the other side of the village.

Bethoc heard Olaf canter off towards the noise.

'Move now!' the man ordered, dragging her to her feet and forcing her to run in the opposite direction. Once far enough away, he removed his hand from her mouth but kept a tight hold of her arm. 'Don't even think of making a noise,' he hissed. 'There are many more of us in these woods.'

Bethoc had no intention of making a noise. Whoever this man was, he was far less frightening than Olaf right now. She raced through the possibilities in her mind, a glimmer of hope flickering into life at his last words. She tried to steal a glance at her captor. He was about her height with dark hair and by the looks of him he was a few years older. His skin was patterned with dark markings.

'Keep moving,' he said, pushing her on.

They reached a clearing filled with heather and stopped. The man gave a quick imitation of a bird whistle. At once another called back and a figure lifted up from the bracken.

'Were you followed?' the woman asked, checking the way they had come. She was dressed in muted colours and sported the same intricate patterns tattooed on the back of her hands as the man had, though her face was unmarked. She had clearly been waiting in the wet bracken for quite a while.

The man shook his head. 'He was alone, Irb led him away towards Rosal. Has anyone been this way?'

'All quiet,' she gave Bethoc a long look. 'I take it you got to her first?'

Her voice was firm but she spoke with a lisp. The man nodded as he released Bethoc's arm and she sank to the ground, glad to be able to rest her feet.

'Why were you hiding from Olaf?' he snapped at her, watching as she flinched at the sound of his name. 'If you are so keen not to be found why did you stomp around Grumbeg leaving a trail easy enough for a child to follow?'

Bethoc flushed, she had thought she was being so careful keeping away from the main paths. It had never occurred to her she was leaving tracks behind.

'Well?' the man said, 'let's hear it.'

Bethoc tried to think, these people knew Olaf but it was clear they did not like him. Were they the painted scum he had talked about? Hope flared but still, she was not going to trust them until she knew for sure. She decided to keep to the truth but make it as vague as possible.

'I am trying to find my family, I hear they are hiding out here somewhere. I have news. Olaf killed my mother and they would want to know.'

The pair looked at each other and back at her. The woman frowned.

'Well any enemy of Olaf Feilan's is a friend of ours but why on earth would that bastard have killed your mother? Come to think of it, if you have family here why have we never seen you before?'

'My mother was from this area,' Bethoc answered. 'Olaf found out who she was after we were engaged but...'

'You were engaged to Olaf?' the woman interrupted, flinging up her arms in disbelief. 'Tagaled, she is deranged. This is all we need.'

Tagaled glared at Bethoc, 'You mean you were his lover?'

The hope died.

'No!' Indignation coloured her cheeks. 'We were engaged but then he attacked my mother and was coming after me. So I ran, this is the only place I have any family.'

She searched their faces but all she could see of what they were thinking was disgust. The response was more than a little unnerving but she had to try again.

'Are you the ones hiding here... from the villages?' she asked, looking from one to the other.

Instead of answering her they moved to one side and lowered their voices so all she could hear was the odd hiss as the woman spoke.

'Look, I don't know what the problem is here,' she called over to them. 'I need to see the people from Grumg-Mhor, I have come such a long way.'

They stopped talking and looked over at her. Hope flared again. Coming back over, Tagaled asked, 'If your family were from Grumg-Mhor, why were you looking around Grumbeg?'

'Grumbeg? Then it wasn't Grumg-Mhor?'

Tagaled shook his head. 'And why did you make it so easy for Olaf to follow you?'

The thought of him following her sent more shivers down her spine, she could feel herself starting to shake but she was not going to let these people know that. If she couldn't convince them to help her she would be left alone out here with Olaf not far behind.

'I've had to travel a long way to get here,' she said. 'I have never been here before. In fact I only found out this place existed a week ago. I thought I would be safe here away from Olaf.' She shrugged, 'Obviously I was wrong.'

He raised his eyebrows as if to indicate what an understatement that was. She ignored him and looked at the woman. 'All I know is I have family somewhere in these hills. Please, can you just take me to see them?'

'What do you think, Edana?' Tagaled asked. 'We need to make a decision.'

Edana shook her head. 'I'm not sure,' she looked Bethoc up and down once more. 'It could be a trap, but who in their right minds would make up such a pathetic story?'

Bethoc lost patience. She was scared, tired and hurting. She had had enough. 'Look, why not tie my hands? Blindfold me? Do whatever it takes to make you happy but please take me to my family.' She held out her hands and waited.

***

They tied her hands in front of her and Edana pushed her forward.

'Move,' she told her. 'We have a long way to go. It is another two days' walk and I don't fancy spending the night anywhere near here if Olaf is on the prowl.'

Bethoc felt her shoulders droop at the thought of another two days travelling. Her legs ached and the blisters on her feet were burst and weeping. She was getting chilly from being so wet and the rain still showed no signs of abating. From what she had seen of Olaf's behaviour these people were right to be wary but she had hoped for a touch of friendliness. Still, her mother hadn't raised her to be resilient for nothing. She swallowed any complaints and walked on.

The hill began to level out and the trees grew more sparse. Ahead of them was a small lochan. Bethoc's companions grew more cautious once they were out of the protective cover of the forest. A number of times they made her stop and wait whilst one of them went ahead to check the way, calling them on with a low whistle when they knew it was safe. They passed another lochan as the ground sloped gradually downwards, smaller than the last and with no surrounding cover at all. They ran across the open ground after Tagaled, pausing for breath as they entered another strand of trees. By now Bethoc's stomach was gnawing at her, she hadn't eaten all day and it was starting to take its toll. It was a relief when Tagaled informed her they would be stopping to make camp soon.

The campsite they chose looked like an ordinary glade of trees until Edana pulled away at a clump of grass and revealed a much used firepit. From a hollow opening at the base of an old oak tree she removed a handful of dry kindling and a few larger sticks. Deftly she set about laying the fire, striking her flint to get it burning before the rain could dampen the spark. The site was well chosen, there was a good thick canopy of leaves overhead that kept the worst of the rain from reaching them and nearby she could hear the faint sound of running water. Edana pointed out a bush nearby covered in blueberries. She hobbled over and gathered enough for them all with her wrists still bound.

As they sat round the fire later, watching the hare Tagaled had caught roasting on a spit, they fired more questions at her.

'So tell me,' Edana started. 'Why are you here?'

Bethoc held her stare as she answered. 'Olaf killed my mother when he found out where she was from. He would have killed me too, so I ran.' She swallowed at the lump rising in her throat at the words. These were probably her people, she must remember that.

'But why come here? There is nothing here anymore.'

'Some of my mother's people are left and hopefully that means I still have family.'

Tagaled eye her with suspicion, 'If you knew you might have family here, why wait all these years to come and find them? It doesn't make any sense.'

Bethoc sighed, her feet were throbbing and she needed to let them breathe. She pulled at her leather laces and removed her boots, revealing the damage. She found her salve and dabbed some on the sores whilst she answered.

'My mother had no idea anyone had survived the Norse attacks, she was made to run away as the second village was burning. I believe she would have come back had she known. I only found out myself when I overheard Olaf ranting about it. When she died I had nowhere else to go.'

She finished applying the salve and started to wind strips of linen to her feet. They watched her as she spoke. She had not uttered a word of complaint despite the pain she must be in. She hadn't even asked for her bindings to be removed. Maybe there was more to her than they thought? Still, her story was a strange one and they were not about to relax their guard. Edana nodded to her salve.

'You a healer?' she asked.

Bethoc nodded. 'My mother taught me.'

Edana threw a sharp glance at Tagaled, he responded with one of his own. The looks were not lost on Bethoc.

'Just who was your family?' he asked her.

'My father was called Donal...'

'Liar!' Tagaled thrust his knife into the ground in front of him, still dirty from cleaning the hare, and glared at her.

'I am NOT a liar!'

'Enough!' he barked. 'The food is ready, we need to eat and sleep. It is a long walk tomorrow and by the looks of your feet it is going to be a slow one.'

After that they ate in uncomfortable silence. Bethoc could almost feel the waves of anger coming from Tagaled. She could not understand why they were acting with such animosity. As soon as the meal was finished the women lay down to sleep whilst Tagaled stomped away to take the first watch.

***

The rain cleared in the night and they woke to a dry, bright morning. Whilst Tagaled re-covered the fire pit and Edana found more sticks to replace the ones they had used in the store, Bethoc attended to her feet and rewound the linen. She found some parsley piert nearby and gathered some of the root to make a decoction when they next stopped. She could soak her linens in it to help dry up the blisters.

They carried on west, pushing Bethoc in front of them. She could hear them muttering together. Before long it was clear they were arguing. She kept her eyes forward and pretended not to notice.

Edana had become increasingly concerned throughout the night. She pushed Tagaled to change their plan but he was not for budging.
'But if she is a healer, couldn't her mother have been...'
'It is all lies,' he cut in, closed to any idea of reason. As soon as she had mentioned Donal's name he had gone cold. He had been a boy of nine when the Vikings had come, burning villages and screaming for the woman. His mother had pushed him away into the trees and told him to run and hide. He had done as she bid, bumping into Irb, a year older than him, already cowering in the bushes. Together they watched the thick black smoke rising over the houses. Many hours later they had crept back to their village only to find everything decimated. He could still remember how his insides had felt like they were tearing out of his body. Shell-shocked, the two orphaned boys had joined the other surviving villagers and raced for the safety of the broch. Theirs was the third village in as many days to be burnt, their arrival was not a complete surprise. Sheilagh had welcomed them in and barred the door behind them, sealing them inside. Her face was a mask of hardened emotion and Tagaled remembered being frightened of the fierce woman. Not long after their arrival her husband

came galloping into the courtyard with a body slung over the withers of his horse. She rived open the door and raced outside. Dungall had returned the previous day from his trip to see Moddan only to find Grumg-Mhor burning and his son missing. None of the survivors had seen him at the village so Dungall had been scouring the area ever since. They had already lost one son to fever when he was only twelve years old, he was not ready to lose another.

Dungall lifted his son's body from the horse and laid him on a cart. It was the first unburnt dead body Tagaled had ever seen. The sight of all the blood shocked him to the core and the sound of Sheilagh's distraught keening had never left him. Edana's voice cut through his thoughts.

'But if she is telling the truth and we make her do this?' she grabbed at his arm. 'I have thought of another way, one that will prove if she knows this area. Let me at least try, if she fails we will do it the usual way.'

It was clear she was not going to give in.

'Alright,' he relented throwing his arms up in defeat. 'Let's try your way.'

***

Edana led the way for the next hour, keeping the pace steady to allow for Bethoc's feet. When the trees came to an end and a huge moorland area opened up in front of them she turned to Bethoc.

'This part is tricky, you lead, we will follow. The way is wet and it will test your feet sorely, it is best if you set the pace.'

There was a distinct softening to the woman's manner today, in sharp contrast to the attitude of Tagaled who had barely said a word. Bethoc looked at the moor, it didn't look bad to her. In fact without the presence of the dreaded bonxies she thought it looked a far easier prospect than the high moor she was used to on Haey. She could see big patches of cotton grass dancing in the breeze and knew the way would be wet. For some reason the sight of it always made her smile. 'Sheep grass' she had called it as a child because it reminded her of minuscule sheep grazing in a field. At least she could grab some to help tend her blisters later. She hitched her bag back up onto her shoulder, wriggled her fastened wrists to make the binding more comfortable, and set off. Had she paused to look back she would have realised that her companions had hung a good way back before following.

The ground was indeed misleading. Where it had looked only slightly wet at a distance it was in fact treacherous and boggy underfoot. Tussocks of grasses stood proud from pools of peaty water and the ground in between that had looked dry enough to take her weight disappeared the moment she stepped on it. She realised why Edana had told her to set the pace. Every step on the uneven ground twisted her boots against her raw skin, even the cold mire water seeping in through the seams did not cool the pain. Soon she was struggling to remove her feet from sucking ground, mud blathered up to her thighs and more than once she had ended up on her knees.

'Can we stop this madness now?' Edana glared at Tagaled. 'It is clear she does not know the way. Her feet must be agony and I am sick of this mud.'

'Fair enough, you win,' he relented, watching as Bethoc fell once more.

Bethoc stopped at his call and turned. She struggled back to them, weighed down by her sodden clothing.

'What's wrong?'

Edana was smiling and even Tagaled's face seemed to have softened somewhat.

'Come on,' he told her. 'Now we can go the proper way.'

He retraced their steps back to drier land before heading to a small stream they had crossed just that side of the trees. The stream led the way over the marshland towards another strand of trees. It had a hard pebble bed and walking up it was the only way across the marsh. Anyone who knew the area well would know this old trick, it was clear that Bethoc did not. She was amazed, she would never have thought of walking in a stream for any other reason than to cool her feet on a hot summer's day.

Leaving the marsh behind, they entered another area of woodland, behind which a jagged mountain rose up like the spiny head of a great dragon. From this distance Bethoc counted three spikes but as they emerged on the other side of the wood yet another peak appeared. The ground was starting to rise sharply to form a much smaller hill. Here the going was rocky and sharp stones jabbed through the thin leather of her boots, causing her to wince every few steps.

'Not long now,' Tagaled told her. She smiled, not really sure why he had changed his mind about her but relieved all the same.

She risked a question. 'I thought it was at least another day's walk?'

'That it was but Edana pleaded your case and begged to bring you the quick way. You clearly have no idea how to move around this area.' He chuckled. 'Only a fool would walk right into a mire like that.'

Bethoc wasn't sure she liked being called a fool and she bristled slightly, 'Well if you had warned me how bad it was I wouldn't have walked in it, would I?'

'Then it wouldn't have been much of a test now would it? We are not going to lead you straight to where we are staying if we don't know you can be trusted.'

'Well it is lucky for me we didn't have bogs like that back home then or I might not have passed your test,' she answered, a little mollified.

'Where was home anyway?' he questioned just as Edana let out one of her bird calls.

'Orkneyjar.'

***

The wind was forced out of her as she was slammed back into a large rock.

'What did you just say?' Tagaled demanded. His hand pushed on her shoulder, whilst his other reached for his knife.

Bethoc's head smacked off the rock and the pain blinded her for a few moments. She blinked the dazzling array of colours out of her vision and tried to calm her frantic heartbeat. What had she said now? This man was as prickly as a holly bush and far less understandable.

'I... I said Orkneyjar, my home was Haey, one of the islands there.'

Tagaled growled in response and was just lifting the knife to her throat when a strange voice barked an order and his arm was pulled away.

The stranger, a man a few years older than Tagaled, glared at the pair of them and back to Edana, who looked as shocked as he did.

'What is going on here?'

'We saw Olaf Feilan up to no good and followed him to Grumbeg. We found this one hiding from him in the trees. Irb led him off the other way and I grabbed her,' Tagaled answered. 'She has a fine story to tell and she acts it well...'

'Tagaled,' Edana burst in. 'I thought we had agre..'

'She is from Orkneyjar.' He cut her off. 'She just admitted it.'

Edana rounded on Bethoc, her eyes wide with shock.

'Is this true?'

The pain lanced through Bethoc's head as she nodded. 'Mother said she thought she would be safer hiding where the Norse already were. She said they burnt villages looking for her, she had to get away.'

Tagaled's arm fell away from her and he stumbled backwards.

'Who is your mother?' the new man asked.

'Her name was Oonagh, she lived at Grumg-Mhor.'

For a moment or two there was silence. The three faces looked at her in utter shock, there was no doubt they knew exactly who her mother was.

'Please,' Bethoc begged, 'Are any of my family still alive? Do you know them? Can you take me to them?'

'My name is Gurum,' the new man told her, cutting her ties. 'You had better come with us.'

He led the way round the large rock and suddenly seemed to disappear. Edana urged her forward and at the last moment she realised there was a slight fissure behind the rock just large enough to let a man pass through. Once inside, Bethoc could see it was the entrance to a long passageway. Gurum had a torch already burning and he passed another to Tagaled, who brought up the rear. The passage got so low at one point that they had to crawl for a few yards before it opened up into a small chamber. From here were three choices, Gurum chose the one to the left. Eventually they reached a huge, long cavern with a hearty fire burning in a large pit near the centre.

Gurum swung his arm wide and bowed his head. 'Welcome to our home.'

The cave was taller than any tree Bethoc had ever seen, much taller in fact. From what she could make out, the roof rose up to a great fissure through which the smoke from the fire filtered away, leaving the air beneath clear and easy to breathe. Away from the centre were numerous stalactites in a variety of sizes. Beneath these were ever-hopeful stalagmites stretching their way up to meet them. In a number of places they had actually met and formed majestic columns, making the cavern a surreal and magical place.

'Wonderful, isn't it?' Edana said. 'There are a number of entrances, which keeps the air fresh. We spend most of our communal time in here but we sleep in the smaller chambers. This whole mountain is riddled with caves and tunnels. So far, the Norse have no idea this place is here.' She led the way into the heart of the space. 'Come on, there is someone you need to meet.'

Bethoc hobbled after her. Her feet were going to take some time to recover from all the abuse she had given them.

Sitting on a thick blanket, leaning against one of the shorter stalagmites, sat an older woman. From a distance she looked old and crooked but the closer they got, Bethoc could see she was not quite as old as she appeared. A young girl sat with her and they both looked up with interest as the group approached.

'Doada, we have brought someone to meet you.' Edana crouched and squeezed her hand. 'I think it will make you very happy.'

The woman looked up at Bethoc with interest. Her face was heavily lined but her eyes were bright. She indicated to the blanket next to her and Bethoc sat down.

'Tell her what you just told us,' Edana urged.

Other people started to gather round and Bethoc waited until everyone was settled. Not really sure where to begin but knowing that her mother's name had made all the difference outside, she decided to start with that.

'My mother's name was Oonagh.'

A moan escaped the old woman, she raised a trembling hand to her face. Dots and lines covered the back of it, right down to her fingertips. Bethoc paused, the woman gave a slight nod and she carried on.

'She told me she lived at a village called Grumg-Mhor where she loved a man called Donal. One day they were up in the woods when they came across some Norsemen. Donal made Mother hide but they caught him and killed him. She managed to get away on his horse and they chased her through the forest. She heard they were going to burn the village to get her so she led them away over the hill.'

Every face was fixed on Bethoc. She glanced at Edana who nodded encouragingly at her.

'She tried to get back to the village but stopped at another first. A man there, a drover I think she said. He told her that her village had been raided and burnt and that he thought everyone was killed. He was going to take her back to see but the Norse arrived and started burning that village too. The man made her run, so she fled. Not daring to go anywhere near a village she went to Orkneyjar where she hid amongst the Norse, pretending to be from the Sudreyjar. I was born not long after she arrived. We lived happily until not long ago. I had become engaged to a man named Olaf.'

At his name the air around the audience grew tenser. Bethoc paused again. This was the hardest part of the story and one she knew she would have difficulty relating.

'He was not the man he had pretended to be. When Mother got sick she began to speak about here and about my father. I had no idea what she was talking about. When the fever broke I got her to explain. She admitted all about her true past and how all her family had been killed. I must have mentioned what she had been saying to Olaf because he sent me to another island to attend a dead woman.' Realising how strange that sounded, she added, 'I am a healer just like my mother.'

At this Doada smiled, her eyes had become watery and her hands still trembled but she stayed silent as the young woman in front of her eased the burden she had carried for twenty years.

'When I returned, I found the house smashed and my poor mother lying dying on the bedroom floor.

She told me my Olaf had done this to her and that he was not the man he was pretending to be. At first I did not believe her but my mother would never lie, she could barely breathe so I knew it must be true.'

Bethoc hung her head. The floor of the cave began to swim and a large teardrop fell to her lap.

'My mother died in my arms, beaten to death by the man I was supposed to be marrying.' She scrubbed at her face with her hand and rushed on, desperate to get it all out before someone interrupted.

'I was outside when he came back so I hid beneath the window. I heard him talking to her body, laughing at the fact she was dead and telling her she had ruined everything. He was like a different man completely. He told her that people from the village were still here hiding but that the Norse would defeat them all and take over Cait. He said he was coming back to get me too so I ran. I came here to find my mother's family and let them know what had happened to her. I have nowhere else to go.'

She lifted her head again and looked at the people gathered round. Each face held the same look of utter shock.

Doada reached her shaking hand forward and Bethoc took hold of it. The old woman was smiling despite her tears.

'Thank you my dear,' she said. 'Thank you for coming all this way and telling us this news. You have indeed found your family. I am your grandmother, Oonagh's mother. I have wondered all these years what became of my eldest daughter.'

***

No one had ever been able to find out what had happened to Oonagh, she had just disappeared without trace.

They had searched for days, until the Norse arrived in such numbers they were forced to retreat inside the broch. Unable to penetrate the defences, the Norse settled in for a siege. A small camp grew up around the entranceway and all excursions were brought to a halt. Food was not an issue, Sheilagh had prepared well, but arguments started to break out and resentment grew like spores of mould.

The biggest cause of contention had been Oonagh. A small but vocal number of people felt she had directly brought the wrath of the Vikings down on them. They blamed her for the loss of their loved ones and homes, refusing point blank to accept that she was a victim too. They had been walled up in the broch for six weeks when tensions snapped. Anger and resentment fuelled by intense frustration boiled over into a huge argument, fists flew, furniture smashed, and somehow Dungall ended up at the bottom of the stone stairs with a broken neck. Sheilagh raged and stormed, her fury ferocious. The dissenters retreated to the courtyard and kept their heads low.

The 25 people left were all united in their belief that Donal and Oonagh must have disturbed the

Norse in the woods. Led by one man, they formed a plan. Taking it in shifts to dig from the courtyard out under the retaining wall, they aimed to come out at the narrow strip of beach between them and the loch. Finally, under cover of darkness, they broke through just the other side of the outer wall, a few feet short of the water's edge. The Norse, busy guarding the far side, carried on with their rowdy noise. Blinded by the brightness of their campfires and the belief that the entrance in front of them was the only means of escape, they were oblivious to the people silently swimming away.

Once out of the water the villagers quickly melted into the trees. The trouble-makers headed straight out of the area but the 25 formed groups of two or three and over the next few days everyone made it safely to their new hideout in the caverns under Ben Law. There they were safe and, possibly more importantly, able to move about, to hunt and to get word out to Moddan.

It took the Norse five days before they realised their quarry had left. They wasted no time taking over the broch. A small garrison took up residence, everyone else was sent out to search the hills, but the people were long gone. Thorstein was furious.

***

For the rebels in the cavern, Bethoc's news was nothing short of miraculous. For almost twenty years they had kept their cause alive, always praying for a breakthrough. Over that time a number of them had been lost, through clashes with the Norsemen or illness. Sheilagh had been one of the first, she had never recovered from her grief.

The first few months in the hideout, she had wasted away, finally breathing her last on a particularly cold February night. The man who had led them from the broch had proved to be a good leader but he had died in a skirmish between the Norse and the rebels at Dun Yrredell. The blond warriors had come in force and with a new mission. The rebels had lost their leader and five of their strongest men. The Norse had taken Dun Yrredell and made Moddan a hostage in his own cell. Still, they would not give in, they held on to the hope that one day everything might change.

For Doada the news was bittersweet. The joy at learning her daughter had indeed survived after all was cut through with the need to grieve for her all over again. Yet, on top of all this was the unbelievable truth that this young woman in front of her was Oonagh's daughter and hence her granddaughter.

***

She was not the only one to be so moved by the news.

'Was Oonagh happy in this strange life?'

One of the men had stepped forward. The tattoos on his face made his age hard to fathom, though Bethoc guessed he was in his mid-30s. His hair was peppered with grey and he carried a nasty scar down the side of his face. His voice wavered slightly as he spoke.

'This is my son, Angus,' Doada explained. 'I had six children including your mother, as you may know, but I lost two in the fires, along with my husband, and another was killed later by the Norse.'

Bethoc smiled at her uncle and glanced around the others to see if she could recognise his sibling. She must have made it obvious.

'My sister Ffiona is not here,' Angus explained. 'She has young twins and this is no place to raise a family. She lives far away by Loch Beannach, a safe area. Her husband Kineth visits regularly with news and supplies.'

So this was what a family was like? Extended lines of people who cared so much. Bethoc was moved by the strangeness of it.

'My mother settled well on Orkneyjar, we lived on an island called Haey. She was their healer and they respected her.' Bethoc paused and looked to her grandmother. 'She told me she learned her skills from you and you from your mother.'

Doada nodded, 'Aye, tis a long-held tradition. It fills my heart with joy that she continued it.'

Bethoc smiled at her and turned back to Angus.

'She didn't mix much, but the people she did mix with were good friends to her and I believe she was happy in her own way. I do know she hated to talk of her past, it was just too painful for her. Always she had said her family was killed on Sudreyjar and

that she missed them more than she could say.
There were days she would seem to drift off into
her memories, then she would be very sad and
quiet.'
Angus shook his head and glanced at the woman
by his side, she squeezed his hand.
'My husband has always described Oonagh as a
being full of life, always happy to be in the
company of others. It has cost the family dear all
these years wondering what happened to her.'

Respectful of the family, most of the people had
moved away. Now only four remained: Doada,
Angus, his wife and a boy a couple of years
younger than Bethoc.
'This is my wife, Moiraugh and our son, Anfrud.'
Angus explained. 'One of my sisters was also called
Moira, she was next in age to your mother.' His
eyes clouded with sadness. 'She was killed in the
fires along with my brother Taran.'
'It must be a shock for you,' Anfrud said. 'Just
finding out you have a family after all this time.'
Bethoc nodded her head, their faces began to blur
as unshed tears threatened to fall. Her emotions
were conflicting. These people seemed good and
they were so eager to hear her news, yet they were
still strangers to her for all they were related. She
longed to have her mother beside her, to rid herself
of the awful gnawing emptiness she and Olaf had
left inside her. More than anything, she hated
missing his company and the closeness they had
shared. For the months they had been together she

had felt part of something, like she had a reason for being. Now, even though she knew it had all been an illusion, that Olaf was a hateful, evil man, she was forced to admit that he had opened up a part of her that would now always feel hollow and lost. She felt an arm around her shoulders. Blinking away the tears, she saw worried faces looking back at her. Moiraugh gave her a hug and held out a cloth for her face.

Anfrud shuffled his feet, looking abashed. 'I am sorry, I didn't mean to upset you.'

Bethoc nodded up to him, feeling embarrassed. She hadn't expected to make a fool of herself in front of everybody.

'You have had a terrible ordeal followed by a long journey,' his mother stated, breaking the awkward silence. 'Let's get you something to eat and then you must rest. We have plenty of time to learn each other's news and get to know one another.'

Doada turned to her grandson. 'Anfrud, will you ask Elinn to prepare a sleeping area for Bethoc? Somewhere quiet I think, for now.'

He scuttled off. Once they were alone, Doada patted Bethoc on the arm. 'You have the look of my daughter,' she told her. 'I will always feel she is still with us now you are around.'

***

Bethoc woke the following morning to the faint sounds of the dawn chorus working their way into the cave from the hills beyond. She stretched and

173

took her time replaying the events of the previous evening. From spending her life believing the only family she had was her mother, she now found herself with two aunts and uncles, three cousins and a grandmother. Not to mention a whole host of rebels all as eager as her family to get to know her. If truth be told she felt more than a little overwhelmed by it all. So much so she realised she had completely forgotten to mention the necklace.

They had found her a place in a small chamber close to the main sleeping areas and close enough to the main cavern that she did not get lost finding her way back. Once there she saw her grandmother talking to a girl and two men. The eldest of these turned to her as she approached.

'I did not get the chance to introduce myself last night,' he began. 'My name is Aiden, I am your father's younger brother and now the leader of this sorry tribe. This is my daughter Elinn, she is a little young to live here with us but we lost her mother last year.'

'I am sorry to hear that, I hope it was under more peaceful circumstances than my mother's death.'

Bethoc felt a strong pull of sympathy for the girl, who looked even younger than Anfrud.

Elinn shook her head, 'She was killed by a Norse raid on our farmstead. She just had time to push me into the food cellar out of the way before they burst in. They had heard we were in league with the rebels and thought to get information from us.'

'Luckily they didn't search or torch the place or I would have lost her too,' Aiden gave a wry smile. 'Finlay here, though, lost his mother to the fever when he was only three. He is another child of the cave.'

Finlay grinned at her, 'Your grandmother has raised me ever since. My father was killed in the burnings when I was just a babe.'

He was about Bethoc's age with wild, dark curly hair and a cheeky face. Just like Anfrud, his face was clear of any tattoos. Bethoc liked him at once.

'Finlay here was the last baby your mother and I delivered before the burnings,' Doada explained. 'He came on Beltane morning, just after she returned from meeting your father at the ritual. I have had a soft spot for the little bugger ever since.'

Make that four uncles, three aunts and four cousins, Bethoc thought as someone handed her a bowl of thick, sticky porridge.

After the food she turned to Aiden. 'I have more news I think you will be interested in, I completely forgot to mention it last night in the shock of meeting you all.'

His attention was roused, 'Go on.'

'Mother said my father took a necklace from the Norsemen, she took it, and they chased her. She told me it was more important than she had realised. She buried it in the woods above the village and forgot all about it until Olaf came looking for it. She told me they must not find it, that she told Olaf she had dropped it when really she had buried it under a marker stone on the hill above Grumg-Mhor.'

Aiden frowned. 'A necklace again... I wonder? Did she say what the necklace was?'

'Only that it was made of black stones and like half a moon but broken. She seemed surprised it was so important.'

'You said that Thorstein had stolen something from a grave, Father, and that is what started all the problems. Do you think it was this necklace?'

Aiden looked at Elinn and nodded, 'It could just be... I shall have to think on this news, Bethoc. Not for the first time I wish Moddan was here.'

'Who is Moddan? I heard he was a prisoner somewhere now,' Bethoc asked, remembering from her journey.

'He is the Maormar, the lord of the whole area. My father was Maor, his underlord. Now Thorstein has taken over Dun Yrredell, his broch and has Moddan as his prisoner.'

So this was the important work Thorstein had been doing all these years. No wonder he rarely had time to visit Haey.

<h1 style="text-align:center">13</h1>

The sun was shining on the rocky area outside one of the entrances to the caverns. Bethoc sat enjoying the warmth on her face, her feet dangling in the cooling water. She had been there just over a week and although she got on well with everyone she was not used to being around so many people so she had taken to spending an hour or two on her own whenever she got the chance. Her blisters were healing well and she had been given a new pair of boots to replace her ruined ones. If only her internal wounds could heal as quickly.

Little things got to her the most. Every time she witnessed a loving touch between a couple, her heart tore at her chest. Worse though were those times when she heard Doada humming to herself. Oonagh used to hum to herself all the time but it was something she herself had never done. This silly little quirk made her feel even more remote from her mother. Often when she was alone like this she would try to hum a tune in the vain attempt it would make her feel less outcast.

A noise startled her. She turned to see Finlay and her grandmother edging their way out from behind the waterfall that hid the cavern entrance.

'You're sounding a little happier,' Doada said, as Finlay helped her to take a seat. 'Your mother used to laugh at me for my humming, she said it was like living with a giant bumble bee.'

'I like your humming, Doada,' Finlay winked at Bethoc. 'It means I always know where you are and you can't sneak up on me.'

The old woman pointed a finger. 'You watch it, terror, or I will put you forward for extra guard duties. Go on now, leave us two to talk. Come back and get me in a little while if you would.'

He placed a light kiss on Doada's cheek, grinned at Bethoc, and skipped back behind the falls.

Doada shook her head. 'He has kept my heart young,' she confided. 'I did not want to take on another child but he had no one else. His mother, Katiana, had suffered a lot, losing her husband only months after Finlay was born. All her other family perished too, so I took her under my wing but she never recovered from her grief. The fever took her only three years later and I, well I ended up with that rapscallion.'

'You had your own grief to bear.'

'Aye lass, I did that but something in a healer's make up means we can dig deep and get on with things we never thought possible when we are needed.'

Bethoc thought back to the incident at the quarry. Maybe Doada was right.

'I sense a deep struggle in you though, lass,' her grandmother continued. She waved her hand at their surroundings, 'Oh, I understand the need for your own space. We all went through something similar when we were cooped up in the broch. Trust me, this place is heaven compared to that but this is different. It's not just about losing your mother, either. I know you do not know me very well yet but can you find your way to trust in me and tell me about it? You never know, I might be able to help.'

So, she had not been as careful as she had thought at hiding her feelings. Bethoc flicked a fly from her leg and pulled a stray hair from her face. Where on earth should she start? She took a deep breath, then another, keeping her eyes on her feet. Doada watched her struggle for a moment.

'I am guessing it has something to do with Olaf?'

Bethoc's eyes flew to her grandmother's face, had she been so transparent?

'Everyone seems to have overlooked the fact you said you were engaged to him.'

The pained look in her granddaughter's face told her she had hit the mark.

Bethoc nodded. With her eyes back on her feet she finally opened her heart.

'He wasn't like the Olaf you all know. The one I see now too. He was... different, caring and...' She shook her head. 'I thought we were in love. He was my world. He even stopped living with his father and stayed on the island just to be with me. I just don't understand how someone could do all that when they were lying the whole time.'

Doada reached forward and took hold of her hand.

'Olaf is a rotten man from a rotten family, he was grown that way. It is no reflection on you, my dear.'

Bethoc took an even deeper breath, she wasn't sure she could voice this properly but it was slowly eating away at her so she had to try. 'I hate him for what he did,' she admitted. 'But I can't help but miss what we had. I don't miss him.' She added quickly, as Doada made to answer, 'At least I don't miss who he really is but...'

'But you miss the man you thought he was?'

Bethoc nodded her head again, not looking up in case her tears showed. 'I thought I had found perfection but I realise it was just an illusion. I know it is wrong but I miss that illusion so much.' The tears could not be held back and they fell onto her knees in great droplets.

'Come here, child.' Her grandmother's arms were open to her and she gladly folded herself inside them. She stayed there until she thought she could sob no more. Pulling away, she looked at Doada.

'I think I would kill him if he ever came near me again. So how can I hate someone so much, yet miss them too? I just have to think of him being with me and I want to be sick but my mind will not let go what we had.'

'Oh my dear,' Doada was crying too. 'It is no wonder you are filled with so much pain. He tricked you into believing he was exactly what you wanted him to be so he could get near your mother and find this necklace. You would not have fallen in love with him if you had known the real person he was. You fell in love with the illusion because that is what he wanted you to do. You must remember you are his victim too.' She frowned. 'I wonder how he found out you were there?'

Her grandmother's words put her heartache into perspective. She was a shrewd woman, it was no wonder she was loved so much by the rebels.

'Thorstein, his father, has a home on Haey but he is barely ever there. He apparently does a lot of work in Cait for Sigurd who is Jarl of Orkneyjar. They came back for the Winter Thing last year and the next Beltane Olaf gave me his feather and we were never apart from then.'

Doada looked surprised. 'Did your mother ever meet Thorstein?'

'Only once that I know of. Why?'

'Thorstein is one of the three Norse that killed your father and burnt the villages. He is the one that has Moddan prisoner and thinks he rules this area. I am surprised she never recognised him.'

They both agreed it was strange. There was so much to all this they would never know for certain. Too many people had died before they could say what they had seen. A noise from behind the waterfall warned them of Finlay's return.

'There is one more thing I must tell you, child,' Doada told her softly. 'Apart from the months he was with you on Haey, Olaf lives here in Cait. He moved into Caisteal Bharraich three years ago where he lives with his wife and their two children.' She reached forward and placed a kiss on Bethoc's forehead. Then tactically retreated into the cavern.

***

'Hey!' a voice called out.

Bethoc wiped her face on the back of her hands just as Finlay sat down next to her.

'Do you mind some company? Doada said she had to give you bad news. You ok?'

She looked at him, her smile not quite reaching her red eyes. 'Yeah, I guess so.'

'It is a tough life,' Finlay told her. 'There ain't one of us who hasn't had to go through something traumatic. We all understand.' He flicked her on the leg. 'You ain't that special you know.'

Now she really did laugh. He put his arm around her shoulders and gave her a quick squeeze. 'And as for that shit, Olaf Feilan. He will get his dues.'

Edana came and sat on her other side. 'Irb said when he came back that Olaf had fallen off his horse the other day, you know when we found you.' She grinned. 'He led him into an area of really low trees and one of the branches knocked him clean to the ground.'

It felt good to sit there with those two, laughing even as her tears continued to fall. There was a conspiratorial lightness that was just what Bethoc needed. Maybe she really did belong there after all?

Later that evening she got the chance to meet yet another relative. Kineth arrived just before nightfall with a cartload of precious supplies. His Maormar, Ruaridh, was very sympathetic to the rebel cause and often sent cartloads of food their way along with any messages he might have. Today he sent word that the Norse had raided another fishing village on the north coast. Kineth also brought his own news, Ffiona was expecting another child.

'It looks like I am the bearer of fantastic news both ways,' he grinned at Bethoc. 'Your aunt will be so upset she cannot come and meet you herself.' He checked himself and apologised. 'I am sorry, you are still grieving. Naturally the news about your mother is terrible, I know Ffiona will take it hard. She was very close to her big sister, I don't think she has ever really got over losing her.'

Bethoc tried to smile but it failed to reach her eyes. All these years so many people had been longing for news of her mother, yet she had lived her life believing herself and Bethoc to be all alone in the world. It was just too sad for words.

Kineth changed the subject quickly. 'It is interesting news about the necklace though, Ruaridh mentioned he had news about one the other day.'

Aiden turned to him, 'What do you mean?'

Kineth shrugged. 'I'm not sure, he was going to meet with someone who had information for him. He should be back by the time I get home, I will go see him straightaway.'

The leader clapped him on the back. 'Thank you my friend, we could use the information as soon as possible.'

'I was planning on spending a couple of nights here but I will leave at daybreak.'

***

183

The next evening, Bethoc was sitting with Doada and the other younger members of the rebel group. They seemed drawn to her grandmother and it didn't take her long to see why. Doada was witty, had a wealth of stories to tell, and always had time for them. The others in the cavern were the more active members of the group, ranging in age from their mid-twenties to early 30s. The only exceptions to this were Eila at 23 and Gurum at 42. Eila had joined them when a ranging party consisting of Tagaled, Irb and Cailtran had rescued her from the hands of the Norse. She had been travelling with her father when they had been attacked. Her father had died defending them and she was pinned down beneath a warrior when Cailtran had emerged behind him and sent him flying into the next world with one swing of his sword. They had been a couple ever since, regularly pairing up on patrols together. Bethoc had still to meet them, they had called back to the cavern only once since she had arrived but she had been outside by the waterfall at the time.

'What was Haey like, Bethoc?' Elinn asked her.

'Beautiful,' she answered. 'A lot like here really but with cliffs and sea all around.'

'Do you miss it?'

'No. It would never be the same if I went back,' she shook her head. 'I miss Groa, my friend, though.'

Anfrud looked thoughtful. 'Was she a Norse?'

Bethoc nodded, 'I suppose she was. Her family were very close to Mother and me, they were the first friends Mother made when she arrived on the island.'

'It seems strange that she would make friends with them after what they did here.'

A flash of annoyance crossed Bethoc's face but she reeled it in. All Anfrud had ever known was the caves and the Norse as enemies, it was a natural reaction.

'They are nice people,' she explained. 'Not all of them are like Thorstein and Olaf. In fact I never met anyone else like them. Everyone else I knew was just normal, though they did have some silly superstitions. They were wary of giants and trows, always worrying about offending them or having their babies spirited away in the night.'

Elinn's eyes widened. 'Really, did you ever see any?'

Bethoc laughed and shook her head. 'Never. Though now I think about it this place is a great hiding place for us, the Norse would never come here. It is the perfect home for a giant. There was this one rock on the island not far from our home that was said to have been pulled down from the cliff by a giant, who carved a great tomb inside. In it he locked a dwarf, who is supposed to be still there to this day. There is a huge rock across the entrance. Everyone on the island takes a wide berth if ever they have to go past it.'

'I take it you used to dance on the stone?' Finlay laughed at her. He was the oldest of the small group at twenty. He had started to join the older rebels on short missions but he still spent a great deal of time with Doada.

'Oor Bethoc, the dwarfie dancer,' her grandmother joked. 'I bet you had no idea you had such a brave cousin, Anfrud?'

'Well I certainly wasn't afraid of dwarfs and giants. There were a few strange things though, you know, things you couldn't explain. Strange lights on the top of the Ward Hill and talk of selkies in the water.'

'If you want to see something strange and wonderful, come with us.' Elinn held her hand out to her and pulled her to her feet. Doada waved them away with a smile and the four of them ran off down one of the tunnels. Anfrud and Finlay carried torches and held them aloft as they entered a side cave in front of the girls. Bethoc rushed in after them and came to an abrupt stop at the sight waiting for her. The waterfall that had once cascaded down the wall had slowly formed itself into a series of calcium bowls, the outside of which trailed with calcified ribbons. Musical tinkling sounds of the water filled the cave as it still trickled through the falls, filling the bowls with crystal-clear water. The effect was stunning. The whole scene lit up with the torchlight glistening off the shimmering stone and turning the pools of water into perfect mirrors. Bethoc felt as if she had been caught in a spell.

'We call it the fountain,' Elinn said.

'But don't worry, we get our water from the stream that runs outside by the north entrance,' Anfrud said, laughing. 'So you won't turn into a stone while you stay here.'

They stayed admiring the fountain for a while longer before returning to the cavern where they spent the rest of the evening discussing different superstitions and scaring each other with spooky stories. For the first time, Bethoc didn't feel like she was on the outside looking in.

14

Cailtran and Eila did not arrive back the next day as planned and the atmosphere in the caverns was edged with trepidation. They had not lost anyone to the fighting for almost a year but no one was complacent. By the time mid-afternoon arrived, Gurum was all for going out searching but Aiden urged caution, just in case they had been forced to lie low for a while. There could be any number of Norsemen out there looking for the necklace by now. They all knew the rule. No rangers were to return to the caverns whilst there was a chance they were being followed.

When they still had not arrived back the next evening, Aiden bowed to pressure and agreed to let Gurum go out scouting. At daybreak the next morning he darted out of the caverns and was soon gone from sight. He arrived back late that evening with news.

'I got as far as the Loch of Islands,' he began, accepting a hot drink from Moiraugh with a nod of thanks. 'In the far distance I could see Norsemen. Lots of them, crawling all over the place. I watched for a while, they seemed to be very intent on something but I could not make out what. I thought it best to come back and warn you all before risking getting closer.' He paused to take a sip of his drink.

'Do you think Cailtran and Eila have been captured?' Aiden asked.

'I would hazard a guess that our friends spotted them and have chosen to use one of the longer routes back. Either between lochs Law and Craggie or else round by Loch an Dherue. Failing that they will be lying low until such time as they can safely find a way back to us.'

Aiden rubbed his elbow, nodding. 'We'd best wait until such time as they show up before making plans.'

The next evening the pair arrived back, dirty, dishevelled and cross. They had been forced to make a wide detour and come into the hideout from the west side.

'Olaf has men everywhere,' Cailtran informed them. 'We were lying low just south of the strath out of the way when we ran into Kineth. He explained they were looking for a necklace?'

Aiden nodded. 'This thing keeps popping up to infuriate us.'

Eila frowned and mumbled something about torture. Aiden stopped her with a glare but Bethoc had already heard.

'Tell me?' she insisted.

Eila was immediately contrite. 'I am so sorry, Bethoc. We haven't even met properly yet and here I am being unthoughtful.'

Bethoc waved her words away. 'Please just tell me what you meant.' She looked at the faces around her. No one wanted to meet her eyes, she looked back at Eila. 'I saw what Olaf did to my mother, don't forget. I know how serious they are about this necklace... I need to know.'

Eila was only a few years older than Bethoc. She remembered how determined she had been when her father had been murdered. She let out a sigh. 'All right but I am keeping it brief.' She glanced at Aiden, who nodded reluctantly.

'We had a couple of people caught by Thorstein a few years ago,' she began. 'He tortured the woman for news about a necklace. The man was forced to watch before they were both killed and thrown out on the midden pile. Luckily for us the man was not quite dead and he managed to signal for help and get the news out to us before he died. We could never work out what on earth this necklace was. We had heard it mentioned a few times before and since but no one has ever been able to find out anything more.'

Aiden stepped forward. 'Clearly we cannot let this go any longer. We need to find out what exactly this necklace is and then find it before Olaf does.'

***

The pace of life in the cavern was an easy one but there was always something to keep people busy. Early the following morning, Irb took Anfrud out to Loch an Dherue, fishing. They left by a long tunnel that led out of one of the smaller adjoining caves and deep under the rising bulk of Ben Law. Eventually it emerged into a craggy, seemingly impenetrable, area of rock face on the mountain's western side, not too far from the northern end of the loch where the best fishing was to be had. Moiraugh, Edana and Elinn were weaving baskets whilst Gurum and Tagaled polished their swords. Doada was busy kneading dough ready to set out on the warm rocks at the back entrance to prove.

A low call filtered through to the main cavern from the southeastern entrance tunnel. Aiden rushed off to meet Eila, waiting where the tunnels joined.

'Thought you would want to see this,' she told him with a glint in her eye.

He followed her out to where their eastern lookout point emerged from the mountainside, high up over the Law Road. A large group of Norsemen were hiking back up the road. Drifts of conversation floated up to them but it was not enough to make out any words. The men sounded happy though.

'Do you think they found it?'

Aiden felt his heart sink, 'I don't know but whenever they look happy, I feel worried.'

A small stone bounced down behind them and they turned to see Cailtran coming down from a higher vantage point.

'Thorstein came thundering down the road a while ago and the next thing I knew the men were starting to head back up. Looks like he has pulled them from the search.'

He waited with his eyes on the road before jumping down the last section and landing lightly next to them. The lookout was safe from view so long as they kept low but parts of the route heading further up the mountain were more exposed and needed much more care to navigate. As they watched, two horses came into view. Thorstein and Olaf were on their way back. From this distance it was impossible to make out their faces. Thorstein's horse pranced and threw his head around, eager for another gallop. It suddenly surged forward, nearly catching Thorstein unawares. After a couple of strides he had his control back and the horse reined round in a tight circle. It smacked into Olaf's horse and Thorstein shoved at his son's shoulder, pushing him out of the way. Up at the vantage point they heard the growl of his voice, if not the actual words. Olaf did not answer, he edged his horse further over and kept his eyes down.

Eila grinned and Aiden relaxed slightly. If Thorstein was this angry with Olaf, they could be sure the necklace had not been found.

'Better brace ourselves, Thorstein is mad and that usually means trouble is not far behind,' Cailtran said quietly.

Aiden looked at his friends. 'As soon as he gets back, tell Irb it's time for him to leave. One man on his own will be better for this watch.'

Cailtran made to interrupt but the leader cut him off. 'I will send you two out again when we have his report back.'

15

Elinn burst into the main cavern and raced over to her father, 'Someone is coming down the long tunnel, I heard hooting. It sounded like Kineth's call but he wouldn't use that entrance.'
Aiden dropped the plate he was holding and grabbed his dagger.
'Wait here.'
He whistled to the other men and headed off to the tunnel entrance. Slight noises could be heard coming from inside; whoever it was was getting nearer. The low hoot that was Kineth's safe call sounded again and all stood ready. For years they had used various bird calls to warn others of their safe approach or a hawk cry to warn of danger. If they were to hear a cuckoo call they immediately knew it was the enemy approaching and they had one of them prisoner or worse. The system had worked perfectly well for years and had saved a number of lives.
What had them so worried now was the fact that Kineth lived to the south of the area, there was no reason at all that he should be using this entrance. The tunnel was only ever used to access Loch an Dherue or to get to the village of Arnaboll which sat to the west of Caol Thunga. The eastern side of the long sea loch was used by the Norse to land their vessels. Thorstein had built himself a tower roughly halfway up the loch, high up on a rocky knoll overlooking the harbour. Caisteal Bharraich,

as it was known, was imposing and formidable. Access was up a wooden ladder to the first floor, which could be raised if ever the tower came under attack. As soon as he had taken Moddan prisoner a few years later, he had left Olaf the tower and moved his family to the Maormar's fort.

At the southern end of the loch stood a disused broch that had once been home to the local Maor and was one of the first casualties of the invasion. A number of large wooden ships had swept into Caol Thunga, bringing with them hundreds of warriors. Whilst a number of these had headed straight down to reinforce the siege, the rest under Thorstein's command had over-run the Thunga communities and established the area as their headquarters. The broch, now abandoned to the elements, was only used occasionally by nearby sympathisers who, not knowing the whereabouts of the hideout, would sometimes leave food or secret messages for the rebels to find.

A glow of light grew steadily brighter as whoever was in the tunnel approached. The waiting party stood ready. Again the hoot came and again there was no mistaking Kineth's tawny call. He followed the sound out of the tunnel and stood dishevelled, though none too surprised at the sight of his greeting party.

'Bloody Norse are still crawling everywhere,' he stated, looking around the concerned faces. 'It has taken me over a week to get to you, every time I thought I could risk approaching I would see another patrol. In the end I had to deliver my cover message to Thunga and under the pretext of having another to go to Arnaboll, I headed down Coal Thunga. The route was empty, all the men must have been diverted to the searches. I called in at the broch and found this for you,' he handed over a bag full of salted meat and cheese. 'I must leave again soon and carry on round to Arnaboll and down Strathmor, I don't want to arouse suspicion plus I want to get back to Ffiona as soon as possible, she will be worrying.'

Aiden relaxed his poise and sheathed his dagger, the others followed suit. 'I don't know how to tell you, but the searches are finished, the men were all called back yesterday.'

Kineth grimaced. 'Bloody typical. I will have to go all that way round now for nothing.'

***

The group made their way back into the main cavern where the women were gathered together behind Edana. At the sight of Kineth they whooped with joy.

Doada handed Kineth a mug of spiced ale and a chunk of bread. Whilst he ate, the rest of them formed a ring in the centre of the cavern floor and readied themselves to hear his news.

'Turns out that the necklace is Hildr's necklace, the one from Haey. It is what Thorstein stole from the barrow tomb when he first came to Cait.'

Aiden looked confused. 'Hildr's necklace?'

195

He turned to Bethoc.

'I've never heard of it,' she said.

Kineth placed his mug on the floor. 'Neither had I but it turns out it is the stuff of legend. Many hundreds of years ago a woman named Hildr crafted the necklace from jet and coal to calm the anger between her husband and her father. She wove many spells into its making but her father had a magic sword and he had already drawn it when the necklace was given to him. The sword had to have blood and so a battle began between the two men's armies. The necklace was lost in the turmoil. Many years later it was found and given to an important leader, who gave it to his wife. They moved to Cait and it was buried in her tomb when she died. Thorstein tracked the necklace to the tomb and stole it, thinking to use it to overpower the people of Cait.'

'That robbery was the first thing they did if I remember right,' Aiden told him. 'I remember they had been seen scouting around the area but then they ripped open the tomb and Moddan put the word out that they must be caught and brought to trial. But I had no idea about the necklace, I don't think anyone did at the time.'

A flash of recognition lit up Moiraugh's face. 'Come to think of it there were rumours of such a necklace when I was a girl, I remember thinking I would love to own a magic necklace.'

'Oh come on,' Angus said, laughing. 'Do you folk really believe a necklace can hold the power to subdue us?'

Bethoc got to her feet, 'It doesn't matter what we believe. What matters is Thorstein believes it, he believes in it so much he burnt all your villages and then sent his son to get to my mother all these years later. This necklace holds power whether we believe it or not.'

All eyes turned back to Kineth. 'The guy Ruaridh went to see was one of his more northerly Maors, he had heard some interesting rumours. It turns out he had been contacted by Olaf regarding the necklace, asking if any such item had been offered for sale. He claims he himself had it made as a gift to his wife after being away so long but that one of his men lost it on the journey back. He is offering a handsome reward for the person who finds it and hands it in. He was very clear that the necklace is to be given to no one but himself or his father and that word of its existence is to be kept quiet.'

The rebels laughed.

'Poor little Olaf would appear to be running scared,' Angus called out. He clapped Bethoc on the back, 'Our Oonagh really put the cat amongst the pigeons, did she not?'

Bethoc answered with a sad smile.

Kineth continued. 'Ruaridh now believes that they want to keep the necklace's true identity secret because Thorstein never told anyone about it. The two men he originally brought to Cait were both sent back to their homeland as ashes soon after. Thorstein claimed to have caught them stealing coin but Ruaridh has reason to doubt that claim.

Not long after the Norse had taken over Thunga he had been visited by an envoy seeking amicable relations. He housed the man and his guards for a week. After they had left, one of Ruaridh's men informed him about a drunken story one of the guards had told. He claimed Thorstein had been in such a rage about a pretty trinket that he had burnt village after village. Then he had killed the two men who helped him when he overheard them laughing about it.' Kineth kicked his boot against the other and raised his eyebrows. 'He says he is sorry he never thought that news was of any importance before now.'

Aiden pulled a face. 'We have all heard snippets about this necklace, none of us was able to realise how significant it was either. What's done is done.'

'If this necklace was made to bring peace, how is it that all it has brought us is death?' Eila asked, looking around at everyone.

Gurum was more blunt. 'It is fighting that's going to stop all this, not some stupid necklace. Jewellery didn't kill all those people and put us in here, the Norse did.'

'If it is important to them then surely it should be important to us too.' Tagaled argued.

Kineth held his hands up for calm and gradually everyone stopped talking again. 'I think we need to look at the possibility that Ruaridh is right and that Thorstein and Olaf are acting alone on this.'

Aiden agreed. 'I think I need to risk a trip over to see Moddan again.'

Bethoc was puzzled, 'But I thought Moddan was a prisoner?'

'Aye, he is that lass, but the fools have him in a dungeon cell built into the enclosure wall. It faces out over a river. They watch the water but forget about the overhanging banking. I have only dared use it twice before but I must find out what he knows about this.'

The group slowly began to dissipate and Kineth came over to speak to Bethoc and her grandmother.

'Before I forget, your aunt Ffiona has sent you this,' he took out a small wooden doll clothed in a tiny plaid dress.

Doada gasped, recognition revealing itself in the crinkles at her eye corners. 'Her dolly,' she cried. 'Your mother made her this when she was naught but a nipper. Always getting under our feet and wanting to play, she was. Oonagh made the dolly and from that day onwards she was smitten with it. I never realised she still had it.'

Bethoc took the little doll and blinked back the emotion it brought.

'She wore it on a thong around her neck for years,' Kineth explained. 'But the moment I told her about you she took it straight off and asked me to give it to you. So you will never feel lonely, she said.'

'I will wear it too,' she told her uncle. 'Please thank her for me, one day I hope to come with you and thank her myself.'

***

A little later, Aiden sought out Bethoc and Finlay who were enjoying the summer sun on the heather-covered slopes overlooking Loch Loyal.

'I have just been talking to your grandmother.'

Bethoc smiled, it was so good to hear those words. She could still scarcely believe they were real but the old woman had made her feel so much like part of the family.

'It seems Olaf went to quite some trouble to befriend you and try to find this necklace.'

Her smile faded. The name that once sent shivers of excitement down her spine now sent hair-raising dread racing across her skin.

'I cannot believe that all the time he was with me he was married and had children. What kind of a man does that?'

Aiden shook his head and pulled a face, 'One with no morals and a bastard for a father. If it helps any, I cannot imagine his wife was very pleased about it either.'

Bethoc looked at him blankly, 'I never even thought about her. I hope she gives him hell.'

'Oh I am sure that is exactly where he is right now,' Aiden said and smiled. 'He failed the task, not only that, but he killed the only person who could tell them where the necklace is. His father looked to be furious with him when they passed here, Thorstein is notorious for his temper. He isn't known as Thorstein the Red for nothing.' Aiden's eyes flashed with mirth. 'Like father, like son, it would

200

appear. They both seem to have a knack of failing to successfully complete their missions. It was Thorstein that was in charge of the incursions into Cait.' The smile left his eyes. 'He is allied with Jarl Sigurd of Orkneyjar, who you probably know.'

She nodded, 'I always found him to be a kind and courteous man. It's hard to recognise this side of him.'

'From what I understand he was given the Jarldom by his brother, who didn't want to give up his life elsewhere. He uses Thorstein to do his dirty work here in Cait whilst he lives the grand life on the islands, keeping his own hands fairly clean. I have no doubt he is a good leader to his own folk.' Aiden batted a wasp away from his face. 'But a good leader should not expect people to do anything he wouldn't do himself.'

'Did the two of them get on?' Finlay asked. 'I mean, if Thorstein messed up the invasion by losing the necklace, Sigurd must have been mad at him.'

Bethoc shook her head. 'To be honest I only ever saw them together once and they seemed to get along just fine. Thorstein was hardly ever on the islands and Olaf only came in the last year or so.' She picked at the heather, 'Olaf never mentioned his family very much at all, I can see why now.'

Something jarred with Finlay. 'If this necklace is as important to them as their actions make it seem, I find it hard to believe they were as friendly as they made out. Probably why Thorstein didn't go back much.'

'You could be right there,' Aiden said. 'Though I must admit, I am starting to wonder...' his words trailed off and he frowned.

'What?' Bethoc asked him. 'It can't be any stranger than everything else?'

'The only times we have ever heard the necklace mentioned were when Thorstein or Olaf were involved. Now with what Ruaridh has remembered it would seem they are determined to keep it very quiet. Which makes me wonder why. After all, if it was the plan behind the invasion all along, surely we would have heard more about it before now?'

'So you mean Sigurd may not even know about it, only Thorstein and Olaf?'

Finlay was thinking fast. 'Maybe Thorstein is wanting more than just Cait? Maybe he found out about the necklace and its powers and thought he could use them to defeat us here in Cait then move on south to Fidach. Maybe even take on Sigurd himself?'

'That is exactly what I am beginning to wonder.' Aiden patted Finlay on the shoulder. 'You have a fine head for strategy, lad, I like that. I am not sure just how far Thorstein intended to take things if he had managed to retrieve the necklace but one thing is for sure. Without it, he is struggling to expand his reach any further.'

It was a dreich day, full of low-lying mist and overcast skies. The constant drizzle ensured anyone outside was soon soaked to the skin. For midsummer it was a definite disappointment but for Aiden and Gurum it was perfect. There was much less chance of anyone being out and about. They left the caverns through a narrow slit in the rock that led out into the craggy west side, almost on top of a group of small lochs. They skirted the northern shores and made their way almost due west to where Dun Yrredell sat in between the river and the route that ran down the base of Strathmor. This strath ran into the west end of Loch Nabaros and together with the length of Strathnabaros formed a huge U shape. Each tip ended in the North Atlantic Ocean.

The going was hard in places, steep and unforgiving mixing with bog and marsh. Eventually they came to the point where the land headed down towards the road. They had aimed for slightly south of the fort, just out of sight of the walls where they could cross and get down into the riverbed without being seen. From here they would have to be extremely careful; one wrong move and they would give themselves away. The area between them and the road was full of loose stones and boulders. Waiting until they were sure there was no one on the road, they headed down as quickly as they could.

The scree was difficult to negotiate at the best of times but in the wet the loose stones were treacherous. Gurum slipped halfway across and was thrown down the slope, stones and all, into a waiting blackthorn bush. Aiden scrambled down after him and helped untangle him from the wicked branches. The band in his hair had caught on the thorns and snapped and he had a number of tears to his clothing and skin. He was just arranging himself again when they heard the unmistakable sound of hooves and wheels on the road ahead. Just coming into view was a shabby pony and cart, driven by an old trader. Behind him his goods were hidden under a waxed cloth to keep the worst of the rain off.

Quickly the pair threw themselves behind the largest of the boulders that had rolled down off the hillside and held their breath. Anyone with half an eye would surely be able to see them. The old man and his cart slowly plodded by, the pony's hooves never altering their pace. They heard him muttering to himself all the way past, grumbling about his damp clothes and water-spoiled goods. Aiden risked a peek and watched as the cart disappeared round the bend. The man was hunched down miserably in his seat, letting the horse make its own way. He never once lifted his eyes from under his hood.

'I couldn't have planned this weather any better myself,' Aiden said, grinning.

'Aye, the gods are surely smiling on us today, mate,' Gurum answered, shaking the drips from his hair and using a leather thong from around his wrist to re-tie it at the nape of his neck. He pulled a face at the mess of his arm then shrugged. It was nowhere near as bad as what the Norse would do to him.

They waited a moment or two longer to reassure themselves then darted across the road and the open ground to the river before leaping down the muddy banking and catching their breath.

Creeping along the side of the river under the overhanging banking, they made their way towards the fort. The enclosure wall ran right down to the riverside, allowing them easy access to the window of the cell that housed Moddan. It was the only window on that side of the fort. The Norse had been sadly lacking in ingenuity when they took over this broch. They had changed nothing of its layout or defences and its former occupants had not bothered to mention the flaws they knew were there.

***

As soon as they were alongside the window, Gurum rolled his tongue and made a sound reminiscent of the oystercatchers that bred all around those parts. Three times he called and a moment after, a single call returned from within the stone walls. Aiden bounded over the banking edge and up to the tiny window, leaving Gurum stayed in the riverbed to act as lookout.

The figure inside the cell was tired-looking and grubby but his eyes were bright with a steely determination that his captors had not yet managed to destroy. He looked eagerly out at his visitor, knowing full well that it must be something important to risk coming. Thorstein had been decidedly more relaxed of late and Moddan had been dogged with a strong sense of dread. Over the last week, however, the mood of the fort had changed palpably. Angry voices had been raised numerous times, drifting into his cell, though he could not make out any words. Something had obviously gone wrong with Thorstein's plans. Now the leader of his rebel force was here, he could only hope it meant things were finally going their way. As soon as Aiden told him about Oonagh, the necklace, and what Kineth had told them, everything began to fall into place.

'There is nothing more important in the minds of these people than the actions of their forebearers,' he explained, keeping his voice low so he didn't attract the attention of any nearby guards. 'They are full of superstition and tales of magical items are commonplace. I have overheard Thorstein and Olaf discussing such things many times, including a necklace, but I never considered it to be relevant, just superstition that had no bearing in fact.'

'What did they say about it?'

'From what I understand it was made to calm forces who were about to battle each other but another, stronger, magic had already been let loose and the necklace was lost in the fighting. They say that battle is still ongoing and will be until

Ragnarok, whatever that is. They mention that a lot, like it is something to be scared of.'

He paused for a moment to think. 'I can only assume now that Oonagh's necklace and the one I thought was just a story are in fact one and the same. So while ever it remains lost, the fighting will continue.' He shrugged, 'Maybe that is why you have never given up hope no matter how slim the chances of winning have been.'

'So, it really is that important?' Aiden's hopes were beginning to rise. 'If that is true then if we can get to the necklace first we will be able to subdue them and gain our land back. No wonder they killed my brother and started a war.'

Moddan held up his hand to quiet his guest, there was a noise outside his door. He waited until the footsteps passed, 'Tell me more.'

Aiden explained what they now knew about his brother finding Thorstein with the necklace and how Oonagh buried it and ran to Orkneyjar.

'She thought to hide in the one place they would not look for her but how could she have ever realised how linked these two places really are?'

Moddan nodded, 'It must be the magic at work, she had held the necklace so maybe she felt it pulling back to Orkneyjar? Once that got into her mind she would not have known it was the necklace's and not her own idea. Does her daughter know where she buried it?'

Aiden grimaced and explained the rest of the story. 'All she managed to tell Bethoc was that she buried it under a marker stone up the hill away from

Grumg-Mhor, though she told Olaf that she had dropped it in the wood as she ran. Bless her, even in her final moments she managed to point him in the wrong direction.'

'That necklace is the key to everything,' Moddan said. 'Until one side has it, peace can never be restored, but we have time to wait. Let Olaf wear himself out looking in the wrong place. Lie low until spring, you don't want them to get any hint of where the necklace really is. The ground will be easier to search once the summer's growth has died off and the winter frosts gone. The necklace has been safe all these years, another few months will not matter. In the meantime see if you can garner any more support from outlying areas. Once the necklace is found we may need every man, jack and his wife to make our own army. I will try to find out all I can here, the guards don't bother to still their words in my earshot. They don't believe I can ever be a threat to them now.'

Aiden saw the sense in the Maormar's words. As frustrating as it was to leave it, it stood to reason not to try anything whilst Olaf and his men were so close.

Their hiding place was safe enough and they were used to winters in the caverns now, plus it would give them time to plan and gather more support.

'One other thing,' Moddan added. 'How many of you know where the necklace was buried?'

Aiden thought for a moment. 'Only myself, Bethoc, Elinn, Finlay and Doada. Why?'

'Keep it that way for now.' The Maormar's face was lined with worry. 'I've just realised. Thorstein is going to stop at nothing to get this trinket back, everyone has now become a target of his wrath and we know to our cost what he is capable of. We must protect the whereabouts of the necklace at all costs.'

Aiden nodded his agreement. 'I will speak to the other four and let them know. I am going to tell Gurum and Angus, though. Should anything happen to me, Angus will take my place. He needs to know what is going on and I think we need one of the more active members to know just in case anything urgent happens out in the field. We can work out an excuse for not going after the necklace until Spring on the way back. The others will see straight through us if we don't.'

Moddan agreed, 'I will see what I can find out here but I can't be of any more use to you until you have the necklace and can risk another visit.'

Just as the hidden sun was reaching its highest point they took their leave.

'I think the best bet would be to tell everyone else the truth up to a point,' Gurum told Aiden after he had relayed all the new information to him. 'That way no one is offended. Just tell them the exact whereabouts are being kept a secret in case anyone gets captured but that we will be going to get the necklace in the Spring. If it makes it any easier, you could say only you and Bethoc know where it really is.'

Aiden grinned and clapped him on the back.
'Brilliant. I hate the idea of secrecy between us even
though I accept it is the best way to go.'

17

Bethoc settled into cavern life, gradually getting to know more about each person there. It was easier now they were keeping their heads down and waiting for Spring. Scouting trips still went out to keep an eye on the villages and see what further support they could muster but other than that everyone was staying more or less in the hideout. Elinn and Finlay soon became her good friends and Doada found a special place in her heart. She was the matriarch, wise woman, healer and surrogate mother to them all. She liked to laugh and joke, keeping everyone's spirits high and at times Bethoc even thought she caught a glimmer of her mother peeping out at her through her grandmother's eyes. Despite her bright and uncomplaining demeanour she would sometimes take herself to one side and spend time just sitting with her memories wrapped around her like a favourite blanket. At these times everyone kept their respectful distance.

Each person in the caverns had suffered incredible loss, they all dealt with it in their own way. One of the favourite places for quiet reflection was the area they called the Castle. This was the highest of the four peaks that made up Law Mountain, it gave an excellent view over to the neighbouring Bay Mountain whenever the cloud cover allowed. It was a craggy peak and offered excellent hiding places from any sharp-eyed Norse who may be nearby; useful as both a retreat and a lookout.

One afternoon, when Bethoc was feeling particularly claustrophobic, she made her way out along the passageway from which she had first entered the caverns. When she arrived at the small cavern with the three passageways, she made for the one on the left. This passage was much narrower, it emerged from the mountainside slightly further north of the marsh tunnel. The two entranceways were separated by a huge outcrop of rocks, falling away steeply below. Ahead of her the rocks formed a barrier, perfectly hiding the entrance. She peered over and could see down the easier, forested slope to Loch Law, which ran the full eastern side of the mountain. A handful of warriors were making their way down the road that ran adjacent to the loch. She watched as they slowly disappeared from view before turning and making her way up to the Castle.

This eastern route was the easiest way up the mountain but it was also the most conspicuous. There were a few places where the cover was not so good and there was a chance Bethoc could be seen from below. She kicked herself for choosing this route now. It wasn't so bad when there were two of them. By the time she arrived on the safe, rocky pinnacle, she was out of breath, as much from concern as from exertion. She found a flat rock and threw herself down.

The view was outstanding and soon drove her worries away. It was the perfect antidote to the hemmed-in feeling that had been growing in her for the last few weeks. She needed to be outside, feeling the breeze on her face and seeing the horizon far away. Outside by the waterfall was all very well but it was so sheltered that the wind barely reached it and there was no way to see out over the surrounding area like this. An eagle quartered the mountainside in his search of prey and she could make out deer, high up on one of the other peaks. Ptarmigan were common on the higher slopes and she watched one pottering amongst the stones. Its summer plumage provided almost perfect camouflage, only its movement giving it away. Eventually it moved out of sight and she leaned back against the rocks, enjoying the pure air and sense of peace. There was a feeling of complete unity up here. Problems and worries seemed to melt away in the face of such panoramic beauty. She hoped that, wherever her mother was now, she had such a good view of the world.

She must have dozed off for a while because she was jolted awake by a shower of small pebbles falling down around her. Jumping to her feet she saw Gurum making his way down from further up the peak.

'Sorry,' he called out to her. 'I didn't realise you were up here too. Everything ok?'

Bethoc smiled, feeling a bit shy. Gurum was not the most approachable person and one she had barely got to know yet. 'I was just needing to escape for a bit, I'm not used to living all cramped up and on top of each other.'

'It does get a bit much,' he agreed. 'But you do kind of get used to it.' He sat down and she did the same. 'Can't beat the view from up here.'

'It's amazing, so peaceful and calm. Makes it hard to believe trouble even exists in the world.'

'Yeah, kind of why I'm up here,' he admitted, rubbing his face in his hands. 'All this sitting around until Spring. Bhah! It's not me, I need to be getting on with things. Thinking, planning...' his voice trailed off and he stared at his feet.

Bethoc was at a loss as to what to say. He looked up at her and smiled. 'Family trait, sorry.'

When she still looked confused, he explained.

'It was my father who led us here in the first place. Six weeks trapped in the broch was driving everyone stir crazy, there was fighting and trouble.' He grimaced, 'Not everyone was happy with your mother and Donal.'

'Why ever not?'

'They felt it was their meddling that had brought down the wrath of Thorstein on us. Stupid really but people were so caught up in their grief, they just needed a scapegoat. Since they couldn't take it out on the Norse they turned on each other. It was a sad day when your grandfather was killed, though I suspect it was a relief to him. He never did get over losing Donal. Poor Aiden, each time one of his brothers died, all hopes were laid at the next one's door. Now it's his turn but he has no parents left to be proud of him.'

'What happened to the other folk? The ones that caused the trouble?'

Gurum shrugged, 'Dunno. They left the area pretty smart when Da sorted the way out. Not a word of thanks to Sheilagh, just upped and out. Still, they would have had a hard time finding us if they had come back.'

He fell silent for a while, lost in the memories of so long ago. Bethoc waited patiently, entertained by a late ring ouzel that was making the most of the warm weather before flying off to its winter home.

'Yea gods, I haven't thought about those times in ages,' he finally announced, rubbing his face in his hands again. 'I'm glad Ma never lived to see it all.'

'Was she killed in the burnings?'

Gurum shook his head.

'No, she was took by the fever a few months before. Never thought at the time that it would be the best thing for her.' He picked up a stone, tossed it up and caught it again in one hand. 'She would never have coped through it all.' He stood up and threw the stone as far as he could. 'It was my wife and child I lost in the fires but I don't talk about it,' he added quickly before she could say anything.

It was clear to Bethoc why Gurum was the way that he was. All that pent-up emotion just bursting to be free. It had never occurred to her that he must have been married before, though he was after all the oldest man there. Suddenly she felt a fool to be upset about the loss of a fiancé who was only a fraud. All these people had lost genuine partners, people they had loved for many years. Then again, when she thought about it honestly, it wasn't Olaf she was missing at all. It was her mother and the promise of a happy future. Olaf, she realised, hadn't come into her thoughts in any kind of longing way since just after she had arrived here. Her spirits lifted even more.

'I can see why this place is used so much,' she said, grinning. 'It really does clear your head, doesn't it?'

Gurum patted her on the back, 'Sure does.' Then, almost as if he could read her mind, he added, 'Olaf was a bastard to do to you what he did, lass. Quite apart from what he did to your mother.'

***

Meal times were usually a communal affair. Moiraugh's role in the group was cook and she took great pride in ensuring they were well fed. Irb and Anfrud had been providing plenty of fish but now everyone was getting tired of it. Vegetables and other staples were running low, there was nothing for it but to risk venturing out to re-stock. Everyone was eager to be chosen to leave and in the end Aiden decided on three parties to go three separate ways. Tagaled and Edana chose to go down to the other side of Loch Law and see what they could rifle from the outlying farmsteads, whilst Angus took Anfrud down across the Strath Mor. The last group consisted of Gurum, Bethoc and Finlay, who were to head up to Arnaboll. This left enough rebels to protect the caverns and keep their usual watch over the Law Road.

Each group left from a different exit. Gurum, Bethoc and Finlay went up the long tunnel. It was Bethoc's first real expedition from the caverns and she was excited.

***

Since her conversation with Gurum up on the Castle she had lost her reticence around him. The air of quiet disdain she had picked up on before had settled into the barely concealed pain she now understood. They made good time up the wilderness to the edge of the road. Though 'well-worn path' might have been a better description, Bethoc thought. She had been imagining something much more substantial but she had noticed the word 'road' seemed to be used for almost any kind of path in Cait.

They made it to the derelict broch without any trouble, finding inside another bag of salted meat and some hard dry biscuits to collect on the way back.

From there they left the road and went over land, it was a tougher if shorter route but much safer. The ground climbed slowly away from the lochside as they made their way over a small hill and down towards yet another patch of water. To their left the great Bay Mountain watched over them, the steep north face of the monolith rising grandly over the desolate moors. As she watched, a tiny speck

217

flew out from atop the cliff face. *An eagle,* she thought, smiling, but she was wrong. Only a moment later another bird that dwarfed the first flew out from almost the same place. *Buzzard,* she corrected herself, chuckling. The buzzard changed course and headed down towards the foot of the mountain whilst the eagle carried on effortlessly rising on the invisible thermals.

As they rounded the northern tip of the small loch, there in front of them was Arnaboll Steading. Sitting a short walk away from the rest of the village, the smallholding was home to an ally. Out of sight, they waited whilst a mother and her child passed by. As soon as the pair were out of earshot, the group quickly covered the short distance to the steading and dived into an old outbuilding. Gurum called out the signal and a moment later came a hoot to indicate the way was clear. The steading door opened and they were greeted by a stout man around Gurum's age and a couple of large, shaggy lurcher dogs who quietly fussed around the visitors, looking for titbits.

They were led into the cool interior and given refreshments by a friendly, ruddy-faced woman who was obviously the man's wife. She rushed off eagerly to pack provisions for them.

'Best not hang about too long,' the man advised them, 'Thorstein's been like a bull with a sore head these past few weeks. You do right to lie low.'

Gurum pulled a face in response and the man chortled. 'Aye, I ken that's not what you want to be hearing now lad, but it's for the best.'

Bethoc and Finlay suppressed their own giggles, they were not used to anyone calling Gurum 'lad'. He did not seem to mind, however, merely nodding his agreement.

'Tis frustrating, I admit but I know it is for the best.'

'Well you can always count on us for help, you know that. The missus here will stock up on staples for you, you can manage most of your own meat and your fish. And the autumn harvest is just around the corner, the young uns will enjoy scrumping. Oh and there's a slab o meat in yonder broch too.'

One of the dogs barked a warning and immediately they were on their feet. The man ducked out of the house and could soon be heard chatting to someone outside. His wife led them through a low door to where the animals were housed in the winter. Hay was piled up in the corner and they took their bags of stores and scrambled underneath it. Heart in mouth, they waited in silence until the dogs came sniffing around them and the man called them out.

'Tis all clear, twas only the laddie from down the road with a message about a beast of mine that's wandered too far.' He clapped Gurum on the shoulder, adding, 'Now you stay safe, do ya hear? This thing is all going to blow up in the coming months and I can't handle losing you too.'

Gurum winced at the words but nodded all the same.

'My brother-in-law,' was all he said after they had left, in answer to Bethoc's puzzled look.

***

They were just coming down the hill towards the broch when Finlay noticed a pair of warriors lying by the road beneath them. Ducking back into the trees, they crouched low and waited. Bethoc's heart was in her mouth and her pulse raced with a mixture of excitement and dread. The warriors appeared to be sleeping, it was lucky they hadn't walked right onto them. There was nothing they could do but sit it out and hope they didn't hang around for too long. The days were still warm but the evenings drew in chilly now and the shadows lengthened early amongst the mountains.

After what seemed an age, the men woke and began to talk quietly, they seemed in no hurry to leave. Bethoc's legs were cramping, she risked stretching them out in front of her but her heel caught on a twig and it snapped. Freezing, she held her breath. Gurum's and Finlay's hands went to cover their swords. The men just kept on talking and after a moment they relaxed again.

'Sorry,' she mouthed to them, not daring to move again. Finlay nodded over to the loch, the water that had been calm when they arrived was now turning choppy. Dark clouds were scurrying across the sky, bringing cooler air and the threat of rain. Gurum rolled his eyes, it looked like they were going to get wet. They held their places and willed

220

the Norsemen to notice the changing weather. It took the first drops of rain before they finally realised. With no real speed they got to their feet and slowly headed down the road towards the Thunga settlement. As soon as they were out of sight, Bethoc was able to stretch out fully before clambering to her feet. The other two were already moving off. There was still a long way to go and it didn't look like a quick shower.

***

The distinct smell of smoke filtered into the caverns. Starting as a mere hint but quickly filling the air with the peaty smell of burning heather. Not far behind it came thick, acrid smoke that sent alarm through the inhabitants. Quickly, they rushed to the various entrance points and lookouts to see a huge area to the southeast in flames. A call came from up at the eastern entrance overlooking the Law Road, the sharp, mewing cry of the buzzard. A warning! Aiden raced to see. Cailtran stood pointing down to the roadway. Norsemen with scarves wrapped around their faces were making their way back up to Thunga. It was clear they were in no panic. The two men looked at each other in alarm, surely they had not started the fire on purpose? A muirburn was one thing, burning off the tough old heather to make way for fresh growth in the spring. Usually done every ten years or so, they were guarded well to ensure they did not get

221

out of control. But this fire was clearly raging out of all control, even the autumn trees were ablaze.

At the caverns they were not in any danger, the wet ground to the south would soon halt the fire in its tracks and the loch to the east would do the same. Their main problem was the smoke. The main cavern and some of the smaller caves to the south were filled with the cloying smell. It lay heavy in the air, clinging to every surface. Only a few of the caves and tunnels to the north were still inhabitable for any length of time. They took to wearing scarves over their faces to make breathing easier and spent as much time as possible out in the sheltered area by the waterfall.

Tagaled and Edana returned from their scouting trip and the news was not good. From the shores of Loch Nabaros north, the land was burning uncontrollably. The wind had whipped up the flames, sending them racing through the dry, dying leaves of the trees on the hillside. There was no doubt that this fire had been started deliberately, they had seen torches strewn everywhere. The men at the broch were unperturbed by the fire, a handful of them were busy beating back any flames that chanced their way but the timing of the burn had been exact. The wind ensured the flames stayed moving north away from the loch, ensuring the danger to the building was slight. They had witnessed no attempt to control the fire let alone any to put it out.

'Have you any idea why they have done it?' Angus asked. It made no sense at all.

'Maybe they thought to flush out Bethoc, if she was hiding in the area?' Edana said.

'But they have been searching it for weeks now, surely they must know she cannot be there?'

Tagaled's frown was even worse than usual, he threw himself down on a seat. 'Sheer madness, that's all it is.'

***

The fire burned for three days before storm clouds raced in from the east and blanketed the sky. The deluge that followed soon put paid to the flames but not before the area was virtually stripped bare. For another two days the rain threw its worst at the hillside. Ash mixed with groundwater to run in sluggish black rivulets and everywhere the air hung thick with the charred smell of the remaining trees. Upon the hill, the scene was one of devastation. Irb and Finlay picked their way carefully amongst the remains. It was soon clear to see that the intensity of the fire had not been uniform. In some places the ground cover was burnt right back, exposing the topsoil whilst in others plenty of unburnt material remained. In areas where the autumn leaves had been the driest, charcoal silhouettes of once thriving trees stood testament to the fire's intensity. Here and there, patches of flowering ivy gave an insight to the life that had once been all around. The wildlife that had managed to move fast enough had escaped the worst of the fire but there were plenty of part-cremated remains littering the ground. A plaintive bark alerted them to a victim still trapped in the debris, a young buck with a broken leg had become entangled in briars. Irb quickly ended the animal's misery, bringing his dagger swiftly across its neck. They left him where he fell, knowing something would be grateful for the feast.

The air was unnaturally still and quiet. The birds that had fled had still not returned. A lone gull flew overhead, it called out once but flew on. In this blackened, crisp landscape it was impossible to move quietly and they heard the men coming long before they saw them. There was no easy refuge, all they could do was flatten themselves out behind the remnants of some low level bushes and watch as the two Norsemen came into view, heading down towards the broch.

'I don't see how this will make it easier,' one of them commented to the other. 'Olaf is out of his mind destroying all this.'

'I heard Thorstein is like a raging bull ever since Olaf returned. Wherever he had been, he got things badly wrong and his father is furious with him.'

'When do the searches start? I don't fancy raking over all this ground, it's gonna be filthy work.'

His friend agreed, 'I think the plan is to wait for a few weeks for everything to settle, then we can get to work. Without the ground covering we should find whatever it is he needs. It would certainly be easier if he told us what it was.'

The men's voices gradually faded into the distance. Irb and Finlay crawled out from beneath the cremated bushes, not knowing whether to laugh or cry.

***

Autumn gales finally blew out the last of the smell from the hideout, leaving the air sharp with the threat of oncoming frost. An early winter would mean the ground would have no chance to recover before spring.

'I just don't understand why they had to burn it?' Elinn asked on a bright November morning when they were up on the Castle.

'Looks like they figured it would be easier to search for the necklace without the undergrowth getting in the way. The stones won't burn,' Finlay answered her. 'After all, they think it was dropped almost twenty years ago.'

'It's such a waste.'

Her father sighed and put his arm around her shoulders. 'You're too young to remember the last time that hillside was burning, love. It's not just the loss of the area that we are grieving.'

Bethoc was reminded of how her own home had gone up in flames. 'So much grief and all so pointless, I thought the Norse only wanted Cait to grow grain and crops.'

'Most of the land isn't even any good for that!' Finlay grumbled.

'Exactly.' Aiden gazed over towards the silent scar on the horizon. The odd bird flew over but none had returned to settle. There was no food left there

225

for them now and only a few unburnt trees to perch on. He thought for a moment.

'I suppose we should take advantage of the unexpected offering though.' He looked round at the young faces and grinned. 'Charcoal. The hillside will be full of it, we should go harvest some before the weather turns again.' He glanced up at the sky. 'The frost has been threatening for a few days, best go now. Who wants to come?'

***

The four of them set out within the hour, taking Anfrud with them as well. Aiden had purposely left all the older members behind. Morale was already quite low, the sight of the hillside in such a state would only cause more distress. They picked their way through the worst burnt places, filling their bags with blackened, twisted stalks of heather and any other wood charred enough. As gut-wrenching as it was to be amongst so much destruction, it was heartening to see tiny signs of life all around. The thick blanketing moss that covered vast areas before the fire was still evident in many places, if a little singed. There were also signs of life down at the base of the heather, not all of it was tinder-dry and dead. Bugs crawled amongst the debris and the odd bird picked at the ground, hoping to catch one. Every sign of life made them smile, it would take more than this fire to eliminate life here, nature was proving as hard to remove as the local people.

Finally their bags were full and their hands black. They set off home in much better spirits. Even Aiden was glad he had ventured out there. The burden of leading this group laid heavy on him at times. He knew another winter in the caverns would be hard on them all. Never in their wildest dreams had they thought they would be there so long when Old Gurum had led them from the shelter of the broch all those years before. Now though, they had more hope than they'd had for years, if only they could cope with the pent-up frustration of having to wait so long to make their move.

Aiden rubbed at his elbow. Realising what he was doing, he smiled. His wife Plantula had always commented on this habit of his. She would take his arm and inspect the elbow before placing a kiss on it, followed by another on his lips. Her image was blurred now in his mind, she had been gone too long. He shook the image away and looked over his brood. This younger generation would see the end of this battle, they would be in houses again soon. Surely this would be the last winter they would spend in the caves. He resolved to make it the best one ever.

18

Tiny lights dotted the inky black sky above. More and more appeared every minute until it felt as though the vastness of it all might crush her.

Bethoc laid on a blanket up on the Castle, watching the heavens open up their secrets to her. She had often done the same with her mother, lying out at the top of the Ward, watching the familiar constellations take shape. They would take turns to name them and make stories about them. Her favourite had always been to pretend Lepus the hare was chasing the two dogs Canis Major and Canis Minor to hide behind Orion the Hunter and shake with fear before racing off to play with Leo the Lion. She smiled at the memory and wondered whereabouts in the heavens her mother would choose to look down on her from if she could. She waited for a long time until she could pick out Libra and imagined her mother sitting on the scales, watching for Olaf to be judged. *I will make him pay for what he did to you, Mother, I promise, and I will make Thorstein pay for killing my father and all those other people.*

The sound of someone approaching made her jump. It was Doada making her way slowly towards her. She waved away Bethoc's offer of help.

'I wondered if you ever used to do this with Oonagh,' she said, laying her own blanket down next to Bethoc's. 'We used to lie out by Loch Nabaros and watch the stars come out. It was one of those fun winter things that made the long, dark nights more interesting. Of course, we couldn't see as much of the sky as we can up here but it was enough all the same.'

'I forgot Mother said she used to do it when she was a child. I was just thinking about us lying on the hill near our home and making up stories about the constellations.'

'My favourite is Cassiopeia because it is the first one I learned to spot as a child. Every night I look for that big zigzag in the sky and when I see her I know everything will be ok.' Doada chuckled, 'I still do it now.'

Bethoc watched her grandmother's tattooed hand pointing out the stars.

'Why did my mother not have her hands tattooed?'

Doada looked at her hands and traced the line of dots right up and over her knuckles. 'We get our first markings when we get married, right over the bones here. It hurts more there, just to show how painful and hard married life can be, even though it appears beautiful.' She pointed to the markings down the fingers of her left hand. 'These are for our children, showing how they point the way into the future and away from us. See how this one is fuller than the rest.' She held up the finger next to her little one. 'That finger is for the twins.' She rubbed at the line sealing the pattern off from her fingertip. The same mark was on one of her other fingers but the one on her thumb looked freshly done.

'What does that line mean?' Bethoc asked

Doada sighed. 'It means the child died.' She looked at her thumb. 'I refused to add it to your mother's line until I knew for sure.'

They were silent for a while before Bethoc asked. 'Why do the men have markings on their face but not the women?'

'Ahh,' Doada laughed. 'Now that depends on who you ask. The men will tell you it is a display of their ranking within their group structure. Women will tell you secretly that it is their bravado painted there for all to see. We of course prefer to keep our strengths hidden.'

Bethoc started to laugh but a thought hit her.

'I wonder if that is what gave my mother away? Thorstein would have seen that she had no markings despite the fact she claimed to have been married.'

'You must miss her terribly, child.' Doada took hold of Bethoc's hand and held it to her chest. 'I know she is still with us, I feel her around you, watching.' She gave a cough and struggled to sit up. Bethoc helped her to her feet and gathered up their blankets, wrapping one around her grandmother and the other around herself.

'I miss her more than I can say,' she admitted. 'And I love to think of her hanging around and watching over us, though right now I think she would be telling us that you need to get down into the warmth.'

They made their way down into the caverns and headed for the large hearth to warm their chilled bodies. There had been a good hazy orb around the bright half-moon and the sharp feel of frost was keen in the air. Their breath hid itself again as they neared the heat and they gratefully accepted a mug of herbal tea from Moiraugh, wrapping their icy fingers around the hot mugs. The evening was spent around the fire, telling stories and singing songs. Cailtran had a beautiful singing voice and could often be convinced to give them a tune. The venison they had eaten for their dinner that night had put everyone in a good mood. It was succulent and rich, braised to perfection with plenty of wild garlic and bread to go with it.

***

The autumn days slipped into winter and before they knew it the first snows were decorating the ground. Light and quickly disappearing at first, then becoming more persistent and instead of melting with the winter sun the coverings would stay for a day or two. Bethoc was surprised to find the temperature of the caves stayed the same despite the drop in temperature. Finlay explained when she mentioned it.

'The caves are so far underground that they keep a constant temperature all year round. It is how everyone can stay here even in the depths of winter. Just think of that huge mountain above us as a big blanket.'

231

Kineth arrived again, bringing with him essential supplies to see them through should they be snowed in. Dried fruits, salted meats and pickled vegetables were all stored away in one of the small caves and more chickens were added to the few left in the coop. He left at first light, loaded up with tea blends for Ffiona to help ease the unrelenting nausea she was suffering. He promised to return as soon as he could though he didn't expect it would be before Yule.

The temperature outside became much colder, icicles formed around the entrance ways. Fingers stiffened and chilblains bit hard, keeping Doada and Bethoc busy making warming salves. The older woman was coughing more and more and Bethoc was starting to be concerned. After numerous failed attempts at getting her grandmother to rest, she had a quiet word with Moiraugh. The other woman was not surprised.

'She is getting old, too old to live this harsh life. Of course being stubborn doesn't help. She is so used to being the matriarch of the group that she fails to accept her own vulnerabilities.'

She paused, seeing Bethoc's worried face, and patted her on the arm. 'Try not to worry yourself too much, I will have a word with her. I have an idea that may help'

She made her way over to where Doada sat mending clothing. She sat down next to her, chatting about this and that. As soon as Doada mentioned Bethoc, Moiraugh pulled her face into a worried frown.

'Is something wrong with Bethoc?' Doada asked.

Moiraugh hid a smile, her plan was working. She sighed. 'I don't know if I should say. She did mention something to me but...'

Doada eyed her granddaughter with concern. 'I thought she was settling well here. Is it anything I can help with?'

Looking uncomfortable, Moiraugh took one of Doada's hands and squeezed it gently. 'I don't really know how to say this but,' she glanced over to Bethoc and back to Doada. 'I think she may be under the impression you don't really trust her to look after the rest of us.'

'Whatever gave her that impression, I..?' Doada broke off to cough.

'Well, that for a start,' Moiraugh answered, handing her water to her. 'She is worried about you and she knows she can take so much of your work off your shoulders so you can rest but you won't let her.' She gave Doada's hand another squeeze. 'So she thinks you don't trust her abilities.'

Doada harrumphed, put the cup down and straightened out her mending. Then she glanced at Moiraugh with a resigned look on her face. 'She has pestered a few times about my cough, that girl is smart. I am starting to struggle a bit.'

Moiraugh nodded. 'There is no shame in taking things a bit easier just now until you are feeling better.'

Doada harrumphed again. 'You know that is not my way.'

'No but it is Bethoc's way to help people... and,' Moiraugh rushed on where Doada would interrupt, 'she wants to prove herself to you. She can't do that if you don't let her help.' She played her final card. 'The poor girl has lost her mother, she doesn't want her grandmother getting ill too.'

Doada blew out a large breath. 'I will take things easy,' she said. 'Let me finish my mending and I will go and lie down for a bit. Bethoc can deal with the salves today. Can you ask her to come and talk to me, I can't have her thinking I don't value her work.'

Moiraugh nodded and made to leave. 'Thank you. It will take a great weight off her shoulders to see you resting more.'

***

Firewood was in constant need now they kept fires in the outer caves as well as the main cavern. Those on watch duty needed somewhere close where they could chase the threat of frostbite away. Every few days a small group would go out to gather more; Finlay and Bethoc got the job of collecting wood from the eastern slope by Loch Law. They already had three piles ready to go up to the lookout entrance and were busy gathering more for a fourth. Bethoc had grown complacent, she was so busy enjoying herself that she forgot to be cautious. When she found a long, unwieldy pole that she didn't want to leave behind, she laid it against a large boulder and slammed her foot down on the

234

unsupported part. The wood broke with a loud crack. Suddenly a whistle rang out from the direction of the road. Norsemen!

Hands grabbed her from behind, dragging her forcibly to an area of holly and blackberry. With just enough time to yank her hood over her head, she was shoved inside. Finlay held his hand over her mouth to keep her from protesting and flicked his eyes towards the area they had been in moments before.

Already they could see two men rushing through the undergrowth, searching for the source of the noise. They were quickly followed by another two.

'I am sure it came from here,' one of them yelled, casting around him for signs of anyone. He grabbed one end of the pole and inspected the broken end. 'This is fresh, they can't be far. Spread out.'

Finlay pressed his weight down on Bethoc, keeping her shielded from view. She could feel his breath next to her face and her pulse began to race. She no longer felt the scratches from the bramble or the sharp leaves beneath her, her senses were overwhelmed by the man on top of her. She fought them for control, forcing herself to think of the danger they were in. If the men found the piles of wood they would know there was a hideout nearby. A cry of shock came from somewhere to their left, followed by loud crashing sounds as someone fled noisily through the woodland. The men followed, cursing at the distance between them and their prey. The two rebels stayed in their prickly hollow for a good while, hearts racing, not daring to move. A call came from nearby, curlew - safety. They scrabbled from their den and came face-to-face with Eila.

'Quickly, let's get this wood moved before he loses them and they come back.'

There was no time for questions. Keeping her eyes averted from Finlay, Bethoc followed in silence. Methodically, she grabbed a handful of wood and started up the slope with the others who had come to help.

The Norsemen came back down the road shortly afterwards, not bothering to even glance at the woodland on their way past. Cailtran had done his job well, he had led the men far enough away to give everyone time to clear the area. He would take his time now, making his way back to the caverns through another entrance. The eastern one would not be used again for a long time.

'How did you know?' Finlay asked Eila when the work was done. 'We had seen no sign of them.'

'Irb was up on the Castle keeping watch when he saw them running down the Law Road. He knew you would never see them in time so he sent down a warning.'

Finlay looked over to Bethoc with a sheepish grin, 'I am sorry for shoving you in the bushes like that.' His eyes twinkled as he spoke and she felt a shiver run down her spine. Her skin felt clammy all of a sudden and she wanted to be sick. Making her excuses, she raced off to the waterfall and heaved until her stomach was empty.

She sat for a long time, watching her breath escape in clouds of steamy condensation. She did not want this, she did not want to feel anything about anyone. To love people was to feel pain. It was to know the greatest happiness in the world and have it torn away. When she had felt Finlay's body pressed so close to hers, felt his chest rise and fall as he drew each breath, it had stirred something deep inside her. A primeval lust that almost as soon as it had arrived had filled her mind with unwanted memories. The revulsion she had felt was only slightly less than the fear of being caught and it had taken all her strength to stay in that place and keep quiet.

How could she not have seen this coming? Finlay was a friend, a good friend, but there was no way it could be anything more. She could not risk becoming the simpering wimp she now saw herself as with Olaf. Love and lust were just a way of someone controlling her, using her feelings to ride roughshod over her. She wasn't going to let anyone, good or bad, get the chance to fool her like that again.

She hated the way her body had betrayed her, the way she had wanted him to kiss her right there in the holly before she had come to her senses. She needed to find a way to sort this out or once more she was going to have to forget a friend and start again.

A few days later, Kineth turned up unexpectedly. He had been sent on an urgent errand for Ruaridh that took him near enough to the caverns for the impromptu visit. Bethoc jumped on the opportunity to escape. Her grandmother was keeping to her promise to rest more, even admitting how much better she was feeling for it. Bethoc made up a good supply of herbal preparations and left instructions with Elinn as to what plants needed collecting and when. Edana agreed to cover any other chores that would need doing and Moiraugh as always could be trusted to fuss over Doada and keep her from doing too much.

The next day, Bethoc left with her uncle. The sky was overcast and heavy with snow clouds. They made their way quickly down the stream until they reached the place where Kineth had left his cart hidden. Bethoc tucked herself underneath a cover in the back as they ventured onto the road. She began to relax as more and more distance was put between her and Finlay. She had managed to avoid him over the last few days but it was clear he could see there was a problem. A few times she had caught him looking at her with a hurt expression. It tugged at her heart-strings but she firmly shut her mind to it and turned away. She forced herself to forget about him now, listening as Kineth spoke to the various people they passed. By midday they were far enough down the road for her to come out from the cover and take a seat beside him. She glanced up at the sky.

'Do you think we will make it in time?'

'Hard to tell,' he answered, 'I hope so. Though we still have a way to go.'

To their left, a high mountain towered up from the road, standing as a sentinel to the safer lands of Beannach. Bethoc craned her neck to see the top but it was shrouded in heavy cloud.

'That's Benn Klibreck, probably the highest one you will have seen,' Kineth said. 'She is the highest we have around here. Not that there is much competition in these parts; if you want to see the real mountains you have to travel much further south.'

Bethoc tore her eyes away and looked at him. 'You mean they get even bigger?'

'Not only that but they cluster together so that even the ground between them is higher than most of the land here. It's like living in the heavens, you're so high up. I've only been once but the memory has never left me. Beautiful, it was; everywhere you looked, the mountains were gathered. Eagles were as common as curlews and the hares were milky white. But the snow was something else, and the wind. It could whip around the peaks like a raging storm, when down near the bottom it was calm. Even in June you could still see white patches of snow on the sheltered tops.' He glanced across at her. 'Aye lass, if ever you get the chance to go you should take it.'

'I would love to,' her eyes were wide. 'It sounds amazing. When did you go?'

'Oh, twas a long time ago, not long after the burnings. I was one of the few who sheltered away from the broch, so I wasn't part of the initial group who moved to the hideout. Not knowing about them, I decided to leave the area and make my fortune somewhere else. A few of us set off south to see what we would find. We got to an area called the Blue Mountains, a long way down. It was the most beautiful of places. We spent a long time there but the work was not for me. You can see so far on a clear day from the tops of the mountains that I would imagine I could see Bay Mountain standing all alone. I started to long for home. Eventually I left my friends and returned. I found Plantula, who was from my village, and she introduced me to the rest of the rebels. I fell in love with your aunt and settled. As soon as she fell pregnant though, Doada insisted I take her away where it would be safer and so we came down here. This place has become home now.'

'Is Ffiona happy here away from her mother?'

'She misses her badly, but she has long since stopped asking her to come down here and join us. Doada will never leave her homeland till she is floating in heaven. Even so, it's a good area down here when you get used to it. You can see why Thorstein keeps himself up in the north though.'

He waved his hand to the landscape around them. Vast swathes of moorland covered in heather and rocks stretched far off into the distance. Closer inspection, however, showed it was in fact an enormous blanket bog, the heather inhabiting only the drier areas whilst the rest was left to the various mosses that thrived in the inhospitable conditions. On the horizon more mountains could be seen, giving the impression they were travelling through the bottom of a huge, uneven basin. A great flock of golden plovers flew over the bog in tight formation, rapid wing beats flashing golden as the light caught them. Their thin, musical chattering shattered the silence as they passed. Beneath them, the odd curlew that had chosen not to winter nearer the coast probed the peaty ground with their funny curved bills, looking for food. Small animals must be abundant, even if they could not see them, as hen harrier and short-eared owl were common even when the breeding season was over.

'You don't want to be leaving the road unless you know this area like the back of your hand,' Kineth told her. 'Or you will end up under the mire and never seen again. But it has its own unique beauty and we do have other parts that are more hospitable. A little way over to your right we have Loch Shin.' He waved his hand to emphasis his point. 'The largest loch in these parts and runs all the way down to below where we are heading. Like a big, long serpent in the land, she is. Plenty of salmon in her though and you will see many folk living near her shores, Loch Beannach by comparison is just a dot.'

'There are no trees,' Bethoc was surprised. 'I have never seen such a huge area without trees before. I can see for ever but I'm no higher than most of the other land.'

Kineth grinned at her. 'It keeps us safe though, anyone coming down from the north has to cross this morass and the road is the only safe way for them as doesn't know these parts. No one can sneak up on us, that's for sure.'

'But what do you burn to keep warm?'

'Ah...' Kineth held his finger to the side of his nose, grinning. 'This bog may look useless and desolate to strangers but the peat that lies beneath the moss is fantastic fuel once it has dried out. We cut lumps of it and leave it out to dry.'

'You burn mud!' Bethoc was convinced he must be joking but sure enough, before long he pointed out a row of brown lumps a distance away from the road.

'The last of this year's cut,' Kineth explained. 'They should have been collected by now but the autumn storms meant some never got inside in time. No matter, they will do for next year.'

***

They crossed a stream that cut across the road and wound its way across the moor, forming little grassy islands as the peat banking was worn away. The fast-running water reached well over the ponies' fetlocks but the stream bed was firm and the cart rolled through with ease. The water tinkled and sang its rushing song, causing Bethoc to smile at the sound. It was hard to feel anything but calm by the side of such a stream. She cast her eyes over its course and caught sight of a white-bibbed dipper just re-appearing from under the ripples. Water droplets ran off his feathers as he shook himself. Then the noise of the cart got the better of him and he took flight, his black body staying low above the water. He landed a short way off and bobbed as he watched them pass.

Kineth was good company, he kept the conversation light and entertaining, so that even when the first snowflakes began to fall, Bethoc still enjoyed herself. Finally they reached an area of trees with a track veering off the main route. The pony headed down the track without any guidance. His ears pricked forwards and his head lifted as he flared his nostrils and blew. His step picked up and before long a small loch came into view.
'Loch Beannach,' Kineth announced, 'we live just a short way from the water. There are a few other homes nearby but the neighbours are not nosy, they keep themselves to themselves. The majority of people in these parts live further over to the west by the tip of the serpent loch. The ones on the far side are not at peace with the Norse and their Maormar does not agree with Ruaridh's stance. He walks a fine line at times, trying to keep everyone happy.'
The little cottage came into view. Two small children were hurling themselves down the path towards them.
'Ah, meet my little monsters.'

Kineth jumped down from the cart and swung the girl up into his arms, squeezing her as she planted kisses all over his face. 'This is Reega,' he placed her into the back of the cart and lifted up her twin. 'And this is Thain.'

The boy was just as happy to see his father but he didn't smother him in kisses the same way his sister had. Instead he stared at his father's companion with interest.

'Who is she?' he demanded as he was placed next to his sister.

'Manners,' Kineth scolded. 'This is your cousin Bethoc.'

Reega's eyes widened. 'Oooh, the one from the island?' she asked, looking at Bethoc with renewed interest.

'Hello you two,' Bethoc said, smiling. 'I hope you don't mind me visiting?'

Two little heads shook vigorously.

'I am sure we will have lots of fun together.'

The heads nodded but before they could speak again another voice spoke.

'Bethoc, my dear. I am so glad to finally meet you.'

Bethoc swung around to see a younger version of her mother standing by the cart. The sight shook her for a moment but she quickly gathered herself and jumped down to hug her aunt. Once up close she could see the subtle differences between the sisters. Where Oonagh's hair was very dark, her younger sibling's was lighter brown, with none of the filaments of grey that Oonagh had developed in her final years. She was a little taller too, and her face had a much less strained look, though the eyes were almost identical. Right now those eyes were filled with unshed tears.

'All these years I thought Oonagh was gone and now here you stand, looking so much like her.' Ffiona's hands rubbed up and down Bethoc's arms as she spoke. 'She was about your age the last time I saw her, it was like seeing a ghost, watching you sitting up there on the cart. You must forgive me for being so silly.'

***

They made their way into the house whilst Kineth and the children dealt with the pony and cart. It was a cosy little home full of the loving touches Bethoc missed so much in the caverns. Ffiona kept the place clean and tidy but even so, evidence of the twins was everywhere. The toys they had been busy playing with were scattered on the kitchen floor - wooden skittles with a small wooden ball to knock them over. A rope was strung above the hearth, covered in the children's freshly washed clothes, and yet more was soaking in a tub. Evidently her aunt had been in the middle of doing laundry when they arrived. She indicated a seat at the table and put the water over the fire to boil, then she pulled her own chair out and sat down, rubbing her expanding belly.

'Phew, this one is a wriggler,' she laughed. 'Goodness knows what it is doing in there but it never stays still.'

'When are you due?'

'I think I have another two moons to go but I was early with the twins. The women in our family are prone to giving birth early, remember that when it is your turn.'

Bethoc gave an involuntary shudder. Ffiona pretended not to notice, instead she leaned forward and let her fingers trace the dolly hanging around her niece's neck. 'I'm glad you like it, it seemed right that you should be the next one to have it.' Her eyes glazed for a moment and she turned away. 'You will be hungry after your journey.' She put some bread and cheese onto plates. 'I know Kineth always is, he could eat like a horse, that one.'

The door burst open and in raced a whirlwind of arms and legs, running around the table and grabbing at the food. Ffiona slapped the hands away. 'Oh no you don't,' she scolded, 'These are for your Pa and Bethoc. You two will wait until supper.'

The children groaned and their father laughed and rubbed their heads. 'Now be nice in front of your cousin, maybe you can make her believe you are loveable instead of the horrors you are.'

Four eyes widened as their mouths dropped open. 'But Pa,' Reega said, 'We is loveable.'

She looked at Bethoc and flashed her best smile, then she turned to her twin and the two of them burst into a fit of giggles.

***

It was lovely to be back amongst a family group again, it reminded Bethoc of the times she spent with Groa on Haey. She soon realised that whilst Ffiona was very similar in looks to her mother, their natures were very different. Where her mother had been quiet and reserved, her aunt was predominantly cheerful and very quick to laugh. Her bubbly personality was infectious and Bethoc felt the anxieties of the last few days melting away. She was going to enjoy a few weeks in her aunt's presence. Her young cousins were a handful, boisterous and noisy, forever getting into mischief. Bethoc learned very quickly to be wary whenever she heard their giggling nearby.

The first week flew past and soon enough they were preparing for the midwinter celebrations. The children were busy sorting which of their toys they would be taking and Bethoc helped Ffiona prepare the food they would need. She noticed her aunt was uncomfortable and rubbing her chest a lot.
'Aunt, do you have pain in your chest?'
Ffiona nodded and grimaced, 'I think I am having a hairy one alright, started about this time with the twins too and they were both born with full heads of hair.'
'It's a good thing I don't go anywhere without my herb bag, let me prepare something for you.'
Bethoc brought out some dried pale green marshmallow leaves mixed with chopped roots and asked the twins to go and pick her some of the mint she had seen growing nearby. 'This should

help,' she told Ffiona, placing a cup of steaming tea in front of her. 'Let it steep for ten minutes or so then sip it whenever you need it.'

Ffiona stretched out her spine, pulling her shoulderblades back and releasing a small burp. 'Sorry.' She winced. 'I guess we get this to let us know what the baby will be feeling every time we don't burp it right. I always find it the hardest thing about being pregnant. Some days no matter how much I wriggle about I cannot get the pain to ease.'

The twins giggled as they writhed around pretending to be her.

'Mother's a worm,' Reega shrieked.

'No, a snake,' Thain cried and hissed as loud as he could.

Ffiona raised her eyes in exasperation. 'I always wanted to be a healer just like Oonagh but I didn't get much chance to learn how after the burnings. Mother taught me the basics, enough to sort most of the scrapes these pair get into but mostly I have to wait until Kineth brings me something back from her.'

'Is there no healer nearby?' Bethoc was shocked.

'The nearest lives a fair way down from here, near a big waterfall. She is quite a hermit and none too friendly so most folk don't bother her unless they are desperate.'

'What about when the baby comes?'

'With the twins, Mother came when my time was near, this time I am due in the winter and the journey will be hard for her. I don't know what I am going to do.'

Bethoc thought for a moment. 'I am not needed in the caverns until the spring, I would be glad to stay and help.' She didn't add that it would also delay having to go back and face Finlay again. She felt a sliver of guilt at leaving her grandmother for so long but she knew she had left plenty of herbal concoctions, salves and blends ready prepared. Anything else could be easily sorted by one of the others.

She was answered by a huge grin and a swift hug. 'I would be so grateful,' Ffiona admitted. 'I was getting quite worried.'

They sat down for a break and Ffiona began to sip the tea. After a few minutes she sighed with relief, 'I can feel it working already. Can we bring some of this with us tomorrow? I am sure I will never manage on ale all day.'

***

The midwinter celebrations were held at nearby Alltbreac, home of Ruaridh. They set off at mid-morning, the children and Ffiona riding in the cart whilst Bethoc and Kineth walked beside. The broch was in the middle of a dense wood on a small knoll. A worn trackway led them to the main entrance, crossing through a stream filled with strange mottled stones on its way. The ancient thick walls had stood for hundreds of years. Here and there they had been mended and the newer stones had not yet weathered enough to blend in perfectly with the rest. At the sides of the entrance

249

passage stood two guard chambers. The guards smiled as they passed and bent their heads briefly to Kineth, who led his family around to the side of the enclosure, where he hobbled the horse. Everyone took a bag of food to add to the huge amount already piling up on groaning tables.

'I took my turn as cook last year,' Ffiona whispered to Bethoc. 'It was such hard work but great fun, we drank so much ale as we worked that I am sure I was as pickled as the onions.'

The adjoining enclosure was where the cooking took place. Two large fires were already burning and an enormous pile of wood stood ready to keep them going all day. They made their way over to the far side where a number of barrels of ale waited. With their mugs filled, they proceeded out of the food area and down into a large oval enclosure, already thronging with people. This area was sunken into the ground a few feet and was surrounded by a natural embankment, forming the perfect amphitheatre for rituals and gatherings. Near the centre stood two men and a woman. Kineth made a beeline for them. Nodding to the druid, he turned to face his companion, a middle-aged man with salt and pepper hair who stood about Kineth's height. He stepped forward and embraced him, clapping him on the back as if they had not seen each other for years.

Ruaridh had obviously been enjoying the ale for a while, his naturally shining eyes were glistening in the winter sunlight as he moved to embrace Ffiona and pat the twins on the head.

'My lord, this is my wife's niece, Bethoc.'

Ruaridh turned to her and grasped her hand. 'It is a pleasure to meet you my dear,' he boomed. Leaning forward he added in a much lower voice, 'I would love a chance to chat with you sometime. You have an interesting story to tell, I understand.'

Bethoc felt herself smiling back at the man almost without thought. She had expected the Maormar to be austere but the person in front of her was a pleasant surprise. The short, mousy woman behind him was a surprise for a different reason. Looking for all the world as if she longed to be elsewhere, she stood wringing her hands. Bethoc noticed they were covered in the tight, vicious scars caused by severe burns. Her fingers were stubby and deformed where they had been damaged and she appeared to have problems moving them properly. Bethoc smiled at her.

'My wife, Caitir,' Ruaridh introduced.

Caitir smiled briefly but made no attempt to move forward or speak, instead her eyes focused on Thain. The colour in her face drained and her hands worked together frantically. As unobtrusively as possible, Ffiona moved herself into the woman's line of vision.

'You have a fine gathering here my lord, we will leave you to speak with my husband if we may. There are a number of people I wish Bethoc to meet.'

Ruaridh nodded, seemingly oblivious to his wife's discomfort. 'Of course, my dear. Do the rounds, converse with the many,' he waved his arms around him, 'we will not be starting for a while yet.

Ffiona ushered them quickly away, 'I should have warned you about Caitir,' she told Bethoc when they were out of earshot.

'Ouch Mother, you're hurting me!' Thain squealed, trying to wiggle out of his mother's grasp.

She released her hold on his shoulder, 'Sorry darling.' She bent her head closer to her niece. 'She didn't used to be so strange but there was a fire years back and their three children were killed.'

Bethoc shivered and glanced over to where the woman stood, still hiding behind her husband. 'I noticed her hands.'

Ffiona shook her head. 'She tried to save them but she was beaten back by the flames.' Glancing down at her son she added, 'The eldest boy would have been about Thain's age at the time, then there was a younger daughter and a baby boy. The fire might as well have taken her too for all the shell of a person she has been since.'

Kineth caught up with them again and took his wife's hand in his. 'She will only stay for the formal part of the day, love, then Ruaridh will let her go back inside and hide again.'

He was one of the few people who understood that for all the man's bombastic nature the Maormar was struggling to cope not only with the loss of his children but also the crippling mental anguish of his wife.

The day passed quickly and Bethoc loved being amongst a large group of people again. The midwinter celebration was just as social as the ones she was used to on Haey. After the formal sacrifices and ceremony there was storytelling and singing. Folk who had brought instruments gathered together, filling the air with music as the last rays of the shortest day filtered from the sky. A great cheer went up as Ruaridh announced the feast was ready and for the rest of the evening they ate, drank and danced. Wearily, they made their way home, arriving well after midnight, exhausted but happy. Clouds were starting to gather and the frosty air spoke of icy rain not far off.

It found its way to earth with a vengeance early the next morning; the streams filled and the loch swelled. Huddled indoors for days on end, the twins grew restless and even more annoying. Bethoc kept the children entertained with stories by the hearth, giving their mother a chance to rest. Her growing bump was making her more and more tired yet she struggled to sleep, with the relentless indigestion.

20

Kineth had been gone a day when Ffiona's waters broke. Bethoc busied herself making fresh raspberry tea, she would change to motherwort and vervain when the contractions began. The twins ran about singing, 'Mother's having the baby, Mother's having the baby.'

'The baby will never come out if all it can hear is lots of noise,' Bethoc told them. 'You will frighten it. You need to stay nice and quiet so it doesn't get scared.'

Two small faces nodded, eyes wide with excitement. 'Can you help me get the cotbed ready?'

The sound of Ffiona retching brought Reega running over, 'Mother, do you need a bowl?' Not waiting for an answer she raced to get one, holding it still as Ffiona was sick. Her brother stared, looking worried.

'It's ok, Thain,' Bethoc said. 'Your mother's body is getting ready to do some very hard work, it's going to feel scary for a while so you are going to need to be a very brave boy. Can you do that for me?'

He nodded, looking unsure. Bethoc cast around for a job to keep him busy.

'We need to keep the room warm and water boiling. You can be in charge of that. I will be too busy helping your mother.'

Thain looked relieved, he liked fires. 'Shall I get some more sticks and peat?'

At Bethoc's nod, he ran out of the house, eager to be doing something. On the other side of the room his twin was busy wiping her mother's face with a damp cloth and encouraging her to sip the tea. Her little face was full of concern.

Bethoc smiled at the sight and called over. 'The contractions should start soon.'

It took another hour but once they started, they came thick and fast. The motherwort wasn't needed but Bethoc brewed the vervain which Reega again took charge of, giving her mother sips of it every so often to help keep her calm and to take the edge off the pain. Bethoc gave Thain a supply of fragrant herbs to sprinkle in front of the fire where the heat could release their scent, keeping the room fresh. He hovered by the hearth, watching as Ffiona grew increasingly uncomfortable. The speed of her labour was starting to take its toll, sweat poured from her brow as the pain intensified. She had already broken one stick biting down as the contractions reached their height.

'Can you place the wrappings over the rope to warm?' Bethoc called over to Thain, nodding to a pile of linens in the corner. The fire was burning well, the water was boiling and he had run out of things to do. She could see he was getting upset about his mother's cries. 'The baby will be here soon. Would you like to wait outside?'

Relief washed over his face, he hung the linens and made a break for the door. 'Don't leave the sight of the cottage,' she warned. Glancing at Reega guiding her mother through her breathing, it was clear that Thain's twin would not be wanting to join him.

The contractions were powerful, almost end to end, giving Ffiona no time to relax in between. She kept her eyes on her daughter and breathed along with her. Suddenly she turned to Bethoc, 'I feel all panicky.' She gasped, her eyes pricking with tears. 'Something isn't right.' She winced as another tide of intolerable pain washed over her.

'Aghh!' she cried out, 'God, it stings.'

'It's ok, Mama,' Reega soothed, placing a cool cloth on her forehead. She showed no signs of panic for all her tender years. She would make a fine healer when she was older.

'I'm going to have a look,' Bethoc told Ffiona. 'Try to keep calm, I am sure everything is alright.'

It was immediately clear what the problem was, the baby's head had crowned but was moving no further forward with each contraction. Bethoc tried to feel around the head to check her suspicions.

'Ffiona, I am afraid your baby is very large. You are already tearing and the head still has a way to go.' She paused whilst another wave of pain invaded her aunt's body.

Reega looked at Bethoc, 'Is that bad?'

'It means your mother is going to have to push much harder and it is going to hurt much more.' She placed her hand on Ffiona's abdomen and felt the strength of the contraction, it seemed weaker than before. 'She is going to need all our help, make sure she bites down on that stick, pet.'

Reega nodded and held the stick in place, 'It's alright, Mama,' she said.

The next five contractions brought no further movement and now Bethoc was sure the contractions were getting weaker. She urged her patient to push harder but Ffiona cried. She was exhausted, the labour was too intense and she had nothing left to give.

Alarm gripped Bethoc, she had seen this happen a few times before. If her aunt couldn't push this baby out they could both die, already the baby could be struggling. She needed to be strong for them both.

'No,' she insisted, 'You've only been in labour a short while, you're not giving up yet.'

Ffiona tried to shake her head. 'I can't,' she pleaded.

It was time for tough love

'Yes you damn well can, woman,' Bethoc shouted back. 'You will not lose this baby in front of Reega here. Don't be so pathetic.' Another contraction was starting. 'NOW PUSH!'

Ffiona lifted her head and pushed with all her might, the stick snapped again and blood appeared on her lip but her cry was one of relief.

'The head is out, well done.'

Reega grinned at her mother who fell back against the pillow.

'Now slowly this time,' Bethoc guided. 'I cannot see where the cord is yet.' But Ffiona was too tired to push any more.

'One more,' Bethoc called to her, 'Just one more.' Ffiona didn't respond. The shoulders would not come out without her help.

'Please Mama,' Reega pleaded.

With a groan she pushed once more.

Bethoc guided the head as the shoulders emerged and the baby slid out and into her arms.

'My gosh, he is huge.'

'Look Mama, look.'

Ffiona lifted her head long enough to catch sight of the slimy, grease-covered life before she passed out.

When she awoke the baby was clean and wrapped in the linen cloths. Reega held him as if he were the most precious thing in the world.

'Look Mama, he is beautiful.'

'Do you want to try and feed him?' Bethoc asked, coming over from the hearth. She lifted the baby from Reega and placed it at Ffiona's breast. He snuffled around for a moment before latching on.

The door opened and Thain brought one of the large pots back in full of fresh water ready to heat up. His face lit up when he saw his mother sitting up.

'You're awake,' he said. 'Bethoc let me have a cuddle before, he is heavy.'

He put the pot down and went over to the bed.

'They have both been great helpers,' Bethoc told her. 'Reega will make a fine healer one day, she never left your side. And Thain kept the fire going, then helped me wash out all the sheets. I couldn't have managed without them.'

They beamed at the praise. Their mother reached out a weak arm and stroked each of their cheeks. She looked up at Bethoc.

'Thank you. For not letting me give up.'

Bethoc smiled and rested a hand on Thain's head. 'I'm sorry I shouted at you. I just needed to make you react.' She looked at the baby. 'You did so well getting him out.'

'Was I that big?' Thain asked his mother.

She shook her head. 'I think he is bigger than both of you put together.' She answered.

Thain looked disappointed.

'Don't worry,' Bethoc ruffled his hair. 'It doesn't mean he will be bigger or stronger than you.'

Thain didn't look too convinced. He reached out a hand to stroke his new brother. The baby splayed out his own hand before clasping hold of Thain's finger and gripping it tightly. His face was transformed. Reega giggled and Bethoc told him.

'See, he knows who his big brother is.'

***

For all the constant wriggling the baby had done in the womb, he was surprisingly quiet and calm. Reega adored him and Thain was often left kicking his heels, waiting for his twin to come and play. Nothing had ever come between them like this before. Not that Thain didn't love his brother, he would spend ages looking at him with amazement. Whenever he touched him, he would act as if he was made of glass. Reega giggled at him and tried to show him how to hold him properly but Thain just stomped off and sat down with his toys.

'You know he won't always be this small and cute,' Ffiona explained. 'In a few months' time he will be crawling around all over the place, getting into mischief. He is going to need his big brother then to keep him safe.'

Thain looked up at her with a spark of interest.

'Girls love babies, Reega can't help being so engrossed with him but sooner or later he is going to need his big brother to show him the way. To stop him eating beetles and the like.'

'Eugh!' Thain looked disgusted. 'Why would he eat beetles? Is he stupid?'

It was Ffiona's turn to laugh, 'Well you did! I caught you munching on one of those big black beetles one day - one of its legs was hanging out of your mouth, wriggling.'

Her son looked embarrassed and for once was lost for words.

Bethoc came over and joined in, 'But you didn't have a big brother to guide you. I bet you would never have done it if you had.'

'Thain, Thain, beetles bain.' Reega sang from by the cot.

The biggest smile formed on her mother's face, 'You ate a worm!' she poked a finger at her daughter. 'Swallowed it whole, you did.'

Now it was Thain's turn to laugh and his sister's to look horrified.

'I never!'

Ffiona nodded, 'Oh yes you did. You two were forever getting up to stuff like that. I am really going to need you both to help me with this one.'

They both nodded in unison and Bethoc added, 'Reega, you can help with keeping him clean and tidy and Thain can guide him with all the boy stuff. That way you both have a role to play and no one feels left out.'

'Until then Thain can maybe help his father make some new toys.' Ffiona suggested. 'The baby will need things to chew as his teeth grow in. Otherwise he will start biting us.'

The twins fell about in a fit of giggles and ran round the room pretending to chew everything in sight. Just then the door opened and Kineth fell inside with an icy gust of wind behind him. His eyes flew to the cotbed and his face broke into a grin. He rushed over and hugged his wife, nodded at Bethoc, then squeezed both the twins before bending down and gently lifting the sleeping babe out of the cot. He was swaddled in linen so only his face and shock of black hair were visible. Kineth glanced quizzically at Ffiona.

'A boy,' she told him, 'We have been waiting for you to get back before we name him.'

'My, he is a bruiser,' his father said. 'Was the birth hard?'

'Well put it this way, it is a good job Bethoc stayed.' Kineth cast a worried look at his niece.

'Don't you be worrying,' Bethoc scolded gently. 'We managed just fine.' She ruffled Reega's hair. 'This one was wonderful and Thain managed to keep the fire going and the water hot the whole time so I could concentrate on the birth. Ffiona will be tired and sore for quite a while but she is healing well and, as you can see, Baby is healthy.'

Kineth bent and placed a kiss on his new son's forehead.

'I was thinking maybe Brude?' Ffiona said.

Kineth nodded, speechless. Bethoc sensed there was a deeper meaning to the word, she gathered the twins and they made a silent retreat to the other side of the room.

***

Later that evening Kineth and Ffiona explained the meaning of the name. Four years earlier Kineth's friend Brude had been captured by Thorstein along with Sionagh, Ffiona's sister. He had been forced to watch as Thorstein targeted the woman. She had kept her defiant eyes on Brude, willing him not to break whilst her screams of agony filled the room. In the shadowy corner stood Thorstein's son Olaf, watching with a gleam in his eye as Sionagh took her final breath. Brude had somehow survived the brutal beating that followed. When their bodies were thrown out into the midden heap he managed to pull Sionagh's away into the nearby woods and call for the help he knew must be nearby. Sure enough, Angus and Gurum had been waiting, hoping for a chance to attempt a rescue. Back at the cave, Brude had lived only a day before succumbing to his injuries. He was laid next to Sionagh in the rebels' burial ground close to Loch an Dherue. They were the last casualties of the rebellion but by far the worst.

So this was the torture Eila had mentioned. Bethoc's skin crawled as she made the connection. Kineth nodded when she admitted she had heard a little of the story. Back then, he explained, no one had known why a necklace should cause so much hatred. Without any idea of the reasons behind it, they had put it down to Thorstein playing games.

It had been one of the hardest times for Kineth and Ffiona since the burnings. The news had heightened their inner conflict as to whether they should have remained in the caverns with the others instead of hiding in safety. The only thing that kept Ffiona at Beannach was the twins. Her sister Sionagh had lost her own twin, Taran, in the burnings and had never recovered from the loss. Ffiona firmly believed that the thought of being reunited with him was what had enabled Sionagh to keep her silence through Thorstein's torture.

Baby Brude chose that moment to soak his linens.

'Well,' proclaimed Bethoc as she lifted him up to change him, 'that shows just what he thinks of Thorstein and his tricks.'

***

It was a few weeks before the trip back up to the hideout was possible. Ffiona had healed nicely and Brude, being a greedy feeder, was putting on weight well. Even so, Bethoc's mood sank as they prepared to leave.

'I would have thought you would be eager to get back and catch up with everyone,' Ffiona said when they got a minute alone. 'It must be boring being stuck here with us all this time.'

Bethoc turned away but her aunt was too quick for her.

'Is something wrong, dear?'

Bethoc didn't know what to say, she tried to think of an excuse but her mind was blank. In her agitation, she dropped a jar of dried mint leaves which broke, scattering the contents. Cursing, she grabbed the broom. Ffiona watched her with a knowing eye and sat down by the table.

'Do you want to tell me who he is?'

Bethoc dropped the broom and stared at her. Ffiona smiled apologetically.

'It's usually a male,' she explained. 'You know, to make normally sane people act like wrecks.'

Her niece sighed and sat down. She would have to open up now.

'I kind of ran away. I mean, I really wanted to come and see you too.'

Ffiona smiled, 'But?'

'I starting having thoughts about someone but I just can't let myself trust anyone again,' Bethoc admitted. 'I mean, when your true love turns out to be just an illusion how can you ever trust that you're not just falling for a bunch of lies again?'

Ffiona took hold of her niece's hands and kissed them.

'My dear, you cannot think like this. You are not to blame for what Olaf did. He is an evil man and he was very clever but not clever enough because he will lose in the end.'

Bethoc sniffed. 'Was I so desperate to be loved that I couldn't see reason?' She forced back the tears that were threatening to fall. All she seemed to do lately was cry. 'I never thought I was that gullible, now I just don't know what I can trust. But...' she rushed on, needing to get it all out now she had started, 'I ended up squashed together in the bushes with Finlay hiding from the Norse and I... I realised how nice it was to be that close to him.' Her face flushed.

Her aunt looked relieved. 'There is nothing wrong with that,' she said. 'Finlay is a lovely boy, he hasn't had it easy, losing his parents so young.'

Bethoc smiled at her. 'I know.' She eased her hands away and stood up to get herself a drink of water. When she returned she had composed herself a little. 'It's just that when I realised what I was feeling, I was so afraid. I mean, how do I know what I am feeling is genuine and not another lie?'

Ffiona waited, sensing there were still more confessions to come. She was right.

'And how do I know I am worthy of anyone's attention when I am so suspicious?'

So much worry and heartache wrapped up in one person was bound to show itself sooner or later. In a way, Ffiona was glad it wasn't any worse.

'First, I think you have to learn to forgive yourself, everything happens for a reason and I think in some way meeting Olaf was meant to happen... otherwise it wouldn't have.'

'He murdered my mother, how can that possibly be fate?' Bethoc jumped to her feet.

'Bethoc dear, please don't look so wounded, remember she was my sister too. I loved her so much, it broke my heart when we lost her. I would give anything for her to walk in the door now but I have thought long and hard over this. If Olaf had not killed her, you would never have come to Strathnabaros and no one would know about the necklace. This battle could have gone on for years and years. I have to believe Oonagh died for a good reason, I have lost too many family members to cope otherwise.'

Bethoc sat back down in her chair, she ran her hand over her face and thought about what her aunt had just said. It did make it better to think her mother had died for a reason. Ffiona paused to give her a moment.

'None of us can ever truly know how another person is feeling, love. We are all fumbling around in the dark, it is just bad luck that you found a monster.'

Bethoc relaxed a little, 'So you think I am over-reacting?'

'I don't think you're over-reacting as such, more like building your own cell so you can be miserable in it alone,'

Letting her words sink in, Ffiona stood up and poured some hot water into the pot, where dried mint leaves were already waiting. Bringing the tea over, she handed a cup to Bethoc and sipped at her own.

'How does Finlay feel?'

Bethoc shrugged. 'I have no idea, I was so worried that I avoided him and then came down here but we had been getting along just fine. He was my best friend in the caverns.'

Ffiona sat her cup back down and turned to her niece. 'If you want my advice, I would treat Finlay how you would want him to treat you.'

Her words were met with a puzzled look.

'You are complaining about Olaf not being honest with you and letting you fall for a lie yet here you are running away from a man who may well have genuine feelings for you without being honest yourself.' She paused and let her tone soften. 'Be honest with him, love, if he is genuine he will understand. You never know, he might appreciate the chance to look after you. He has gone through a world of hurt too, trust me, he understands what it is like.'

***

Bethoc travelled back up the road with Ffiona's advice ringing in her ears like a lesson. It made her smile whenever she thought about it. The walls she had been building up to keep people out now began to act as her support so she could let them back in. All it had needed was a different point of view. She still had no idea how she was going to approach Finlay but she knew when she did she would face it head on.

The farewell had been a tearful one. Ffiona had held her tight and insisted she return whenever she could. She loaded her with messages for everyone until Bethoc was sure she would never remember them all. The twins were especially upset to see her go; Reega had clung to her legs, begging her to stay, whilst Thain had run away and hidden in the peat store. She sat Reega down and promised her that she would take her as an apprentice healer when she was old enough. Until then she must work hard and learn all her mother could teach her. Her solemn face had brightened instantly and she flung her arms around her neck and promised.

When they had finally found Thain, she had wiped his tear-streaked face and asked him to make her a new stick for when she went out walking in the woods. Kineth had given him his first knife to help make Brude's new toys and he was proving very good at whittling little animals. She had described a seal to him, which made him laugh. He couldn't believe an animal could have flippers instead of legs but he promised he would practice hard and have the stick ready next time she visited. Twins calmed,

Bethoc gave Brude a last cuddle and jumped up onto the cart.

They were taking advantage of a break in the winter weather but even so, they both had to help push the cart through sections of deep snow in a number of places. Even the morass had been unable to soak it all up and was lying hidden under a blanket of white, waiting to entrap anyone foolish enough to think the ground beneath was frozen hard. The sky was a watery blue-grey and the sun shone with all the pretence of a warm day. Although it warmed their spirits, the air stayed bitterly cold.

Near the base of Benn Klibreck a huge herd of red deer hinds dug at the snow to expose the greenery underneath.

'It's usually the stags that come down the lowest in the winter,' Kineth commented. 'That would have been a good sight if they were males all still in antler.'

He rubbed his face, 'Maybe I can take Thain hunting for antlers this spring? He can start to carve them as well, poor lad needs something to keep him busy now Reega has become chief nursemaid.'

Bethoc was just about to agree when a noise alerted them to people on the road up ahead. Quickly, she rolled herself backwards off the seat and into the back of the cart, where she tucked herself under the cover. Whoever it was had no intention of travelling quietly; the deer fled and she heard

Kineth tut to himself. He gave a gruff acknowledgment as the two men drew close.

'Well if it isn't Ruaridh's lackey,' she heard. 'Going flirting with the devils in the north again, are we?'

Kineth cleared his throat. 'I have an errand to run, yes.'

Bethoc felt the cart slow right down as the men blocked the road.

'And I would like to get there before the sun goes down,' Kineth added.

'Ruaridh is mad, dealing with their sort. They will be down here trying to take our lands too before long.'

'And I suppose the Scots of Dal-Riata are a better choice, are they?' Kineth retorted.

'You might do well to hear what their priests have to say,' the other man answered. 'They perform miracles we cannot begin to understand.'

'Right now the only miracle I want is the end of my journey before it is too dark to see.'

One of the horses gave a snort and the cart began to move again. Peeking out through a small tear in the cover, Bethoc could see the backs of the two men riding away. Each of them held a goshawk on their left arm. By the side of each saddle hung a brace of grouse. Obviously a good morning's hunt.

As soon as they were out of sight she pulled back the cover but remained low in the cart.

'I take it they do not approve of Ruaridh's stance with the Norse.'

Kineth shook his head, 'They have been taken in by the Christian missionaries from Dal-Riata and think everyone else is heathen. Ruaridh will not entertain them so they hold a grudge. Still, they like to come up here to hunt the grouse on the moor, hoping to spread their new religion to everyone they see. It is unusual to see them this far up, though.'

They met no one else on the journey, which was as well since Bethoc had to get off the cart and help push twice more before they were done. Leaving the cart hidden in the usual place, they led the pony up the stream bed. He was used to the icy water around his feet but Bethoc was not. Only the thought of a roaring fire to warm her back stopped her moaning.

Moiraugh had sent Gurum and Finlay to Arnaboll for more supplies, not knowing Kineth was about to arrive. Bethoc breathed a silent sigh of relief, she had a little while longer to compose herself. The men went down the stream and retrieved the supplies from the cart. They were quickly stowed away in one of the storage caves and Moiraugh rubbed her hands with glee at all the possibilities. Blizzards had swept in from the east and sealed them off for a few weeks. She had stretched their supplies as much as possible but the last few days had consisted of weak potage and stale bread.

As soon as she had thawed out, Bethoc went to find Doada. She was shocked to find her lying in bed looking grey and washed out.

'Now don't you be worrying yourself, love,' she croaked. 'I have had a touch of the cold, that is all. Angus insisted I rest as much as possible.'

Bethoc rubbed the back of her grandmother's hand. It felt very cold. 'Have you been taking the cold remedy I left?'

Doada nodded. 'It is very good, I like the addition of lemon balm. I usually only put in mint, chamomile and yarrow but it certainly improves the effects if not the taste.' She screwed her face up. 'Blah! Even the honey doesn't take away the bitterness.'

Bethoc laughed, 'It's the way you make it. I will make you some, you'll be surprised. We have brought more onions and garlic with us, so you can have some broth later as well.'

She came back a few minutes later with a steaming mug of tea which Doada frowned at. Ignoring her, Bethoc encouraged her to take a drink and was rewarded with a smile.

'Mother used to leave the herbs in as well,' she explained. 'I used to take them out when she wasn't looking and found I recovered just as well. What's more, I enjoyed the taste so much when it wasn't as strong, I would drink more of it. It took years before I admitted what I was doing.' She giggled. 'When I did, Mother scolded me, not for doing it but for not telling her sooner so she could stop suffering the strong stuff.'

***

The next afternoon, Bethoc took a walk up the Castle, she wanted to get a look over the area whilst it was still covered in snow. She bundled herself up as warmly as she could and carefully traversed the icy pathway. Though the winter sun was bright, the wind was bracing and her throat was soon burning with each breath. The cloudless sky afforded her a magnificent view right over to Bay Mountain and beyond. She remembered what Kineth had told her about the Blue Mountains further south and made herself a promise to one day go and visit them. She stayed up there for quite a while, enjoying the tranquillity. Having spent the last two moons in a small cottage with five-year-old twins, there had not been much time for solitude. Finally, the cold drove her back down to the warmth of the caverns just as Finlay was coming out.

'Hey there, I was just coming to say hello. Did you enjoy it down at Beannach?'

Her breath caught in her throat, it was now or never. 'I owe you an apology.'

He looked at her, confused, 'Why?'

She shivered, 'Can we go inside first? That little chamber where the tunnels meet will do.'

She couldn't remember any of her clever words.

'I owe you the truth, Finlay,' she said. 'It's very hard for me to admit but I didn't just go down to Beannach to see my aunt. I went to get away from you.'

He tried to hide his concern with a joke. 'Am I such bad company?'

'No... It's just that I found myself liking you quite a lot.' She studied her feet for a moment. 'It frightened me.'

Oh, it was hard to be so honest but her aunt's words were ringing in her ears, she owed him this.

He squeezed her hand. 'I like you a lot too but you are my friend first and foremost. If you are not ready for anything more just now then that is fine by me.' He surprised her by flushing, 'I realised I might have worried you so I tried to back off but then you rushed away and I have been kicking myself ever since.'

It hit her how silly she had been. 'I don't know what I can cope with, but I do know I want us to stay friends. I was wrong to run away and not face things.'

He kissed her hand and smiled back at her. 'All you have to do is talk to me whenever you are worried. There is no pressure. We are friends, Bethoc, and we take things at your pace.'

***

For the rest of February and almost all of March the weather kept up its frigid attack. The top of Law Mountain had not been seen for weeks, obstinately invisible behind a wall of cloud. Snow piled higher and higher, becoming more and more unstable. Icicles hung down from every available surface, some as big as a man hung precariously overhead. The incessant wind drove snow into such deep drifts that whole sections of the mountain seemed to disappear beneath them. Walking became treacherous and they took to going everywhere in pairs just in case of an accident.

Bethoc had been back about ten days when they heard the first of many avalanches. The beautiful sunny day that she had enjoyed up on the Castle had melted the top layer of snow, freezing it hard again as the temperature plummeted once more. The days following had deposited another three feet of snow on top. Eventually the load became too much and the resulting avalanche had thundered its way down the mountain. Inside the hideout everyone stopped as the noise rumbled on.

275

It was a huge fall but inside the caves it was impossible to tell exactly where it had happened, dusk was falling and no one was going to risk venturing out to see. When morning came they quickly found out that the northern entrance was completely blocked. The avalanche must have started high above the crags and cascaded down, filling the final few feet of the long tunnel. Many more falls followed. Most were small, lasting only moments, the sound barely registering through the thick layers of rock. Even though they were safe inside the hideout, each fall sent a frisson of excitement and fear through them.

There was not much the rebels could do until the thaw. So they concentrated on enhancing the plans made whilst Bethoc was away. The usual scout trips would resume as normal, they had always been key to keeping them up-to-date with the activities of the Norse whilst also keeping an eye on the strath. They also planned to send teams to Caol Thunga and to Dun Yrredell to see if they could get any early ideas as to what Thorstein and Olaf were planning. Whilst those were going ahead, Bethoc and a couple of others were to make a start looking for the place Oonagh had buried the necklace.

Cailtran and Eila would be one scout party. They couldn't wait to be off, much preferring to be out scouting than in the caverns. The two other teams would be made up of Edana and Tagaled, who would go to Caol Thunga, and Irb, Aiden and Anfrud, who would go to Dun Yrredell.

Anfrud was eager to see more field action, Irb and Aiden were more than happy to take him along. After much debate they managed to persuade his father that he was ready for the challenge. Once they agreed not to take his son right up to the fort but leave him further down the river where he could easily escape if anything went wrong, Angus reluctantly agreed.

Gurum and Finlay would help Bethoc, leaving Angus to oversee the caverns along with Moiraugh, Elinn and Doada. Everyone was pleased with the arrangements except Elinn. At fifteen she was considered too young to go out on patrols but she was so keen to be of help that Edana suggested she be put in charge of watching the Law Road. She would be arranging rotas and logging all sightings and, whilst these things were not really risky, they were important.

***

Frustration began to grow the longer their enforced hibernation lasted. Eila felt it the worst. She started to get ratty with people and had snapped once or twice at some of them. In the end she took to jogging up and down the long tunnel. After a week, a few of the others began to join her and, before long, most of them were wanting to exercise too. She was soon busy arranging a small assault course around the caverns. Even Doada tried to join in some of the lighter exercises. She was feeling much stronger now and had never been one to sit around idle.

The morning Eila ran in to say the tunnel entrance was now passable, everyone cheered. The thaw had set in, places they had still been able to get out to were also showing distinct signs of a rise in temperature. Icicles dripped constantly and the pathway up to the Castle became a stream as the melting snow escaped down the well-trodden path. Small tunnels underneath the snow formed as water sought ways to get down the slope. The mountain was like an ever-changing magical landscape. The red deer began to migrate further up the slopes again, ready to make the most of the new spring shoots that would soon be appearing.

Being able to get outside and enjoy the bright sunny days was such a boost for everyone that they forgot to be miserable in their last few days there. Bethoc felt a new-found excitement growing, she was about to find her mother's necklace and complete a circle started before her birth. What's more, her friendship with Finlay was just as good as it had ever been. She was back to being her relaxed self around him, all worries about the future seemed a world away. Only finding the necklace and bringing peace again mattered now. What happened afterwards wasn't a factor.

She also felt she had a better connection with Gurum. Ever since he had told her about his loss, she had felt much more at ease around him. Whilst everyone had lost someone close, for some reason the man's tortured pain had struck a chord deep within her, making his gruff, tough exterior so much easier to understand. She knew Anfrud and Elinn often felt intimidated by him and sometimes she got the impression some of the others were too. To her, though, he was a lost man. Torn apart by grief but determined to do the right thing by those who were left. He could have raged and screamed, ripping into the Norse at the first opportunity. Instead, he held himself in control, and if his demeanour was a little brusque at times then so be it.

***

The hillside had not yet recovered much from the fire, it was bleak and bare with hardly any shrubbery left. With no cover to rely on, Bethoc's party needed Cailtran and Eila to stand watch for them. They headed out first so they could position themselves near to the broch, ready to call out an alarm should any guards decide to venture out. Aiden had asked them to keep a good distance from the search site, they were still unaware of the fact the necklace had been buried and he wanted to keep it that way.

Gurum planned to start their search by following Oonagh's escape route. Bethoc remembered her mother talking about a lightning tree but she was unsure if it was part of her made-up past or her real past. Gurum, however, knew exactly where she was talking about.

279

The tree stood on a slight rise with others all around it. There was nothing to indicate why it would have been struck instead of the rest, though now the other trees were suffering from various degrees of fire damage, the oak didn't stand out quite so much.

'There used to be so many stories about this tree,' Gurum said. 'Kids would call it the witches' tree and dare each other to walk around it on the eve of the midwinter festival. It is probably why your parents chose this place, it would be nice and private.'

From this spot they attempted to retrace the lovers' steps. They had no idea where exactly they had come across Thorstein and his men but they did know Oonagh had first run back towards the village. The old path was impossible to follow now the ground was scorched and littered with debris so they headed in the general direction of the village until they neared the stream.

'The path must have crossed the burn,' Gurum explained. 'So if we follow it back down to the village we should find it.'

Before they reached the village, they found the ford where the paths split. Bethoc was torn. It was the closest she had been to her mother's old home and she longed to go and look around but the necklace had to be her priority. With a heavy heart, she turned away and followed the others up the narrow track. This side of the stream had escaped the worst of the fire but with no one to walk it regularly over the years, the track was overgrown and hard to follow. Several times they lost the path and had to waste time trying to locate it again. Eventually they found themselves at the remains of the Coire Buidhe settlement. There had only been a handful of houses sitting out of the woodland in a natural dip amidst the heathery moor but even these had been burnt.

'I think everyone here was wiped out,' Gurum told them as they sat amongst the stone footings for a rest, trying not to let their frustration grow. 'If any did survive they certainly did not make it down to the broch.'

They tried not to feel disheartened. It had been twenty years since Oonagh had buried the necklace, the marker stone could be covered by now.

After some food and rest they set off to retrace their steps. This time they collected sticks to poke about in the remains of the undergrowth, just in case the marker stone was smaller than they had anticipated.

Again they drew a blank. The days were still short and dusk was starting to fall as they made camp. In the morning, Bethoc suggested moving further down the stream to look for another crossing. Maybe there was another path Gurum had forgotten about?

***

They drew yet another blank, there was no other path to be found. They were just discussing their options when they heard Eila call in the distance.

They made their way towards their agreed meeting
point. The Norse were on the move, one of their
patrols had left the broch and was doing a round of
the deserted ruins. Time for them to head back to
the hideout. The four of them set off, leaving
Cailtran to cover their backs. He caught up with
them before they reached the loch of islands.
Dejected, they reached the caves and informed the
eager faces there that they had failed. They were
surprised to see Aiden, sporting a nasty gash down
his arm.

'I fell,' he told them, rolling his eyes. 'Cut it on a
sharp rock. There was no way I could carry on with
blood dripping a trail after us.' He glanced quickly
over to Angus. 'It's lucky there were three of us,
Irb was able to continue on with Anfrud.'

Angus made a noise, somewhere between disgust
and annoyance. 'They should have come back so
that I could go with them.'

Gurum tutted. 'Give the boy a chance. He's a
sensible lad, he will be fine. You know Irb will keep
him safe.'

Angus tried to glare at him but one sight of the
exaggerated look on his face and he gave in.

'Oh alright, I know. I can't help being
overprotective.' He exhaled loudly and shook his
head at Aiden. 'Just you wait until Elinn starts to go
out.'

Aiden snorted, 'Over my dead body.'

Moiraugh fed them bowls of steaming stew before
the three men, along with Finlay and Bethoc,

gathered around an area in one of the smaller caves where the floor was sandy. Gurum drew a rough map of the area and showed Aiden exactly where they had looked. The leader shook his head.

'I cannot remember clearly enough.'

'Well it's no wonder, is it?' Doada snapped at him as she entered. 'You were still a child when you last lived there and Gurum, you lived at Grumbeg and rarely travelled that way. Maybe if you had bothered to ask me I could have explained why you went so wrong.'

Taking the marker stick from Gurum, she re-drew the path.

'What you have forgotten is that the path never ran directly up to Coire Buidhe,' she said, her voice heavily laced with sarcasm. 'The only way up to there was from the Grumbeg path. It was this one that crossed the Grumg-Mhor stream but it would appear it has grown over since the last time anyone walked that way.'

Gurum hit his forehead with the palm of his hand, 'Of course it did. I cannot believe I forgot that.'

'I can't believe no one bothered to ask me,' Doada said. 'I've had a bad cold, I'm not dying. There was a time that you all spoke to me about everything. Maybe if you weren't so busy writing me off it would have saved you two days of following a sheep track.'

She tossed the stick onto the map and walked out. They heard her muttering under her breath as she went.

Gurum looked at everyone with a sheepish grin. His face was flushed and he shuffled his feet like a young boy. Finlay broke first, he tried to hide his laugh behind a cough but he didn't succeed. Aiden grinned and Angus clapped Gurum on the back.

'You know it was almost worth upsetting her to see you put in your place, mate. I don't think anyone else would have dared.' He shook his head, 'Seriously though, you had better make it up to her quickly. Mother can be fierce when annoyed.'

***

Much to Angus's relief, Irb and Anfrud arrived back later that night, falling in with the dark. They had nothing of worth to report, Moddan had heard nothing. As far as he knew, Thorstein had gone back to Orkneyjar a few weeks earlier and the place had been operating on a skeleton crew. They had camped out nearby for a couple of nights to see if they could see anything but had drawn a blank.

'We need to take advantage of the hard ground,' Aiden told them. 'Once the ground starts to thaw out there will be no chance of hiding your tracks until the greenery comes through. Best not wait for the others, if there is a problem we will get a message to you.'

Finlay, Bethoc and a very relieved Gurum left the caverns once more. Despite all his efforts, Doada had still not forgiven him. Bethoc had to admire her spirit, even if she did feel a little sorry for Gurum.

Even with the new information, the path took some finding. Eventually it was located, hidden by a tangle of bramble. Even partly burnt and dried out, the thorns were vicious.

'This should guard our back,' Finlay said. 'If we leave it alone and try to get onto the path further up, no one should be able to tell we have any interest here.'

The path was now not much more than the sheep track they had followed before. The marker stone itself was almost missed, lying broken on its side underneath a holly bush.

'This ground is like rock,' Gurum complained as he set about digging, his small trowel making little headway in the frozen ground

'Mother must have used her hands, it can't be too deep.'

After what seemed like an age, Gurum threw the trowel down in disgust. There was no sign of anything buried.

'Maybe it's the wrong marker?' Finlay ventured.

'There was only one up here that I remember, besides, Doada would have told us if there was more than one.'

Gurum looked at the stone again. It was definitely a marker stone, no one would have taken the time to shape it in such a way otherwise. All of a sudden he gave a groan of frustration.

'Does this look broken to you?'

The others looked where he was pointing. The base of the stone was uneven and covered in lichen but when he scraped this away the stone looked much less weathered.

'Maybe it is just where it has been in the ground for so long?' Bethoc suggested.

Gurum shook his head, 'I don't think so.' He pointed to the side, 'See here, this line is where the soil must have been. It is different from the bottom part. I think it must have broken a few years ago and ended up here.'

They set about searching again, finding the base of the stone, not far away. It took a long time to lift it out of the ground but once again their digging proved fruitless.

'God only knows how your mother managed to move that stone by herself,' Finlay stated, looking at the chunk of rock they had dug out. 'I don't see how she could have managed it, even with softer ground.'

Gurum looked at him and frowned, he turned to Bethoc. 'You're sure your mother said "beneath the stone"?'

She nodded, but even Bethoc could see this would not have been possible. The well in their garden on Haey popped into her mind, as it had been doing all morning. She hadn't thought about it in ages and now its persistence was finally getting through to her. She racked her brains to work out why. It came to her in a rush. All their precious offerings, deceased pets and lucky talismans had been buried beneath the well. Except they had never gone beneath the well, they had gone next to the wall in the shadow of the well.

'I've got it,' she exclaimed, quickly telling them what she had remembered. 'Mother must have meant the same thing here.'

Before long, the pieces of the necklace lay before them. The main stone at the front was cracked and a few of the smaller stones to one side were missing but all the remaining stones were still threaded together to form the half-moon-shaped choker. The piece was stunning, all the years it had been buried had not dulled the polished stone. Once the small bits of soil that still clung to it were cleaned off it would be impossible to tell it had ever been in the ground. Bethoc's hands buzzed with excitement as she wrapped it up and tucked it safely into her pocket.

'We tell no one we have got this until either Aiden or I give the word,' Gurum warned them. 'The fewer people that know we have it, the safer it will be.'

Bethoc nodded, without really taking in his words. It had just hit her that she was now carrying the cause of her parents' death. It sat like a great weight at her side.

Finlay slipped his hand around Bethoc's as they made their way back. He gently squeezed her cold fingers and smiled down at her. The reassurance was exactly what she needed.

A screech broke through the silence. Suddenly they were all crouching down, trying to identify where the warning call had come from. A quieter call came from the right and they crept towards it.

Eila was waiting in a shallow scrape in the ground, the surrounding heather hiding her from view.

'We met Tagaled and Edana on their way back from Caol Thunga. Olaf is leading half his men down here to search for the necklace. They have even managed to find someone who used to live in Grumbeg to be their guide, not voluntarily of course.'

Gurum's face was one of thunder that one of his old villagers would be used in such a way. 'Who?' he demanded.

Eila shook her head, 'There is no time for that now. We have to get away, the men are almost here. Another few minutes and you would have walked right into their scouts. I've been forced to move more than once to keep this side of them'.

Hearts thumping and nerves stretched taut, they followed her without another word, keeping low to the ground and letting the heather mask their movements. By the time they were safely away, they were all out of breath and glad of the chance to rest for a moment.

'Do you have the necklace?' Eila suddenly thought to ask.

Gurum shook his head before the others could answer. 'Couldn't find it,' he told her. Bethoc and Finlay exchanged glances. Only now did his earlier words register. What was going on?

A blackbird call alerted them to Cailtran's approach. He gave Eila a brief hug. 'Thank god you are all safe. Edana has gone ahead to warn Aiden, Tagaled is watching the route so we can get back.'

'It was close,' Eila said. 'They nearly had me once, it was lucky a hare broke cover next to me and took their attention.'

'We expected you back before now,' Cailtran turned to the rest of them. 'What took you so long?'

Gurum wiped his brow, 'Couldn't find the damn thing. Spent so much time looking, then we had to cover our tracks.'

A flash of annoyance crossed Cailtran's face but it was gone in an instant, replaced by a shrug. He said no more about it and Gurum offered nothing further. He kept his face neutral and avoided looking at his companions.

The walk back to the caverns was a tedious cycle of moving forward a few hundred yards then waiting until Cailtran or Gurum scouted ahead to check out the next section. Twice they had to take cover whilst Olaf's men passed them by. It was past midnight by the time they arrived back home.

22

A light flickered in the small side cave where the outer passages met. Aiden appeared briefly and nodded to the group.

'A word, you three,' he said, looking at Gurum, Bethoc and Finlay. 'There have been some developments I need to tell you about.'

'I told him about the villager,' Eila admitted, looking guilty. 'I didn't realise to keep it quiet.'

Cailtran frowned at this and glanced at Aiden but instead of speaking he turned and strode away towards the main cavern with Eila hurrying behind.

Aiden watched as they disappeared from view, it was getting harder to hide how worried he was. He entered the small cave and sought Gurum's eye.

'Well?'

'It took some doing but we found it.'

Gurum looked at Bethoc, who removed the necklace from its wrappings and handed it over.

Aiden gave a low whistle of admiration, 'Looks like old Hildr certainly knew what she was doing when she crafted this.' He turned the piece this way and that in the candlelight before quickly wrapping it back up. 'I think I should hang on to this,' he told Bethoc, tucking it inside his tunic.

She felt a pang of regret as it disappeared from sight. Her fingers reached out towards it but Aiden was too distracted to notice. He paused for a moment as if listening for something. Understanding, Gurum went to the entrance and checked the passageways. He nodded the all clear and Aiden relaxed again.

'Is something going on?' Finlay asked, 'All this secrecy, it's not right.'

Aiden shifted in his seat. 'The night Irb came back from his mission he came to me and said Moddan had warned him there may be a mole in our midst...'

'What?'

'Keep your voice down,' Gurum growled from the doorway.

'He hinted it may be Eila or Cailtran as they had the most opportunities to pass on information. I warned Gurum before you left but until now, apart from Angus, he is the only one who knows.'

A familiar feeling of shock and disappointment was building inside Bethoc. Betrayal was nothing new to her but it still hurt. Finlay, however, was shaking his head.

'I don't believe either of them would do such a thing. Why would they suddenly start helping the Norse after all they have lost?'

'That is exactly my thought,' Aiden admitted. 'Cailtran has been with us from the start, he is from Grumg-Mhor. His family all perished, he has no reason to turn on us, but we don't know about Eila's background. She wasn't from any of our villages. Maybe Olaf has one of her family and is holding them hostage? I cannot think of any other reason for her to change sides like this.'

'I take it that it was her information that led to the capture of the man from Grumbeg.'

Gurum sounded angry now. He had known everyone from his village. It was much smaller than the other villages and only a few men had survived the burnings. Not all had run to the broch, he knew a couple of the older men had gone to live with family not too far away. He presumed the hostage must be one of these.

Aiden rubbed at his elbow, 'That is my guess but we still have no proof. Until we do, I cannot risk challenging either of them. I wish I had managed to speak to Moddan, I couldn't have fallen at a worse time.'

'How does Moddan know this?' Bethoc asked.

'Apparently he overheard his guards talking about an informant, someone close to the heart of the rebels.'

'Then it isn't necessarily Eila or Cailtran anyway?' she replied and her spirits sank even further. 'Edana and Tagaled are often out, as is Gurum.'

Aiden gave a deep sigh, the strain showed in the lines of worry around his eyes.

'In all honesty, there are only a few of us it can't possibly be. Obviously you are safe from doubt. You would hardly have come and told us about the necklace if you were working for Thorstein now, would you? Let alone go and find the thing and bring it back here. Gurum is another I could never doubt. As for you, Finlay, you haven't left the caverns on your own for months and when you did you stopped Bethoc from getting caught. It was a fair guess you weren't the one.'

Finlay looked over to where Gurum stood watch, 'At least now I understand why you told us to keep quiet about the necklace.'

'I couldn't tell you any more until Aiden gave the word, sorry.'

'Hey, don't apologise. I am just happy I am one of the few you do trust.'

There was silence for a few moments then Aiden cleared his throat. 'I think we need to start calling in re-enforcements. I want to move on the Norse whilst they are all together, concentrating on their search. I want us to be ready to move by the dark moon, that gives us three weeks. First thing tomorrow though, we need to call a meeting.'

They all nodded their agreement. The stakes suddenly seemed so much higher.

***

For the first time since anyone could remember, they were all in the main cavern together. No one stood guard or manned any of the watch points, instead they formed a semi-circle around Aiden, who stood on a box so they could all see him clearly.

At the announcement the necklace had not been found, a groan went up around the group. They had been banking on a successful mission this time. After Edana had come crashing into the hideout the day before with the news that they now had even more of those invaders to contend with, the acquisition of the necklace was even more essential.

Now, as Aiden described how the necklace had alluded them once more, he could see fear and defeat growing in the eyes of his friends.

No one had been expecting an influx of men to have arrived over the winter months. A total of five new boats had been counted in the harbour beneath Caisteal Bharraich. Four were smaller longships, seating about twenty men each, but the fifth was larger. Tagaled guessed about 30 to 36 men could have been aboard. That meant there were now over a hundred more men added to Olaf's search party. Not only that but now they had a local to guide them.

'What if the Norse already have the necklace?' Elinn asked, voicing the biggest fear of almost everyone else in the room.

Gurum stepped forward. 'If they already had the necklace why would they need the hostage?'

The noise grew as everyone agreed with his point. Aiden raised his hands for quiet.

'We need more information,' he told them. 'If these men are the new search party then we will need to lie low until they leave so we can try again. So I need to ask for volunteers to watch what they do and give us an early warning should they be successful.' He looked round at the faces, trying to weigh up any that did not look genuine, but he saw nothing but fear and disappointment. He tried one last line.

'If they already have the necklace we need to know so we can plan our escape.'

It was the first they had ever heard of him admitting possible defeat and it stunned them. They had come so far, for so long, and now just when they had their fingertips on success they had to accept that it may be snatched away from them. It was not easy news to hear.

Without another word said, almost in unison, Cailtran, Eila, Irb, Gurum, Edana and Tagaled all stepped forward. Aiden accepted all of them bar one. Gurum he charged with another task, they were going to need eyes at Caol Thunga just in case more warships should arrive.

The first five rebels prepared to set off immediately. They loaded themselves up with supplies, it would be a long watch. Despondent faces watched them go, only those that knew the real problems they were facing gave a sigh of relief. Angus followed them to the southern exit and waved them off, watching until they were out of sight down the stream before returning and giving Aiden the nod.

Wasting no time, he called the remaining rebels together again. All were beyond suspicion and were soon brought up to speed with the true events. The response was a mixture of disbelief, upset, and relief, in equal measures. Not one of them could believe that Eila was a double agent but all were forced to agree that she was the most likely candidate. That also brought into doubt Cailtran's loyalty but here Doada was adamant. Cailtran was a Grumg-Mhor lad, he would have no part of such a deception. If Eila truly was a spy, she would have to be acting alone.

***

The race was now on. Whilst Irb kept an eye on Eila in the field, those who were left quickly gathered their supplies and set off to rally their supporters. Angus and Anfrud had the longest journey down to Beannach. Finlay headed for Arnaboll and Gurum made his way northeast, hoping to garner support from the eastern villages. He could also keep an eye on the coastline and watch for any more boats arriving.

Moiraugh and Doada took to sharpening weapons and Elinn manned the lookouts as best she could whilst Aiden and Bethoc planned various strategies for confronting Thorstein. Adrenalin became a constant companion, not yet strong enough to cause any more than a continuous tingling, but enough to keep them conscious of the dangers that lay ahead. It drove away laughter and brought with it a foreboding mood that kept them all on edge. When Finlay returned with news that Arnaboll had been sacked, the mood intensified.

He had found nothing but a smouldering pile of rubble in the place of the steading. Animals were left wandering untended and one of the dogs, hungry and scared, had tried to attack him. The other he found dead in amongst the rubble. There was an unusual smell in the air, a sickening blend of singed hair and cooking meat. Heart in his mouth, he crept towards the smell. Nearing the other houses, he saw the remains of the pyre. It was impossible to tell how many bodies had been on it. A quick search of the other ruined houses brought no joy, everywhere was deserted. He was halfway back to the caverns when he realised the dog was following him. Digging in his pack, he threw the animal what food he had left. The dog swallowed it without thought and crept a little nearer, his tail thumping weakly.

'Come on boy,' Finlay had clapped his hand against his thigh. 'Let's get you home.'

Together they made their way back to the caverns. Man and dog, united victims of the blond invaders.

The sound of someone following them became clearer the closer to the tunnel entrance they got. Finlay's heart began to pound. He scanned ahead, searching for the best place to confront whoever was behind him. Whoever it was, they weren't making much effort to keep quiet. He ducked behind a large boulder, willing the dog to stay beside him and quiet. The person kept coming but just before he passed the boulder, he coughed then called out, 'Are you going to jump on me or just hope I walk right past?'

The voice was kindly and not at all threatening. Surprised and a little ashamed, Finlay, keeping one hand on his knife, stepped out to face the stranger. His hair was peppered with grey and the lines on his face told of a long, hard life, yet he appeared unaffected by the rough terrain they had been traversing. The dog thumped his tail happily, and went straight over to lick the man's hand.

'Hello boy, I see you have found a new friend.' He patted the dog and looked up to smile at Finlay. 'No need to look so alarmed, I made my footsteps loud enough to hear as soon as I realised who you were.' He held his arms wide in a sign of surrender. 'I am Lutrin, druid of these parts. I have come to offer my help.'

Finlay frowned. 'You know who I am?'

'Well, I know you are one of the so-called rebels and by your age I can see you were just a child when the Norse arrived. The only baby that I recall would have been poor Katiana's but I cannot say for sure that is you.' He moved to sit on a boulder and squinted as the sun shone in his eyes.

Finlay frowned at his mother's name and tightened his grip on the knife.

'I could not approach you at the village, I had to be sure you were one of Aiden's men first. I knew he had a hideout somewhere in these parts and I prefer not to attempt to seek it out without invitation.' He lifted his hand to shield his eyes. 'You can let go of your knife, I will not do you any harm. If you prefer, you can blindfold me, tie me, or both.' He smiled and held out both hands.

Finlay stayed alert. 'If you are who you say you are, tell me something only you could know.'

The man's smile deepened, wrinkling the lines in his face and adding a sparkle to his eyes. He lowered his hands. 'You do right to be suspicious, my friend. Now let me see.' He thought for a few moments. 'The only way you can speak to Moddan now is to follow the overhang in the river until you are outside his cell window. You give an oystercatcher's call three times. I myself prefer to use a peewit.' He shrugged. 'No matter. He has had three visits in the last few months, the first was from Aiden himself, the next was Irb and the last was me.'

Finlay relaxed. He moved out of the sun's glare and sat close by.

'I have heard of you,' he told Lutrin. 'Aiden knew you had been in touch with Moddan as well but we never knew where to find you. He will be pleased you are here.'

After a few moments' rest they resumed their journey, without the blindfold.

***

'Eila had no link with Arnaboll.'

Aiden strode back and forth across the small meeting room as he tried to assimilate the news. 'I can't remember that she ever went there. It was always Gurum.' He looked down at Bethoc, 'We try to limit the number of people anyone has contact with, it keeps us safer if anyone gets caught.'

Bethoc nodded at the sense of it. 'Was he close to them?'

Aiden dragged his hand through his hair and sat down. 'Oh gods. That was all the family he had left.' He gave her a sad smile. 'I take it he told you about his family, then?'

She nodded. 'This is going to hit him hard.'

Finlay agreed. 'Are you going to tell him?'

Aiden nodded 'I will tell him when he gets back.' He was not looking forward to it. 'He should be here any day now. At least he has the dog.' He looked down to where the dog had rested its head on his knee. He patted it and was rewarded with a wag of its tail.

'How important was Arnaboll?' Bethoc asked.

'In itself not much,' Aiden admitted, 'but from there a message could be sent out to the west to bring in more help. Now we have no one there who can pass such a message on. It means the west cannot be relied on to come to our aid.'

'Do not be so sure,' Lutrin interrupted, entering the room. 'I was told the news of the attack by a villager who had evaded capture. I sent him on to warn as many as he could, whilst I prepared the pyre. They will be waiting for us near to Dun Yrredell in a few days' time.'

'Those men must be stopped, the guards will see them.' Aiden could feel his temper rising. Too many things were going wrong at once.

Lutrin held up a hand in a peaceful gesture. 'There is no need to worry, it is all in the plan.'

The druid's words did not help. 'I have no idea what plan you are talking about but it is going to ruin ours if you do not stop it.'

Lutrin did not flinch, he fixed his dark green eyes on Aiden. 'I fear your plan has already come undone. There is further news that will alarm you but for that we must speak privately.'

'You may speak in front of these two.'

'That may not be wise.'

'We already know about the mole,' Finlay told him. 'What else could be worse?'

Lutrin stared at him. 'How can you know? Do you have him here?'

'Him?' Finlay frowned, 'Irb told us it was Eila?'

The druid looked back at Aiden. 'When did Irb tell you this?'

'When he returned from seeing Moddan. He said he had warned him to let me know there was a traitor in our midst and that Eila was the most likely culprit.'

'Where is Irb now?'

'Out with the other scouts, keeping an eye on things for me.'

Lutrin sighed. He looked at everyone and wondered how to break the news. In the end he decided to be brutally honest.

'When Irb visited Moddan, he was not careful. He blundered right into a trap laid for him when the Norse saw him coming. He was given the option of sharing Moddan's cell and submitting to torture or helping Thorstein in return for his life. The fact he returned to you should tell you his decision.'

The news sucked the air out of the room and for a moment the listeners sat with their mouths gaping wide. Bethoc was the first to recover. 'What about Anfrud? He was with Irb.'

Lutrin shook his head, his mouth forming a joyless smile. 'Thorstein's ruse could only work if he wasn't involved, that way no suspicion could fall back on Irb.'

For the second time in a few days, Aiden was faced with the betrayal of one of his group. It tasted sour in his mouth. He looked up and noticed Bethoc's face. She understood too well what he was feeling, yet when it had happened to her she had stood strong and done the right thing. He would too. For once he didn't rub his elbow, instead he focused on the druid.

'Do you know what information Irb gave away? Is the hideout jeopardised? We need to get everyone out as soon as possible, if he hasn't told them already he soon will.'

Lutrin shook his head. 'I think they just discussed the necklace, it is the only thing that matters to Thorstein. To know any more we need to ask Moddan. It is time we took our Maormar back.'

Aiden looked at him sharply. 'We do not have the men to storm the Dun.'

Lutrin's face lit up. 'By now Thorstein's men are all away in Strathnabaros, there is only a skeleton guard left at the fort. We do not need many men, trust me. All I need is three men plus myself.'

'Three men cannot possibly take the Dun,' Aiden said, shaking his head. 'Even if they could, I don't have three men to spare.'

Lutrin stood firm, 'I need three men and I can take the Dun. You say you have a good man due back any day?'

Aiden nodded. 'As soon as he arrives we will evacuate this place.'

Lutrin stood firm. 'I will take him, this lad here, and the girl. We can meet you down the road at the end of the strath.'

Aiden shook his head again, 'I cannot let Bethoc go, she is too precious to my plans.'

He finally rubbed at his elbow. They were so close to their goals now. Moddan would be an unexpected bonus and one he sorely needed but even so, he would not risk Bethoc to get him out.

Lutrin grinned at him. 'Then we are in luck, I did not mean Bethoc. I need your daughter.'

23

A whistle rang out from the walls of the Dun, there was no mistaking its intent. The girl smiled to herself and kept the exaggerated sway of her hips going while she slowly walked on. She lifted a morsel of food and placed it seductively into her mouth as a man appeared by the entrance and called over to her.

'What you got there, then?'

With a finger still in her mouth she turned towards the voice, looking every bit the picture of shy innocence.

'Cockles,' she replied. 'My Ma sent me to deliver these to my aunt. She don't live near enough the coast to get her own.' She sauntered over to the guard and showed him the bag.

He looked her up and down, a smile playing on his lips. Who was there to tell if he had some fun with this one? He could always share her with the other two if they complained. She looked young and fresh, just the way he liked them.

'Gonna give me a bite?' he asked her, winking.

Her eyes cast downwards for a moment before flickering back to his face. She smiled and held out the bag. Without taking his eyes off her, he reached in and took one. She licked her lips as he bit the tender flesh and tossed away the shell.

'They are good, aren't they?'

He started to nod then something in his eyes changed. The smile was quickly replaced with fear as his throat began to burn. He reached out to grab hold of her, gasping for breath.

'Help!' she screamed, jumping backwards. 'Help him. Quick!'

Just as he fell to his knees, the other two guards came charging out of the Dun. The girl took a few paces back to give them room. 'I don't know what happened,' she cried. 'He just started choking.'

The men bent down to lift their comrade and never saw Finlay step out from the shelter of the Dun wall with his knife unsheathed. Elinn ran. Finlay's heart was racing, he had never killed anyone before. Keeping his eye firmly on the smaller man's neck he rushed forwards and struck hard. Hot blood pumped out over his hand, the shock made his loosen his grip and as the man fell sideways, he lost hold of the blade. The other Norseman was on him immediately. He'd had no time to draw a weapon but he was a big man. His right fist powered into Finlay's jaw, sending him reeling sideways. Before the Norseman could follow up on the move, Gurum appeared and thrust his dagger firmly into his back, puncturing his kidney and stopping him in his tracks. He spun around. Fury driving him on, he swung his fist towards his new opponent with a great roar. Gurum jumped back out of his reach. The man staggered and fell forwards. Quickly Gurum grabbed his hair and drew his blade deeply across his throat, ending his life in an instant. He looked around him, the three guards lay dead but Gurum felt no joy at their victory. He helped Finlay to his feet.

'You did a good job. The first time is always the hardest but if you're a good man the rest don't get any easier to bear.'

Finlay nodded and rubbed his jaw, rolling it around to check it was not broken. The pain made the whole thing easier to cope with somehow. Looking up, he saw the others coming towards them. He could feel Elinn shaking as she gave him a quick hug. If he was finding this hard it must be so much worse for her. Ignoring the nausea he was feeling, he made a painful effort to grin.

'You did great,' he told her. 'Your father would be shocked to know you can be such a minx.'

'I just thought of Mother,' she admitted. 'For all I know, that man could have been the one who killed her.' She looked down at the bodies, lying in their own blood and vomit, with disgust.

It was easy to forget that Elinn was not the innocent girl she appeared. She had heard her mother raped and murdered whilst she hid in the cellar. Only her mother's last words had kept her quiet. She had regretted it ever since, secretly berating herself for not going to her mother's aid. Now at last she felt she had done something to avenge her.

***

Moddan was easy to find, Lutrin knew the fort well and went straight for the cell. The Maormar was waiting for them. He hugged his old friend and shook the others by the hand.

'You were right, there were only three of them,' Lutrin told him. 'Let's hope they left a bit more weaponry behind.'

Moddan's left eye twitched as he looked at Lutrin. His gaze flicked briefly to the others. Lutrin smiled. 'All is well, my friend. We have a plan in place but you cannot be seen by anyone just yet. What would you like for your disguise?'

A search of Dun Yrredell soon uncovered a number of weapons. Long, thin spearheads with wooden shafts, double-edged swords, axes and bows, along with piles of arrows and round wooden shields. There were even a few byrnies - mailshirts. Clearly Thorstein was not expecting much resistance. That would prove to be a big mistake on his part. They piled their loot onto two wooden carts and hitched a horse to each. By the time midday was on them, they were on their way. They left the bodies to the elements, they deserved no respect. Already scavengers were circling. It would not take long before they began their feast.

The road was well-trodden and easy to negotiate. Before long, they were joined by others eager to take part. The Norse were tolerated but not liked. They had ruled by fear and brutality, it did not engender allegiance. The lone survivor from Arnaboll had done his job well, soon there were almost 40 men behind them. No one recognised the scruffy bearded man under his heavy brown cloak, busy steering one of the carts. He was careful to keep the hood over his flaming red hair and his eyes downcast, speaking only to mutter guidance to the horse.

When they reached the southern end of Loch Meadie, they made camp. Here they would wait for Aiden. The days were still cold and the nights frosty, they were far enough away from Strathnabaros to light fires and soon the air was filled with smell of roasting game. Folks roused each other with tales of injustices and murder committed by the enemy. Battle fever grew amongst men and women alike.

***

Six men and one woman sat around a small fire well away from the main camp, weaving the fate of the next couple of days. The mood of the group was sombre. Moddan kept his hood up and his back to any approaching visitors. Between this group and the main camp, Moiraugh, Doada and Elinn were busy preparing enough food to keep everyone fed. Anyone attempting to get near the private meeting would have to pass by them first. Hidden to the side in the bushes were Edana and Tagaled, keeping a close eye on how everyone was acting. Aiden was taking no more chances.

The pair of scouts had surprised them just as they were all leaving the caverns. They had returned early to let Aiden know their efforts to watch the Norsemen were being hampered at every turn. Two of their hidden camps had been found and overturned and Eila and Cailtran had narrowly missed being captured near Grumbeg. They had no news on the whereabouts of Irb, believing him to be caught.

The news of his double cross had not sat well with them. Being both orphaned from the village of Skail, Tagaled and Irb had forged a firm friendship and he had often accompanied them on scouting trips. He was the perfect antidote to Tagaled's fiery temper, keeping his cool when times were tough. Tagaled was at a loss to understand how he could betray them all now.

Moddan kept his voice low, his distinctive rasping tone would be a sure giveaway to anyone near enough to hear it.

'I was dragged into the room to witness what went on, to reinforce how helpless I was as their prisoner.' His top lip curled with disgust at the memory. 'Irb was faced with two options. Switch sides or face the worst of Thorstein's torture. He capitulated without any further pressure.'

Disbelief flared on everyone's faces.

Moddan continued, 'Thorstein's plan was simple. Extract the information he needed as quickly as possible then send the traitor out to act like normal so you would be none the wiser as to what had happened. The ruse about one of the other rebels was Thorstein's idea to keep you from suspecting Irb when they started to act.'

Aiden asked the one question everyone was thinking. 'Why did he agree to it? What could he possibly gain by keeping quiet? He had every chance to tell me once he returned.'

Moddan re-adjusted his hood before answering. 'Thorstein promised him your father's broch at Loch Nabaros once all this was over. His eyes lit up like greedy gems, Thorstein didn't need to add his threats of what he would do to him if he failed him.'

A noise interrupted them. Moiraugh was whistling, it was her signal that someone wanted to approach. Aiden jumped up and went over to her. In a few moments he was back with three others. Angus had returned with Anfrud and Ruaridh.

'Kineth is waiting with my men lower down the Beannach Road as arranged,' Ruaridh said to them. 'We would have been here sooner but we had to dodge the Norse patrols near the west end of Loch Nabaros...' he stammered to a halt when he realised Moddan was sitting amongst them. Angus's mouth fell open.

'How?'

The Maormar laughed and quickly filled them in with events.

Angus growled at the news, 'The slimy coward. When I think what my sister faced at the hands of that bastard to protect us all, and he knew we were almost at the end of all this. He would only have to hang on a short while.'

Aiden raised a hand to calm him. 'There will be time enough for anger later, my friend. For now let us hear what damage has already been done.'

Angus inclined his head to him and looked at Moddan but his anger was still palpable and the tension around the group intensified at the Maormar's words.

'In order for everything to work, Irb only had time to tell Thorstein a few things and agree to meet him as soon as he was back out on patrol. Anfrud would have known something was wrong if he had been gone too long. He told them where to find old man Duncan and of course he told them about the help Arnaboll had been giving you.' Moddan looked at Bethoc, 'He also told him that you were with the rebels and that the necklace had not yet been found but that you would be setting off to search any day.'

Bethoc felt the familiar cold trickle of duplicity run down her spine.

'It is not the fact that he gave away my whereabouts so easily that bothers me,' she admitted. 'After all, everyone knows what the Norse are capable of. It is the fact that he smiled with me after he returned, acting like nothing had happened.' An involuntary shiver ran through her. 'He sat and ate with us all around the fire. Not once did he attempt to warn us, even though he knew what was happening at Arnaboll.'

No one knew how to answer.

Finlay broke the silence, 'I think we can use that to our advantage?'

Everyone turned to him. 'Irb is cocky, he obviously believes we will never suspect him. I say we bring him back here, spin a false story and let him feed it to Thorstein. Then we hit them with our real plan, defeat Thorstein and Olaf and catch Irb red-handed.'

A smile played on Aiden's lips and he turned to Moddan, 'Didn't I tell you he had a head for strategy?'

The Maormar nodded, his eye twitching in the firelight as he thought fast. 'Send a runner for the scouts to return. Make sure Eila and Cailtran arrive back here first.'

Lutrin looked at Moddan, he recognised that look. 'You have a plan, don't you?'

Moddan nodded.

***

Whilst the men were busy planning battle strategies, Lutrin took Bethoc to one side.

'I have had a look at the necklace,' he told her. 'I am concerned about the break. The magic is powerful but it is not contained as it should be.'

'Does that mean it will not work? Have we done all this for nothing?'

Lutrin shook his head. 'I believe the power of the necklace is far greater than the magic contained within it. Even if there were no magic left inside I think its reputation alone would give us the upper hand and cause Thorstein such fear that he would lose control of the situation very quickly.'

Bethoc let out a sigh of relief.

'Did you feel the magic?' Lutrin asked her.

She looked puzzled.

'A vibration in the stones,' he explained.

Bethoc remembered how the necklace had felt in her hands and she nodded. 'I thought it was my excitement at finding it. Is that why I found it so hard to give it to Aiden?'

A frown appeared on the druid's forehead and Bethoc felt a frisson of fear ripple through her.

'Is that a problem?'

'I am not sure, magic is a tricky thing, there is no way of knowing for certain.'

'What does that mean?'

'It means, when you wear the necklace the magic may become unstable. It could try to control you. Ordinarily I would advise against even trying to wield it but in this case we do not have that option.'

The feeling of fear transformed to one of dread. 'I am not going to let anyone else take the necklace. I have lost too much because of it.' Bethoc was adamant. 'I will be the one wearing it.'

Lutrin nodded his head, 'that is exactly what I expected you to say, my dear. Please just bear my warning in mind.'

***

By the time Irb arrived at the camp, everything was ready. By the light of a multitude of torches, the men were gathering together in groups of twenty, ready to form a strong battle line behind the leaders. Aiden stood by the main fire with Angus and Gurum. They turned as Irb approached them.

'Thank goodness,' Aiden said to him. 'We had heard reports you might have been captured. Are you alright?'

Irb grinned at them. 'I had a close call up on the hill but I managed to get away. I had to head east before I could shake them.' He looked around at the men amassed nearby. 'You have been busy.'

Someone approached and Irb turned to see Bethoc bundled under a thick woollen cloak. She smiled at him. 'That is because we found this.' Opening her cloak, she watched as his eyes fell on the necklace fastened around her neck. For a brief moment panic flashed in his eyes but he recovered well.

'You found it,' he exclaimed and turned to Aiden. 'Does this mean we are moving on the Norse?'

'It does. Though we never found the necklace.'

Irb looked confused.

'This one is just a fake one to confuse Thorstein. It should work long enough for our men to surround his. There are 200 men here and a further 300 ready in the east of the strath. They will come in behind the Norse at the designated time and cut them off before they know what has happened.'

Irb whistled. 'I'm impressed.' He took a step closer and lowered his voice. 'But what about the other matter?' he glanced around. 'I don't see her here.'

Aiden leaned towards him. 'I have sent her up to Arnaboll. For some reason they never answered our call and I am worried.'

Irb nodded, then remembered to smile. 'When do we start?'

'We head out at first light, not long to go now. I just need to sort out a front runner to scout our way ahead.'

Irb' face lit up. 'Let me,' he offered. 'I feel like I haven't contributed anything to all this yet.'

Angus stepped forward and shook his head. 'You have only just arrived back. It is already late, we cannot possibly ask you to head straight back out without any rest. Let one of the others do it.'

Fighting to keep the annoyance out of his voice, Irb tried again. 'I slept most of the day waiting for my chance to get back. I need a moment to grab something to eat and I am ready to go.'

'If you are sure?'

In the bushes, Lutrin and Moddan smiled as they watched him go.

'Now we just need to prepare the decoy and re-arrange the men,' Moddan told his friend.

24

Two hooded figures made their way along the northern bank of Loch Nabaros. A short way behind them walked a rank of men, armed and ready for battle. Ripples of water lapped against the pebble shoreline. Further out, the hills of the southern shore were reflected in the perfectly mirrored surface. To their left the woodland cloaked the rise but as they rounded a slight bend, the trees receded in an arc to allow a clear view of the remains of Grumg-Mhor. Round the next corner, they came face-to-face with the impressive stone tower of the broch, protected by the retaining wall running almost down to the narrow shingle beach. A cry went up and instantly guards moved to surround them.

Thorstein and Olaf appeared from within. Ducking their heads under the low stone lintel, they emerged and walked up to the front pair. Without warning, Olaf lunged forward and plunged a dagger into the belly of the smallest figure. She let out a cry and crumpled to the floor.

'That was not a very good move, Olaf dear.' Bethoc's voice rang out from the trees. 'It would appear your informant was not to be trusted.' She laughed as he wrenched back the girl's hood. Eila glared back at him. Before Olaf could respond, Bethoc stepped out of the trees. She was surrounded by the rebels, all heavily armed. Two arrows pointed straight to Olaf and Thorstein. Held at almost full draw by Edana and Angus, only a fraction of a second between aim and flight. At the same time, Cailtran threw back his own cloak and moved between Olaf and Eila, his sword now revealed and held menacingly close to the Norseman, who wisely drew back a few paces. Eila struggled to get back to her feet, the blade had not pierced far into the mail shirt she was wearing beneath Bethoc's cloak but the force had winded her. She drew her axe and stood tall. Together they slowly backed away to stand by the others where Eila replaced her axe with a bow from Gurum and readied an arrow.

Thorstein recovered his composure first, 'You were a fool to come here.' He called over to her, 'We have hundreds of men around us, you cannot hope to get away.'

'It is not I who is the fool,' she answered. 'I too have hundreds of men but they are not over to the east where half your forces are heading. They are all here. Not only that, I also have this.' She threw back her cloak and lifted her chin, revealing a shining black necklace. Large stones interspersed with tiny beads that shone as the weak April light reflected off them. Even though the necklace was now broken the effect on Thorstein was not diminished.

He cursed and was about to speak when Olaf gave a rough laugh. 'That is not the necklace we seek. We already know you didn't find it, that is just a broken relic.'

An arrow shot through the air at such short range it went straight through its target and pinned him to the tree at his back. Eila's face curled with hatred as she lowered her bow and looked her victim in the eye. Fear shone back at her as Irb realised he was caught. He looked at Bethoc and started to form an apology but his words burbled in the blood rising into his mouth.

Bethoc waved her hand dismissively at him.

'Don't bother, Irb, I've been betrayed by far better people than you. You should have asked for lessons, shouldn't he Olaf?'

She glared at the man she had once believed to be her soulmate, leaving the traitor to die alone and ignored. The love she thought she used to see was now replaced by cold, dead eyes lit only by a sneer of self-importance. She took a few deliberate steps forward, never once taking her eyes from his face. When his eyes flickered under her stare she abruptly turned to face his father.

'You know this is Hildr's necklace, Thorstein, it was after all you who stole it from the tomb further up the valley. You too will have felt the vibration it still carries, the pulse of magic yearning to do its work.'

She could see he knew exactly what she meant, it made her smile. She could feel the power of the stones coursing through her body. She felt invincible, untouchable. Taking a long, deep breath she took one further step towards Thorstein.

She spoke softly, she had no need to raise her voice anymore. 'You have failed. Leave Cait and go back to Orkneyjar or wherever the hell you like but you will not bother us again.'

The magic was getting stronger, building along with the loathing. The crack in the main stone widened, the pressure was too great for the fault. Maybe if the necklace had been worn by someone who wasn't so damaged by the pain that had been done to them it would have coped better. Maybe someone else would have been able to control the pent-up power. From somewhere deep inside her, the overwhelming desire for revenge consumed Bethoc. Her head snapped around to face Olaf once more.

'But not you,' she snarled. 'You will never leave. You will pay for what you did to me. For what you did to my mother.'

Her hand was on her dagger before she even knew what she was doing. She launched forward and plunged it into Olaf's chest. Falling to the ground with him, she stabbed him over and over again.

Chaos ensued all around her as Norse and Pict alike raised their weapons, but she was unaware of it. The stone broke completely and the necklace fell from her neck, snapping Bethoc back into reality. She dropped the blade and looked down, horrified at what she had done. Arms came around her and dragged her from Olaf's body. She became aware that everyone around her was fighting. Moddan and Ruaridh had joined the battle with their men and Norse were pouring in from the woods. Finlay hauled her away, using one arm to hold her and the other to swing his axe. He made no attempt to engage anyone in a fight, only to deflect blows coming their way whilst he got Bethoc to a safer place in the trees. She was white as a sheet and shaking badly. He tried to give her another dagger so she could protect herself but it just fell from her hand. It was no use, she was beyond fighting. He propped her against a tree and stood over her, using both hands to swing his axe at anyone daring to come near.

***

The noise was incredible, cutting through the air like angry thunder. It was punctuated with screams of agony and roars of rage. The smell of fear and blood was overwhelming. A horse whinnied and danced past Aiden. It shoved him sideways, sending him to his knees just as a sword would have taken off his head. The force of the swing pulled Thorstein down onto one knee, landing on a stone. Pain shot into the joint and he dropped his sword. Aiden lunged for it, Thorstein moved quicker. His hand closed on a discarded spearhead and he plunged it hard into the rebel leader's chest. The point pierced the mail and split his heart. Thorstein spat in his face, too breathless to manage any clever words. He staggered to his feet and retrieved his sword, turning just in time for Elinn's arrow to lodge in his stomach.
'That one is for my father,' she screamed nocking another arrow and drawing back the string,

anchoring her thumb to her jawbone. 'And this one is for my mother.' The arrow flew, finding its mark in his neck. His lifeless body collapsed in a heap, unnoticed by his men.

Aiden's vision was getting foggy, his breath laboured and the weight of his head was too much to hold up any longer. He rested it back on the ground and watched as the world above him clouded over. *I am sorry, Donal,* his mind called out to his long-lost brother. *I tried to keep her safe for you.* A tear rolled from the corner of his eye as he realised he had failed. A gentle hand wiped it away and Aiden felt his head lifted onto his daughter's lap. She stroked his hair, kissed his forehead, and together they waited for his last breath.

***

The necklace had been forgotten, the hand that bent to pick it up was unhindered. Slowly, Doada brushed the debris from the stones before cradling the precious jet in her cupped hands. She closed her eyes and prayed, using every fibre of her being to will peace to return. She'd had enough of death, enough of fear and loss, and enough of hiding. She was too heart-sick for revenge and old enough to remember well how lovely life had been before the Norse arrived. She wanted that life back more than anything, she wanted to have her grandchildren around her and watch them grow.

Unbeknown to anyone, she had defied Aiden and followed them to the strath. Something had called out to her, she was needed here. Only her age and wisdom could control the charms now the necklace was broken. She was the last cog in the wheel, the third female of the family. Her daughter had almost broken the chain, her granddaughter had been almost broken by it, now she would be the one to tie the loose threads and make it whole again.

Oh so slowly, the fighting around her stopped. Enemies dropped their weapons, exhausted, and collapsed to the ground. The wounded and the dying lay where they had fallen, responding only when water was poured into their parched mouths by those who still had the energy to help. The vibrations of the stones calmed and soon Doada could no longer feel her hands tingling. She looked around her at the carnage and shook her head. Gathering herself together, she rose and walked to the lochside. Using all the force she could muster, she hurled the necklace as far into the water as she could. Never again would it be used to subdue anyone.

25

Moddan took control of the area with no further trouble. The Norsemen that were left were allowed safe passage from the mainland and they left without argument.

Slowly, the villages started to return. It was a huge task. They started with Grumg-Mhor. A hazel tree in the centre was left as a memorial to those who had died, a strip of linen tied to the trunk in a simple ceremony of remembrance. Separate ribbons were hung for Aiden, Gurum and Edana, who had also fallen in the battle. There was no ribbon for Irb.
Once a handful of houses were re-built, concentration moved onto Grumbeg. Old man Duncan had survived his ordeal with Olaf. He was given the first house along with his remaining family. The other villages followed and the strath filled once more with life.

Initially Bethoc lived with Doada but when Ffiona, Kineth and the children arrived, the wee home became crowded. The answer came out of the blue one evening whilst she was down by the lochside. The quiet babble of the water lapping against the stony shore was the best form of peace she could find. She would often sit on one of the huge boulders that guarded the shingle beach and let her mind go blank. The stars reflected in the smoother surface further out, the inky blackness of the water barely even hinted at the green tinge to the cloudless sky. A slight noise behind her marked Finlay's approach. He smiled at her and sat on the adjoining rock. For a while they sat in companionable silence, each lost in their own thoughts. Bethoc's were dark but Finlay's were bright, if edged in fear.

'Magic is a cruel master you know,' he said eventually.

Bethoc turned to him, puzzled.

'You haven't been the same since the showdown, I am guessing all this alone time has got something to do with that day.'

The familiar feeling of ice-cold dread clutched at her insides with its steely hand, the air became viscous and hard to breathe. She clung to the rock and waited for the feelings to subside.

'You know you weren't yourself that day, don't you?' he continued, tiptoeing gently towards his goal.

She recovered enough to turn her flushed face towards him. 'What are they all saying about me?'

Finlay was thrown for a moment, this was not what he had been expecting her to say. 'It is obvious something is wrong,' he told her truthfully. 'But everyone is just worried about how you are coping. The last time you were this quiet and needing so much time to yourself was when you first arrived. It doesn't take a genius to see you are struggling, even the children have asked why you are not playing with them anymore...'

He strained to hear the words she had spoken. He took her hand in his and urged her to repeat them.

'I am such a bad person, Finlay,' she whispered. Her voice was barely audible and he had to lean in close to hear her.

'How are you bad?' he asked, lowering his voice. 'Because you killed Olaf?'

A stifled cry burst from her as the tears finally came. She had held them back all this time but now they had started she could not control them. Finlay was there in front of her, taking both her arms in his hands.

'You are not bad, Bethoc, you are a good person.'

'All I can feel is the hatred I felt for him when I was stabbing him, it is eating me up inside. I want to be sick, I want to tear my arm off so I can no longer feel the dagger going in, and above all...' she paused to take a deep gulp of thick air, her voice dropped even more. 'Above all I want to stop feeling the intense joy at the sight of his eyes when he knew I was killing him.'

She made to get up and leave but Finlay still had hold of her and he wasn't about to let go. Instead, he pulled her to him and held her there whilst her heart broke.

'That man did so much damage to your mother and you,' he spoke into her hair. He pulled back and took her face in his hands. 'But you must remember, you were wearing the necklace when all that happened. You were under the influence of magic that had failed to fulfil its destiny for hundreds of years. Not only that but it had been broken as well, you were not in control of your actions. Did you feel so strongly once it had broken and fallen off?'

His eyes were full of such empathy and love that she was taken aback long enough to let his words sink in. She cast her mind back to that forgotten moment. To her surprise she remembered feeling indescribable relief as the intense pressure of all that hatred vanished in an instant. For a fraction of a second it freed her mind before reality took over and she saw with revulsion what remained of the man who had hurt her so much. That revulsion had eclipsed everything else, feeding on itself and growing inside her until she could barely cope with who she was.

Confused, she shook her head, unable to speak, but something in her eyes had changed and Finlay knew he had been right.

'This evil person you think you must be would not have stopped the minute the necklace fell off. You certainly would not have let me lead you away. You would have fought anyone and everyone.' He wiped at her cheeks and smiled, 'But you didn't.'

She was trembling. Overhead, the green haze was dancing across the sky. In front of her knelt the one man she realised meant more to her than Olaf ever had. He had always been there to support her whenever she needed it, quietly caring and never asking for anything in return. In the midst of the fighting, when most men's battle fever was roused, he had taken her away to safety and let no one get close to her. She knew it was not lack of courage

on his part; after all, he had endured the thick of
the fighting to get to her and pull her away.
She leaned forward and placed a tentative kiss on
his lips.
'Thank you,' she said. She snaked her arms around
his neck, cupped the back of his head, and kissed
him again.

The Northern Lights danced green and pink
overhead. Doada smiled at the sight of them
silhouetted against the water. She sighed. Finally
she could stop worrying. Turning, she walked back
up to the village. They were going to need to build
a new house.

THE END
*

NOTES

The main area featured in this book is now known as Strathnaver in Sutherland, Scotland. Those of you familiar with the much later highland clearances will recognise that I have 'borrowed' the villages used. In fact I have used my creative licence to ignore all timescales when including buildings, forts, brochs and barrows. If you look on a map of Orkney you will even see Picts Well, exactly where it is in the story. The only invented village is the small hamlet on Stroma (Straumsey). There are plenty of disused dwellings on the island but apart from the two forts and the cave known as the sloup, I have ignored them and invented everything else.

Grummore (Grumg-Mhor) is a place I have many fond memories of from my childhood. I used to stay every year at the tiny caravan park on the shores of Loch Naver (Loch Nabaros), next to the ruins of the old broch. I remember the little loch up the hillside where I would walk, thinking I had almost climbed a mountain. The huge boulders by the side of the loch no longer form the den, where we would hide, but they did give me the inspiration for the caverns under Ben Loyal (Law Mountain).

The necklace itself is based on the jet and cannel coal necklace find from a burial cist near Achcheargary burn, Strathnaver. It is not the necklace from the folklore tale of the Never Ending Battle, fought on Hoy (Haey) but the two of them tied in so nicely I could not possibly pass up the opportunity of linking them. For those of you interested in the folklore of the Orkneys, you can find a lovely version of Hogni and Heddinn's battle on the Orkneyjar website: http://www.orkneyjar.com/tradition/everlastingba ttle.htm.

As for the characters, Sigurd I of Orkney formed an alliance with Thorstein the Red and together they conquered all of Caithness (including what is now Sutherland), extending into parts of Argyll, Moray and Ross. Thorstein was married to Thurid and had one son, Olaf Feilan, and a number of daughters. He is reported to have ruled over the mainland territories as king until he was killed by Cait (Caithness) chieftains. Upon his father's death, Olaf left the islands with his grandmother, who continued to raise him.

All other characters are entirely fictitious, though I leave it up to your own judgment as to whether the trows and dwarves were real.

*

The Albion Chronicles

book 1

The Girl of Two Worlds

by

Nelly Harper

ISBN 798-0-9932748-0-0

Published by Goblin House
www.goblinhouse.co.uk

Available now

**"Gripping and absorbing historical fantasy
cleverly slipping between two eras"**

Debbie Young, author & book blogger

The Albion Chronicles

book 2

The Battle of Brigantia

by

Nelly Harper

ISBN 978-0-9932748-4-8

Published by Goblin House
www.goblinhouse.co.uk

Due for release 2016

For more information about the
author, news on upcoming releases,
and to follow her blog,
visit her website at:

www.nellyharper.co.uk